DOROTHY PARKER

STORIES

About the Author

DOROTHY PARKER, born in West End, New Jersey in 1893, began her career as a writer with *Vogue* and later wrote for *Esquire*. She also served as dramatic critic for *Vanity Fair* and book critic for *The New Yorker*. Her original writings include numerous books of poetry, such as *Death and Taxes, Enough Rope*, and *Not So Deep as a Well*. She also collaborated in writing two plays, *Close Harmony* and *Ladies of the Corridor*. Dorothy Parker died in 1967.

DOROTHY PARKER

STORIES

"AH CANNOT WEE,

AS WELL AS COCKS AND LYONS JOCUND BE,

AFTER SUCH PLEASURES?"

—JOHN DONNE, FAREWELL TO LOVE

WINGS BOOKS

New York • Avenel, New Jersey

Laments for the Living
was dedicated to
ADELE QUARTERLY LOVETT

After Such Pleasures
was dedicated to
ELLEN AND PHILIP BARRY

This edition contains the complete and unabridged texts of the original editions. They have been completely reset for this volume.

This omnibus was originally published in separate volumes under the titles:
Laments for the Living, copyright © 1930 by Dorothy Parker
After Such Pleasures, copyright © 1933 by Dorothy Parker

This 1992 edition is published by Wings Books, distributed by Outlet Book Company, Inc., a Random House Company, 40 Engelhard Avenue, Avenel, New Jersey 07001, by arrangement with Viking Penguin, a division of Penguin Books USA, Inc.

Jacket art recreated from original Vogue *cover courtesy of* Vogue. *Copyright © 1929 (renewed 1957) by The Conde Nast Publications Inc.*

Random House
New York • Toronto • London • Sydney • Auckland

Printed and bound in the United States of America

Library of Congress Cataloging-in-Publication Data
Parker, Dorothy, 1893–1967.
 [Laments for the living]
 Dorothy Parker stories.
  p.   cm.
 "Originally published in separate volumes under the titles Laments for the living . . . [and] After such pleasures—T.p. verso.
 ISBN 0-517-08466-X
 I. Parker, Dorothy, 1893–1967.   After such pleasures.   1992.
II. Title.
PS3531.A5855A6   1992
813'.52—dc20   92-24644
                                                           CIP

8 7 6 5 4 3 2 1

Contents

CONTENTS

The Short Story, through a Couple of the Ages

The New Yorker, December 17, 1927

There was a time, when I still had my strength, that I read nearly all the stories in the more popular magazines. I did not have to do it; I did it for fun, for I had yet to discover that there were other and more absorbing diversions that had the advantage of being no strain on the eyes. But even in those days of my vigor, nearly all the stories was the best that I could do. I could never go the full course. From the time I learned to read—which, I am pretty thoroughly convinced, was when I made my first big mistake—I was always unable to do anything whatever with stories that began in any of these following manners:

(1) "Ho, Felipe, my horse, and *pronto!*" cried *El Sol*. He turned to the quivering girl, and his mocking bow was

so low that his *sombrero* swept the flags of the *patio*. *"Adiós*, then, *señorita*, until *mañana!"* And with a flash of white teeth across the lean young swarthiness of his face, he bounded to the back of his horse and was off, swift as a homing *paloma*.

(2) Everybody in Our Village loved to go by Granny Wilkins' cottage. Maybe it was the lilacs that twinkled a cheery greeting in the dooryard, or maybe it was the brass knocker that twinkled on the white-painted door, or maybe—and I suspect this was the real reason—it was Granny herself, with her crisp white cap, and her wise brown eyes, twinkling away in her dear little old winter apple of a face.

(3) The train chugged off down the long stretch of track, leaving the little new school-mistress standing alone on the rickety boards that composed the platform of Medicine Bend station. She looked very small indeed, standing there, and really ridiculously young. "I just won't cry!" she said fiercely, swallowing hard. "I won't! Daddy— Daddy would be disappointed in me if I cried. Oh, Daddy—Daddy, I miss you so!"

(4) The country club was a-hum, for the final match of the Fourth of July Golf Tournament was in full swing. Many a curious eye lingered on Janet DeLancey, rocking lazily, surrounded as usual by a circle of white-flanneled adorers, for the porch was a-whisper with the rumor that

the winner of the match would also be the winner of the hitherto untouched heart of the blond and devastating Janet.

(5) I dunno ez I ought to be settin' here, talkin', when there's the vittles to git fer the men-folks. But, Laws, 'tain't often a body hez a chanct ter talk, up this-a-way. I wuz tellin' yuh 'bout li'l Mezzie Meigs, ol' Skin-flint Meigs's da'ter. She wuz a right peart 'un, Mezzie wuz, and purty!

(6) "For God's sake, don't do it, Kid!" whispered Annie the Wop, twining her slim arms about the Kid's bull-like neck. "Yer promised me yer'd go straight, after the last time. The bulls'll get yer, Kid; they'll send yer up, sure. Aw, Kid, put away yer gat, and let's beat it away somewhere in God's nice, clean country, where yer can raise chickens, like yer always dreamed of doin'."

But, with these half-dozen exceptions, I read all the other short stories that separated the Ivory Soap advertisements from the pages devoted to Campbell's Soups. I read about bored and pampered wives who were right on the verge of eloping with slender-fingered, quizzical-eyed artists, but did not. I read of young suburban couples, caught up in the fast set about them, driven to separation by their false, nervous life, and restored to each other by the opportune illness of their baby. I read tales proving that Polack servant-girls have their feelings, too. I read of young men who collected blue jade, and solved mysterious murders, on the side. I read stories of transplanted Russians, of backstage life, of shop-girls' evening hours, of unwanted grandmothers, of heroic collies, of experiments in child-training, of golden-hearted cow-punchers with slow drawls, of the comicalities of adolescent love, of Cape Cod fisherfolk, of Creole belles and beaux, of Greenwich Village, of Michigan Boulevard, of the hard-drinking and easy-kissing younger generation, of baseball players, side-show artists, and professional mediums. I read, in short, more damn tripe than you ever saw in your life.

And then I found that I was sluggish upon awakening in the morning, spots appeared before my eyes, and my friends shunned me. I also found that I was reading the same stories over and over, month after month. So I stopped, like that. It is only an old wives' tale that you have to taper off.

Recently, though, I took the thing up again. There were rumors about that the American short story had taken a decided turn for the better. Crazed with hope, I got all the more popular and less expensive magazines that I could carry on my shoulders, and sat down for a regular old read. And a regular old read is just what it turned out to be. There they all were—the golden-hearted cow-punchers, the suburban couples, the baseball players, the Creole belles—even dear old Granny Wilkins was twinkling away, in one of them. There were the same old plots, the same old characters, the same old phrases—dear Heaven, even the same old illustrations. So that is why I shot myself.

It is true that in the magazines with quieter covers, with smaller circulations, and with higher purchasing prices, there are good short stories. Their scholarly editors have extended a courteous welcome to the newer writers. And the newer writers are good; they write with feeling and honesty and courage, and they write well. They do not prostitute their talents for money; they do not add words because they are to be paid by the word; scarcely, indeed, do they violate their amateur standing. But here, just as one did in the old days, does one get the feeling of reading the same stories over and over, month after month. There are no golden-hearted cow-punchers, but there are the inevitable Midwestern farm families; the laughing Creole belles have given place to the raw tragedies of the Bayou; but the formulae are as rigorous. You must write your story as starkly as it was written just before you did it; if you can outstark the previous author, you are one up. Sedulous agony has become as monotonous as sedulous sunshine. Save for those occasions when you come upon a Hemingway or an Anderson or a Lardner in your reading, the other stories that meet your eye might all have come from the same pen.

I do not see how Mr. Edward O'Brien stands the strain. Season after season, as inescapable as Christmas, he turns out his collection of what he considers to be the best short stories of their year. To do this, and he does it conscientiously, he must read and rate every short story in every American magazine of fiction. Me, I should liefer adopt the career of a blood donor.

The Best Short Stories of 1927 is distinguished by the inclusion in it of Ernest Hemingway's superb "The Killers." This is enough to make any book of stories a notable one. There is also Sherwood Anderson's "Another Wife," which seems to me one of his best. But in the other stories I can find only disappointment. They seem to me wholly conventional, in this recent conventionality of anguish. There is no excitement to them; they have all the dogged quiet of too-careful writing. Separate, each one might possibly—oh, possibly—grip you. Grouped together, they string out as flat as Kansas.

Their compiler shows himself, in this volume, to be more than ever the unsung hero. In the back of the book, where he lists all the short stories of the year, and grades them, unasked, without a star, with one star, with two stars, or with three stars, according to his notion of their merits, you may gain some idea of what the man has been through. I give you some of the titles of the stories that he has wrestled with:

"Vomen is Easily Veak-Minded"; "Ma Bentley's Christmas Dinner"; "Archibald in Arcady" (there is always one of those, every year); "Fred and Circuses"; "Willie Painter Stays on the Level"; "Sylvia Treads among the Goulds"; "Betty Use Your Bean"; "Daddy's Nondetachable Cuffs"; "Ann 'n' Andy"; "Freed 'Em and Weep" (I bet that was a little love); "Jerry Gums the Game"; "Blue Eyes in Trouble"; "Grandflapper" (you can practically write that one for yourself); "She Loops to Conquer"; "Yes, Sir, He's My Maybe"; and "Dot and Will Find Out What It Means to Be Rich," which last sets me wondering into the night just what were the titles that the author threw out as being less adroit.

They say Mr. O'Brien makes ample money, on his sales of these stories written by others, and I hope it is true. But no matter how much it is, he deserves more.

The Sexes

The Sexes

The young man with the scenic cravat glanced
nervously down the sofa at the girl in the fringed dress.
She was examining her handkerchief; it might have been
the first one of its kind she had seen, so deep was her
interest in its material, form, and possibilities. The young
man cleared his throat, without necessity or success, pro-
ducing a small, syncopated noise.

"Want a cigarette?" he said.

"No, thank you," she said. "Thank you ever so much
just the same."

3

"Sorry I've only got these kind," he said. "You got any of your own?"

"I really don't know," she said. "I probably have, thank you."

"Because if you haven't," he said, "it wouldn't take me a minute to go up to the corner and get you some."

"Oh, thank you, but I wouldn't have you go to all that trouble for anything," she said. "It's awfully sweet of you to think of it. Thank you ever so much."

"Will you for God's sakes stop thanking me?" he said.

"Really," she said, "I didn't know I was saying anything out of the way. I'm awfully sorry if I hurt your feelings. I know what it feels like to get your feelings hurt. I'm sure I didn't realize it was an insult to say 'thank you' to a person. I'm not exactly in the habit of having people swear at me because I say 'thank you' to them."

"I did not swear at you!" he said.

"Oh, you didn't?" she said. "I see."

"My God," he said, "all I said, I simply asked you if I couldn't go out and get you some cigarettes. Is there anything in that to get up in the air about?"

"Who's up in the air?" she said. "I'm sure I didn't know it was a criminal offense to say I wouldn't dream of giving you all that trouble. I'm afraid I must be awfully stupid, or something."

4

"Do you want me to go out and get you some cigarettes; or don't you?" he said.

"Goodness," she said, "if you want to go so much,
please don't feel you have to stay here. I wouldn't have you
feel you had to stay for anything."

"Ah, don't be that way, will you?" he said.

"Be what way?" she said. "I'm not being any way."

"What's the matter?" he said.

"Why, nothing," she said. "Why?"

"You've been funny all evening," he said. "Hardly
said a word to me, ever since I came in."

"I'm terribly sorry you haven't been having a good
time," she said. "For goodness' sakes, don't feel you
have to stay here and be bored. I'm sure there are mil-
lions of places you could be having a lot more fun. The
only thing, I'm a little bit sorry I didn't know before,
that's all. When you said you were coming over tonight,
I broke a lot of dates to go to the theater and everything. But it doesn't make a bit of difference. I'd much
rather have you go and have a good time. It isn't very
pleasant to sit here and feel you're boring a person to
death."

"I'm not bored!" he said. "I don't want to go any
place! Ah, honey, won't you tell me what's the matter? Ah,
please."

"I haven't the faintest idea what you're talking

about," she said. "There isn't a thing on earth the matter. I don't know what you mean."

"Yes, you do," he said. "There's something the trouble. Is it anything I've done, or anything?"

"Goodness," she said, "I'm sure it isn't any of my business, anything you do. I certainly wouldn't feel I had any right to criticize."

"Will you stop talking like that?" he said. "Will you, please?"

"Talking like what?" she said.

"You know," he said. "That's the way you were talking over the telephone today, too. You were so snotty when I called you up, I was afraid to talk to you."

"I beg your pardon," she said. "What did you say I was?"

"Well, I'm sorry," he said. "I didn't mean to say that. You get me so balled up."

"You see," she said. "I'm really not in the habit of hearing language like that. I've never had a thing like that said to me in my life."

"I told you I was sorry, didn't I?" he said. "Honest, honey, I didn't mean it. I don't know how I came to say a thing like that. Will you excuse me? Please?"

"Oh, certainly," she said. "Goodness, don't feel you have to apologize to me. It doesn't make any difference at all. It just seems a little bit funny to have somebody you were in the habit of thinking was a gentleman come to your home and use language like that to you, that's all. But it doesn't make the slightest bit of difference."

"I guess nothing I say makes any difference to you," he said. "You seem to be sore at me."

"I'm sore at you?" she said. "I can't understand what put that idea in your head. Why should I be sore at you?"

"That's what I'm asking you," he said. "Won't you tell me what I've done? Have I done something to hurt your feelings, honey? The way you were, over the phone, you had me worried all day. I couldn't do a lick of work."

"I certainly wouldn't like to feel," she said, "that I was interfering with your work. I know there are lots of girls that don't think anything of doing things like that, but I think it's terrible. It certainly isn't very nice to sit here and have someone tell you you interfere with his business."

"I didn't say that!" he said. "I didn't say it!"

"Oh, didn't you?" she said. "Well, that was the impression I got. It must be my stupidity."

"I guess maybe I better go," he said. "I can't get right. Everything I say seems to make you sorer and sorer. Would you rather I'd go?"

"Please do just exactly whatever you like," she said. "I'm sure the last thing I want to do is have you stay here when you'd rather be some place else. Why don't you go some place where you won't be bored? Why don't you go up to Florence Leaming's? I know she'd love to have you."

"I don't want to go up to Florence Leaming's!" he said. "What would I want to go up to Florence Leaming's for? She gives me a pain."

"Oh, really?" she said. "She didn't seem to be giving you so much of a pain at Elsie's party last night, I notice. I notice you couldn't even talk to anybody else, that's how much of a pain she gave you."

"Yeah, and you know why I was talking to her?" he said.

"Why, I suppose you think she's attractive," she said. "I suppose some people do. It's perfectly natural. Some people think she's quite pretty."

"I don't know whether she's pretty or not," he said. "I wouldn't know her if I saw her again. Why I was talking to her was you wouldn't even give me a tumble, last night. I came up and tried to talk to you, and you just said, 'Oh, how do you do'—just like that, 'Oh, how do you do'—and you turned right away and wouldn't look at me."

"I wouldn't look at you?" she said. "Oh, that's awfully funny. Oh, that's marvelous. You don't mind if I laugh, do you?"

"Go ahead and laugh your head off," he said. "But you wouldn't."

"Well, the minute you came in the room," she said,

"you started making such a fuss over Florence Leaming I thought you never wanted to see anybody else. You two seemed to be having such a wonderful time together, goodness knows I wouldn't have butted in for anything."

"My God," he said, "this what's-her-name girl came up and began talking to me before I even saw anybody else, and what could I do? I couldn't sock her in the nose, could I?"

"I certainly didn't see you try," she said.

"You saw me try to talk to you, didn't you?" he said. "And what did you do? 'Oh, how do you do.' Then this what's-her-name came up again, and there I was, stuck. Florence Leaming! I think she's terrible. Know what I think of her? I think she's a damn little fool. That's what I think of her."

"Well, of course," she said, "that's the impression she always gave me, but I don't know, I've heard people say she's pretty. Honestly I have."

"Why, she can't be pretty in the same room with you," he said.

"She has got an awfully funny nose," she said. "I really feel sorry for a girl with a nose like that."

"She's got a terrible nose," he said. "You've got a beautiful nose. Gee, you've got a pretty nose."

"Oh, I have not," she said. "You're crazy."

"And beautiful eyes," he said, "and beautiful hair

and a beautiful mouth. And beautiful hands. Let me have one of the little hands. Ah, look atta little hand! Who's got the prettiest hands in the world? Who's the sweetest girl in the world?"

"I don't know," she said. "Who?"

"You don't know!" he said. "You do so, too, know."

"I do not," she said. "Who? Florence Leaming?"

"Oh, Florence Leaming, my eye!" he said. "Getting sore about Florence Leaming! And me not sleeping all last night and not doing a stroke of work all day because you wouldn't speak to me! A girl like you getting sore about a girl like Florence Leaming!"

"I think you're just perfectly crazy," she said. "I was not sore! What on earth ever made you think I was? You're simply crazy. Ow, my hair-net! Wait a second till I take it off. There!"

Mr. Durant

Mr. Durant

$\mathcal{N}$ot for some ten days had Mr. Durant known any such ease of mind. He gave himself up to it, wrapped himself, warm and soft, as in a new and an expensive cloak. God, for Whom Mr. Durant entertained a good-humored affection, was in His heaven, and all was again well with Mr. Durant's world.

Curious how this renewed peace sharpened his enjoyment of the accustomed things about him. He looked back at the rubber works, which he had just left for the day, and nodded approvingly at the solid red pile, at the six neat stories rising impressively into the darkness. You would go far, he thought, before you would find a more up-and-coming outfit, and there welled in him a pleasing, proprietary sense of being a part of it.

He gazed amiably down Center Street, noting how restfully the lights glowed. Even the wet, dented pavement, spotted with thick puddles, fed his pleasure by reflecting the discreet radiance above it. And to complete his comfort, the car for which he was waiting, admirably on time, swung into view far down the track. He thought, with a sort of jovial tenderness, of what it would bear him to; of his dinner—it was fish-chowder night—of his children, of his wife, in the order named. Then he turned his kindly attention to the girl who stood near him, obviously awaiting the Center Street car, too. He was delighted to feel a sharp interest in her. He regarded it as being distinctly creditable to himself that he could take a healthy notice of such matters once more. Twenty years younger—that's what he felt.

Rather shabby, she was, in her rough coat with its shagginess rubbed off here and there. But there was a something in the way her cheaply smart turban was jammed over her eyes, in the way her thin young figure moved under the loose coat. Mr. Durant pointed his tongue, and moved it delicately along his cool, smooth upper lip.

The car approached, clanged to a stop before them. Mr. Durant stepped gallantly aside to let the girl get in first. He did not help her to enter, but the solicitous way in which he superintended the process gave all the effect of his having actually assisted her.

Her tight little skirt slipped up over her thin, pretty legs as she took the high step. There was a run in one of her flimsy silk stockings. She was doubtless unconscious of it; it was well back toward the seam, extending, probably from her garter, half-way down the calf. Mr. Durant had an odd desire to catch his thumb-nail in the present end of the run, and to draw it on down until the slim line of the dropped stitches reached to the top of her low shoe. An indulgent smile at his whimsy played about his mouth, broadening to a grin of affable evening greeting for the conductor, as he entered the car and paid his fare.

The girl sat down somewhere far up at the front. Mr. Durant found a desirable seat toward the rear, and craned his neck to see her. He could catch a glimpse of a fold of her turban and a bit of her frankly rouged cheek, but only at a cost of holding his head in a strained, and presently painful, position. So, warmed by the assurance that there would always be others, he let her go, and settled himself restfully. He had a ride of twenty minutes or so before him. He allowed his head to fall gently back, to let his eyelids droop, and gave himself to his thoughts. Now that the thing was comfortably over and done with, he could think

15

of it easily, almost laughingly. Last week, now, and even part of the week before, he had had to try with all his strength to force it back every time it wrenched itself into his mind. It had positively affected his sleep. Even though he was shielded by his newly acquired amused attitude, Mr. Durant felt indignation flood within him when he recalled those restless nights.

He had met Rose for the first time about three months before. She had been sent up to his office to take some letters for him. Mr. Durant was assistant manager of the rubber company's credit department; his wife was wont to refer to him as one of the officers of the company, and, though she often spoke thus of him to people in his presence, he never troubled to go more fully into detail about his position. He rated a room, a desk, and a telephone to himself; but not a stenographer. When he wanted to give dictation or to have some letters typewritten, he telephoned around to the various other offices until he found a girl who was not busy with her own work. That was how Rose had come to him.

She was not a pretty girl. Distinctly, no. But there was a rather sweet fragility about her, and an almost desperate timidity that Mr. Durant had once found engaging, but that he now thought of with a prickling irritation. She was twenty, and the glamour of youth was around her. When she bent over her work, her back showing white through her sleazy blouse, her clean hair coiled smoothly on her thin neck, her straight, childish legs crossed at the knee to support her pad, she had an undeniable appeal.

But not pretty—no. Her hair wasn't the kind that went up well, her eyelashes and lips were too pale, she hadn't much knack about choosing and wearing her cheap clothes. Mr. Durant, in reviewing the thing, felt a surprise that she should ever have attracted him. But it was a tolerant surprise, not an impatient one. Already he looked back on himself as being just a big boy in the whole affair.

It did not occur to him to feel even a flicker of astonishment that Rose should have responded so eagerly to him, an immovably married man of forty-nine. He never thought of himself in that way. He used to tell Rose, laughingly, that he was old enough to be her father, but neither of them ever really believed it. He regarded her affection for him as the most natural thing in the world—there she was, coming from a much smaller town, never the sort of girl to have had admirers; naturally, she was dazzled at the attentions of a man who, as Mr. Durant put it, was approaching the prime. He had been charmed with the idea of there having been no other men in her life; but lately, far from feeling flattered at being the first and only one, he had come to regard it as her having taken a sly advantage of him, to put him in that position.

It had all been surprisingly easy. Mr. Durant knew it

would be almost from the first time he saw her. That did not lessen its interest in his eyes. Obstacles discouraged him, rather than led him on. Elimination of bother was the main thing.

Rose was not a coquettish girl. She had that curious directness that some very timid people possess. There were her scruples, of course, but Mr. Durant readily reasoned them away. Not that he was a master of technique, either. He had had some experiences, probably a third as many as he habitually thought of himself as having been through, but none that taught him much of the delicate shadings of wooing. But then, Rose's simplicity asked exceedingly little.

She was never one to demand much of him, anyway. She never thought of stirring up any trouble between him and his wife, never beseeched him to leave his family and go away with her, even for a day. Mr. Durant valued her for that. It did away with a lot of probable fussing.

It was amazing how free they were, how little lying there was to do. They stayed in the office after hours—Mr. Durant found many letters that must be dictated. No one thought anything of that. Rose was busy most of the day, and it was only considerate that Mr. Durant should not break in on her employer's time, only natural that he should want so good a stenographer as she was to attend to his correspondence.

Rose's only relative, a married sister, lived in another town. The girl roomed with an acquaintance named Ruby, also employed at the rubber works, and Ruby, who was much taken up with her own affairs of the emotions, never appeared to think it strange if Rose was late to dinner, or missed the meal entirely. Mr. Durant readily explained to his wife that he was detained by a rush of business. It only increased his importance, to her, and spurred her on to devising especially pleasing dishes, and solicitously keeping them hot for his return. Sometimes, important in their guilt, Rose and he put out the light in the little office and locked the door, to trick the other employees into thinking that they had long ago gone home. But no one ever so much as rattled the door-knob, seeking admission.

It was all so simple that Mr. Durant never thought of it as anything outside the usual order of things. His interest in Rose did not blunt his appreciation of chance pretty ankles or provocative glances. It was an entanglement of the most restful, comfortable nature. It even held a sort of homelike quality, for him.

And then everything had to go and get spoiled. "Wouldn't you know?" Mr. Durant asked himself, with deep bitterness.

Ten days before, Rose had come weeping to his office. She had the sense to wait till after hours, for a wonder, but anybody might have walked in and seen her blubbering there; Mr. Durant felt it to be due only to the efficient management of his personal God that no one had. She wept, as he sweepingly put it, all over the place. The color left her cheeks and collected damply in her nose, and rims of vivid pink grew around her pale eyelashes. Even her hair became affected; it came away from the pins, and stray ends of it wandered limply over her neck. Mr. Durant hated to look at her, could not bring himself to touch her.

All his energies were expended in urging her for God's sake to keep quiet; he did not ask her what was the matter. But it came out, between bursts of unpleasant-sounding sobs. She was "in trouble." Neither then nor in the succeeding days did she and Mr. Durant ever use any less delicate phrase to describe her condition. Even in their thoughts, they referred to it that way.

She had suspected it, she said, for some time, but she hadn't wanted to bother him about it until she was absolutely sure. "Didn't want to bother me!" thought Mr. Durant.

Naturally, he was furious. Innocence is a desirable thing, a dainty thing, an appealing thing, in its place; but carried too far, it is merely ridiculous. Mr. Durant wished to God that he had never seen Rose. He explained this desire to her.

But that was no way to get things done. As he had often jovially remarked to his friends, he knew "a thing or

two." Cases like this could be what people of the world
called "fixed up"—New York society women, he understood, thought virtually nothing of it. This one must be,
too, that was all. He got Rose to go home, telling her not
to worry, he would see that everything was all right. The
main thing was to get her out of sight, with that nose and
those eyes.

But knowing a thing or two and putting the knowledge into practice turned out to be vastly different things.
Mr. Durant did not know whom to seek for information.
He pictured himself inquiring of his intimates if they
could tell him of "someone that this girl he had heard
about could go to." He could hear his voice uttering the
words, could hear the nervous laugh that would accompany them, the terrible flatness of them as they left his lips.
To confide in one person would be confiding in at least one
too many. It was a progressing town, but still small enough
for gossip to travel like a typhoon. Not that he thought for
a moment that his wife would believe any such thing, if it
reached her; but where would be the sense in troubling
her?

Mr. Durant grew pale and jumpy over the thing as the
days went by. His wife worried herself into one of her sick
spells over his petulant refusals of second helpings. There
daily arose in him an increasing anger that he should be
drawn into coniving to find a way to break the law of his

country—probably the law of every country in the world. Certainly of every decent, Christian place.

It was Ruby, finally, who got them out of it. When Rose confessed to him that she had broken down and told Ruby, his rage leaped higher than any words. Ruby was secretary to the vice-president of the rubber company. It would be pretty, wouldn't it, if she let it out? He had lain wide-eyed beside his wife all that night through. He shuddered at the thought of chance meetings with Ruby in the hall.

But Ruby had made it delightfully simple, when they did meet. There were no reproachful looks, no cold turnings away of the head. She had given him her usual smiling "good-morning," and added a little upward glance, mischievous, understanding, with just the least hint of admiration in it. There was a sense of intimacy, of a shared secret binding them cozily together. A fine girl, that Ruby!

Ruby had managed it all without any fuss. Mr. Durant was not directly concerned in the planning. He heard of it only through Rose, on the infrequent occasions when he had had to see her. Ruby knew, through some indistinct friend of hers, of "a woman." It would be twenty-five dollars. Mr. Durant had gallantly insisted upon giving Rose the money. She had started to sniffle about taking it, but he had finally prevailed. Not that he couldn't have used the twenty-five very nicely himself, just then, with Junior's teeth, and all!

Well, it was all over now. The invaluable Ruby had gone with Rose to "the woman"; had that very afternoon taken her to the station and put her on a train for her sister's. She had even thought of wiring the sister beforehand that Rose had had influenza and must have a rest.

Mr. Durant had urged Rose to look on it as just a little vacation. He promised, moreover, to put in a good word for her whenever she wanted her job back. But Rose had gone pink about the nose again at the thought. She had sobbed her rasping sobs, then had raised her face from her stringy handkerchief and said, with an entirely foreign firmness, that she never wanted to see the rubber works or Ruby or Mr. Durant again. He had laughed indulgently, had made himself pat her thin back. In his relief at the outcome of things, he could be generous to the pettish.

He chuckled inaudibly, as he reviewed that last scene. "I suppose she thought she'd make me sore, saying she was never coming back," he told himself. "I suppose I was supposed to get down on my knees and coax her."

It was fine to dwell on the surety that it was all done with. Mr. Durant had somewhere picked up a phrase that seemed ideally suited to the occasion. It was to him an admirably dashing expression. There was something English about it; it was the sort of thing you would expect to hear used by men who wore spats and swung canes without self-consciousness. He employed it now, with satisfaction.

"Well, that's that," he said to himself. He was not sure that he didn't say it aloud.

The car slowed, and the girl in the rough coat came down toward the door. She was jolted against Mr. Durant—he would have sworn she did it purposely—uttered a word of laughing apology, gave him what he interpreted as an inviting glance. He half rose to follow her, then sank back again. After all, it was a wet night, and his corner was five blocks farther on. Again there came over him the cozy assurance that there would always be others.

In high humor, he left the car at his street, and walked in the direction of his house. It was a mean night, but the insinuating cold and the black rain only made more graphic his picture of the warm, bright house, the great dish of steaming fish chowder, the well-behaved children and wife that awaited him. He walked rather slowly to make them seem all the better for the wait, humming a little on his way down the neat sidewalk, past the solid, reputably shabby houses.

Two girls ran past him, holding their hands over their heads to protect their hats from the wet. He enjoyed the click of their heels on the pavement, their little bursts of breathless laughter, their arms upraised in a position that brought out all the clean lines of their bodies. He knew who they were—they lived three doors down from him, in the house with the lamp-post in front of it. He had often lingeringly noticed their fresh prettiness. He hurried, so that he might see them run up the steps, their narrow skirts sliding up over their legs. His mind went back to the girl with the run in her stocking, and amusing thoughts filled him as he entered his own house.

His children rushed, clamoring, to meet him, as he unlocked the door. There was something exciting going on, for Junior and Charlotte were usually too careful-mannered to cause people discomfort by rushing and babbling. They were nice, sensible children, good at their lessons, and punctilious about brushing their teeth, speaking the truth, and avoiding playmates who used bad words. Junior would be the very picture of his father, when they got the bands off his teeth, and little Charlotte strongly resembled her mother. Friends often commented on what a nice arrangement it was.

Mr. Durant smiled good-naturedly through their racket, carefully hanging up his coat and hat. There was even pleasure for him in the arrangement of his apparel on the cool, shiny knob of the hatrack. Everything was pleasant, tonight. Even the children's noise couldn't irritate him.

Eventually he discovered the cause of the commotion. It was a little stray dog that had come to the back door. They were out in the kitchen helping Freda, and Charlotte thought she heard something scratching, and Freda said nonsense, but Charlotte went to the door, anyway, and there was this little dog, trying to get in out of the wet. Mother helped them give it a bath, and Freda fed it, and now it was in the living-room. Oh, Father, couldn't they keep it, please, couldn't they, couldn't they, please, Father, couldn't they? It didn't have any collar on—it didn't belong to anybody. Mother said all right, if he said so, and Freda liked it fine.

Mr. Durant still smiled his gentle smile. "We'll see," he said.

The children looked disappointed, but not despondent. They would have liked more enthusiasm, but "we'll see," they knew by experience, meant a leaning in the right direction.

Mr. Durant proceeded to the living-room, to inspect the visitor. It was not a beauty. All too obviously, it was the living souvenir of a mother who had never been able to say no. It was a rather stocky little beast with shaggy white hair and occasional, rakishly placed patches of black. There was a suggestion of Sealyham terrier about it, but that was almost blotted out by hosts of reminiscences of other breeds. It looked, on the whole, like a composite photograph of Popular Dogs. But you could tell at a glance that it had a way with it. Scepters have been tossed aside for that.

It lay, now, by the fire, waving its tragically long tail

wistfully, its eyes pleading with Mr. Durant to give it a fair trial. The children had told it to lie down there, and so it did not move. That was something it could do toward repaying them.

Mr. Durant warmed to it. He did not dislike dogs, and he somewhat fancied the picture of himself as a soft-hearted fellow who extended shelter to friendless animals. He bent, and held out a hand to it.

"Well, sir," he said, genially. "Come here, good fellow."

The dog ran to him, wriggling ecstatically. It covered his cold hand with joyous, though respectful kisses, then laid its warm, heavy head on his palm. "You are beyond a doubt the greatest man in America," it told him with its eyes.

Mr. Durant enjoyed appreciation and gratitude. He patted the dog graciously.

"Well, sir, how'd you like to board with us?" he said. "I guess you can plan to settle down." Charlotte squeezed Junior's arm wildly. Neither of them, though, thought it best to crowd their good fortune by making any immediate comment on it.

Mrs. Durant entered from the kitchen, flushed with her final attentions to the chowder. There was a worried line between her eyes. Part of the worry was due to the dinner, and part to the disturbing entrance of the little

dog into the family life. Anything not previously included in her day's schedule threw Mrs. Durant into a
state resembling that of one convalescing from shell-
shock. Her hands jerked nervously, beginning gestures
that they never finished.

Relief smoothed her face when she saw her husband
patting the dog. The children, always at ease with her,
broke their silence and jumped about her, shrieking that
Father said it might stay.

"There, now—didn't I tell you what a dear, good
father you had?" she said in the tone parents employ when
they have happened to guess right. "That's fine, Father.
With that big yard and all, I think we'll make out all right.
She really seems to be an awfully good little——"

Mr. Durant's hand stopped sharply in its patting motions, as if the dog's neck had become red-hot to his touch.
He rose, and looked at his wife as at a stranger who had
suddenly begun to act queerly.

"She?" he said. He had always been notable for getting much into a single word.

Mrs. Durant's hand jerked.

"Well—" she began, as if about to plunge into a
recital of extenuating circumstances. "Well—yes," she
concluded.

The children and the dog looked nervously at Mr.
Durant, sensing something wrong. Charlotte whimpered
wordlessly.

"Quiet!" said her father, turning suddenly upon her. "I said it could stay, didn't I? Did you ever know Father to break a promise?"

Charlotte politely murmured, "No, Father," but conviction was not hers. She was a philosophical child, though, and she decided to leave the whole issue to God, occasionally jogging Him up a bit with prayer.

Mr. Durant frowned at his wife, and jerked his head backward. This indicated that he wished to have a few words with her, for adults only, in the privacy of the little room across the hall, known as "Father's den."

He had directed the decoration of his den, had seen that it had been made a regular he-man's room. Red paper covered its walls, up to the wooden rack on which were displayed ornamental steins, of domestic manufacture. Empty pipe-racks—Mr. Durant smoked cigars—were nailed against the red paper at frequent intervals. On one wall was an indifferent reproduction of Gibson's pen-and-ink drawing, "The Eternal Question," and on another, a water-colored photograph of "September Morn," the tints running a bit beyond the edges of the figure as if the artist's emotions had rendered his hand unsteady. Over the table was carefully flung a tanned and fringed hide with the profile of an unknown Indian maiden painted on it, and the rocking-chair held a leather pillow bearing the picture, done by pyrography, of a girl in a fencing costume which set off her distressingly dated figure.

Mr. Durant's books were lined up behind the glass of the bookcase. They were all tall, thick books, brightly bound, and they justified his pride in their showing. They were mostly accounts of favorites of the French court, with a few volumes on the private life of the ex-Kaiser, and the intrigues of the Russian throne-room. Mrs. Durant, who never had time to get around to reading, regarded them with awe, and thought of her husband as one of the country's leading bibliophiles. There were books, too, in the living-room, but those she had inherited or been given. She had arranged a few on the living-room table; they looked as if they had been placed there by the Gideons.

Mr. Durant thought of himself as an indefatigable collector and an insatiable reader. But he was always disappointed in his books, after he had sent for them. They were never so good as the advertisements had led him to believe.

Into his den Mr. Durant preceded his wife, and faced her, still frowning. His calm was not shattered, but it was punctured. Something annoying always had to go and come up. Wouldn't you know?

"Now you know perfectly well, Fan, we can't have that dog around," he told her. He used the low voice reserved for underwear and bathroom articles and kindred risqué topics. There was all the kindness in his tones that one has for a backward child, but a Gibraltar-like firmness was behind it. "You must be crazy to even think we could for a minute. Why, I wouldn't give a she-dog house-room,

not for any amount of money. It's disgusting, that's what
it is."

"Well, but, Father——" began Mrs. Durant, her
hands again going off into their convulsions.

"Disgusting," he repeated. "You have a female
around, and you know what happens. All the males in the
neighborhood will be running after her. First thing you
know, she'd be having puppies—and the way they look
after they've had them, and all! That would be nice for the
children to see, wouldn't it? I should think you'd think of
the children, Fan. No, sir, there'll be nothing like that
around here, not while I know it. Disgusting!"

"But the children," she said. "They'll be just
simply——"

"Now you just leave all that to me," he reassured her.
"I told them the dog could stay, and I've never broken a
promise yet, have I? Here's what I'll do—I'll wait till
they're asleep, and then I'll just take this little dog and put
it out. Then, in the morning, you can tell them it ran away
during the night, see?"

She nodded. Her husband patted her shoulder, in its
crapey-smelling black silk. His peace with the world was
once more intact, restored by this simple solution of the
little difficulty. Again his mind wrapped itself in the
knowledge that everything was all fixed, all ready for a
nice, fresh start. His arm was still about his wife's shoulder
as they went on in to dinner.

Just A Little One

Just A
Little One

I like this place, Fred. This is a nice place.
How did you ever find it? I think you're perfectly marvelous, discovering a speakeasy up here in the Forties. And
they let you right in, without asking you a single question.
I bet you could get into the subway without using anybody's name. Couldn't you, Fred?

Oh, I like this place better and better, now that my
eyes are getting accustomed to it. You mustn't let them tell
you this lighting system is original with them, Fred; they

got the idea from the Mammoth Cave. This is you sitting next to me, isn't it? Oh, you can't fool me. I'd know that knee anywhere.

You know what I like about this place? It's got atmosphere. That's what it's got. If you would ask the waiter to bring a fairly sharp knife, I could cut off a nice little block of the atmosphere, to take home with me. It would be interesting to have for my memory book. I'm going to start keeping a memory book tomorrow. Don't let me forget.

Why, I don't know, Fred—what are you going to have? Then I guess I'll have a highball, too; please, just a little one. Is it really real Scotch? Well, that will be a new experience for me. You ought to see the Scotch I've got home in my cupboard; at least it was in the cupboard this morning—it's probably eaten its way out by now. I got it for my birthday. The only other thing I got was a year older.

This is a nice highball, isn't it? Well, well, well, to think of me having real Scotch; I'm out of the bush leagues at last. Are you really going to have one? Well, I shouldn't like to see you drinking all by yourself, Fred. Solitary drinking is what causes half the crime in the country. That's what's responsible for the failure of prohibition. But please, Fred, tell him to make mine just a little one. Make it awfully weak; just cambric Scotch.

It will be nice to see the effect of veritable whisky

upon one who has been accustomed only to the simpler forms of entertainment. You'll like that, Fred. You'll stay by me if anything happens, won't you? I don't think there will be anything spectacular, but I want to ask you one thing, just in case. Don't let me take any horses home with me. It doesn't matter so much about stray dogs and kittens, but elevator boys get awfully stuffy when you try to bring in a horse. You might just as well know that about me now, Fred. You can always tell that the crash is coming when I start getting tender about Our Dumb Friends. Three highballs, and I think I'm St. Francis of Assisi.

But I don't believe anything is going to happen to me on these. That's because they're made of real stuff. That's what the difference is. This just makes you feel fine. Oh, I feel swell, Fred. You do too, don't you? I knew you did, because you look better. I love that tie you have on. Oh, did Edith give it to you? Ah, wasn't that nice of her? You know, Fred, most people are really awfully nice. There are darn few that aren't pretty fine at heart. You've got a beautiful heart, Fred. You'd be the first person I'd go to if I were in trouble. I guess you are just about the best friend I've got in the world. But I worry about you, Fred. I do so, too. I don't think you take enough care of yourself. You ought to take care of yourself for your friends' sake. You oughtn't to drink all this terrible stuff that's around; you owe it to your friends to be careful. You don't mind

my talking to you like this, do you? You see, dear, it's
because I'm your friend that I hate to see you not taking
care of yourself. It hurts me to see you batting around the
way you've been doing. You ought to stick to this place,
where they have real Scotch that can't do you any harm.
Oh, darling, do you really think I ought to? Well, you tell
him just a little bit of a one. Tell him, sweet.

Do you come here often, Fred? I shouldn't worry
about you so much if I knew you were in a safe place like
this. Oh, is this where you were Thursday night? I see.
Why, no, it didn't make a bit of difference, only you told
me to call you up, and like a fool I broke a date I had, just
because I thought I was going to see you. I just sort of
naturally thought so, when you said to call you up. Oh,
good Lord, don't make all that fuss about it. It really didn't
make the slightest difference. It just didn't seem a very
friendly way to behave, that's all. I don't know—I'd been
believing we were such good friends. I'm an awful idiot
about people, Fred. There aren't many who are really your
friend at heart. Practically anybody would play you dirt for
a nickel. Oh, yes, they would.

Was Edith here with you, Thursday night? This place
must be very becoming to her. Next to being in a coal
mine, I can't think of anywhere she could go that the light
would be more flattering to that pan of hers. Do you really
know a lot of people that say she's good-looking? You must

have a wide acquaintance among the astigmatic, haven't you, Freddie, dear? Why, I'm not being any way at all—it's simply one of those things, either you can see it or you can't. Now to me, Edith looks like something that would eat her young. Dresses well? *Edith* dresses well? Are you trying to kid me, Fred, at my age? You mean you mean it? Oh, my God. You mean those clothes of hers are *intentional?* My heavens, I always thought she was on her way out of a burning building.

Well, we live and learn. Edith dresses well! Edith's got good taste! Yes, she's got sweet taste in neckties. I don't suppose I ought to say it about such a dear friend of yours, Fred, but she is the lousiest necktie-picker-out I ever saw. I never saw anything could touch that thing you have around your neck. All right, suppose I did say I liked it. I just said that because I felt sorry for you. I'd feel sorry for anybody with a thing like that on. I just wanted to try to make you feel good, because I thought you were my friend. My friend! I haven't got a friend in the world. Do you know that, Fred? Not one single friend in this world.

All right, what do you care if I'm crying? I can cry if I want to, can't I? I guess you'd cry, too, if you didn't have a friend in the world. Is my face very bad? I suppose that damned mascara has run all over it. I've got to give up using mascara, Fred; life's too sad. Isn't life terrible? Oh, my God, isn't life awful? Ah, don't cry, Fred. Please don't.

Don't you care, baby. Life's terrible, but don't you care. You've got friends. I'm the one that hasn't got any friends. I am so. No, it's me. I'm the one.

I don't think another drink would make me feel any better. I don't know whether I want to feel any better. What's the sense of feeling good, when life's so terrible? Oh, all right, then. But please tell him just a little one, if it isn't too much trouble. I don't want to stay here much longer. I don't like this place. It's all dark and stuffy. It's the kind of place Edith would be crazy about—that's all I can say about this place. I know I oughtn't to talk about your best friend, Fred, but that's a terrible woman. That woman is the louse of this world. It makes me feel just awful that you trust that woman, Fred. I hate to see any-body play you dirt. I'd hate to see you get hurt. That's what makes me feel so terrible. That's why I'm getting mascara all over my face. No, please don't, Fred. You mustn't hold my hand. It wouldn't be fair to Edith. We've got to play fair with the big louse. After all, she's your best friend, isn't she?

Honestly? Do you honestly mean it, Fred? Yes, but how could I help thinking so, when you're with her all the time—when you bring her here every night in the week? Really, only Thursday? Oh, I know—I know how those things are. You simply can't help it, when you get stuck with a person that way. Lord, I'm glad you realize what an

awful thing that woman is. I was worried about it, Fred.
It's because I'm your friend. Why, of course I am, darling.
You know I am. Oh, that's just silly, Freddie. You've got
heaps of friends. Only you'll never find a better friend than
I am. No, I know that. I know I'll never find a better friend
than you are to me. Just give me back my hand a second,
till I get this damned mascara out of my eye.

Yes, I think we ought to, honey. I think we ought to
have a little drink, on account of our being friends. Just a
little one, because it's real Scotch, and we're real friends.
After all, friends are the greatest things in the world, aren't
they, Fred? Gee, it makes you feel good to know you have
a friend. I feel great, don't you, dear? And you look great,
too. I'm proud to have you for a friend. Do you realize,
Fred, what a rare thing a friend is, when you think of all
the terrible people there are in this world? Animals are
much better than people. God, I love animals. That's what
I like about you, Fred. You're so fond of animals.

Look, I'll tell you what let's do, after we've had just
a little highball. Let's go out and pick up a lot of stray dogs.
I never had enough dogs in my life, did you? We ought to
have more dogs. And maybe there'd be some cats around,
if we looked. And a horse. I've never had one single horse,
Fred. Isn't that rotten? Not one single horse. Ah, I'd like
a nice old cab-horse, Fred. Wouldn't you? I'd like to take
care of it and comb its hair. and everything. Ah, don't be

stuffy about it, Fred, please don't. I need a horse, honestly I do. Wouldn't you like one? It would be so sweet and kind. Let's have a drink and then let's you and I go out and get a horsie, Freddie—just a little one, darling, just a little one.

New York to Detroit

New York to Detroit

"All ready with Detroit," said the telephone operator.

"Hello," said the girl in New York.

"Hello?" said the young man in Detroit.

"Oh, Jack!" she said. "Oh, darling, it's so wonderful to hear you. You don't know how much I——"

"Hello?" he said.

"Ah, can't you hear me?" she said. "Why, I can hear you just as if you were right beside me. Is this any better, dear? Can you hear me now?"

"Who did you want to speak to?" he said.

"You, Jack!" she said. "You, you. This is Jean, darling. Oh, please try to hear me. This is Jean."

"Who?" he said.

"Jean," she said. "Ah, don't you know my voice? It's Jean, dear. Jean."

"Oh, hello, there," he said. "Well. Well, for heaven's sake. How are you?"

"I'm all right," she said. "Oh, I'm not, either, darling. I—oh, it's just terrible. I can't stand it any more. Aren't you coming back? Please, when are you coming back? You don't know how awful it is, without you. It's been such a long time, dear—you said it would be just four or five days, and it's nearly three weeks. It's like years and years. Oh, it's been so awful, sweetheart—it's just——"

"Hey, I'm terribly sorry," he said, "but I can't hear one damn thing you're saying. Can't you talk louder, or something?"

"I'll try, I'll try," she said. "Is this better? Now can you hear?"

"Yeah, now I can, a little," he said. "Don't talk so fast, will you? What did you say, before?"

"I said it's just awful without you," she said. "It's such a long time, dear. And I haven't had a word from you. I—oh, I've just been nearly crazy, Jack. Never even a post-card, dearest, or a——"

"Honestly, I haven't had a second," he said. "I've been working like a fool. God, I've been rushed."

"Ah, have you?" she said. "I'm sorry, dear. I've been silly. But it was just—oh, it was just hell, never hearing a word. I thought maybe you'd telephone to say good-night, sometimes,—you know, the way you used to, when you were away."

"Why, I was going to, a lot of times," he said, "but I thought you'd probably be out, or something."

"I haven't been out," she said. "I've been staying here, all by myself. It's—it's sort of better, that way. I don't want to see people. Everybody says, 'When's Jack coming back?' and 'What do you hear from Jack?' and I'm afraid I'll cry in front of them. Darling, it hurts so terribly when they ask me about you, and I have to say I don't——"

"This is the damnedest, lousiest connection I ever saw in my life," he said. "What hurts? What's the matter?"

"I said, it hurts so terribly when people ask me about you," she said, "and I have to say—Oh, never mind. Never mind. How are you, dear? Tell me how you are."

"Oh, pretty good," he said. "Tired as the devil. You all right?"

"Jack, I—that's what I wanted to tell you," she said. "I'm terribly worried. I'm nearly out of my mind. Oh, what will I do, dear, what are we going to do? Oh, Jack, Jack, darling!"

"Hey, how can I hear you when you mumble like that?" he said. "Can't you talk louder? Talk right into the what-you-call-it."

"I can't scream it over the telephone!" she said. "Haven't you any sense? Don't you know what I'm telling you? Don't you know? Don't you know?"

"I give up," he said. "First you mumble, and then you yell. Look, this doesn't make sense. I can't hear anything, with this rotten connection. Why don't you write me a letter, in the morning? Do that, why don't you? And I'll write you one. See?"

"Jack, listen, listen!" she said. "You listen to me! I've got to talk to you. I tell you I'm nearly crazy. Please, dearest, hear what I'm saying. Jack, I——"

"Just a minute," he said. "Someone's knocking at the door. *Come in. Well, for cryin' out loud! Come on in, bums. Hang your coats up on the floor, and sit down. The Scotch is in the closet, and there's ice in that pitcher. Make yourselves at home—act like you were in a regular bar. Be with you right away.* Hey, listen, there's a lot of crazy Indians just come in here, and I can't hear myself think. You go ahead and write me a letter tomorrow. Will you?"

"Write you a letter!" she said. "Oh, God, don't you think I'd have written you before, if I'd known where to reach you? I didn't even know that, till they told me at your office today. I got so——"

48

"Oh, yeah, did they?" he said. "I thought I—*Ah, pipe down, will you? Give a guy a chance. This is an expensive talk going on here.* Say, look, this must be costing you a million dollars. You oughtn't to do this."

"What do you think I care about that?" she said. "I'll die if I don't talk to you. I tell you I'll die, Jack. Sweetheart, what is it? Don't you want to talk to me? Tell me what makes you this way. Is it—don't you really like me any more? Is that it? Don't you, Jack?"

"Hell, I can't hear," he said. "Don't what?"

"Please," she said. "Please, please. Please, Jack, listen. When are you coming back, darling? I need you so. I need you so terribly. When are you coming back?"

"Why, that's the thing," he said. "That's what I was going to write you about tomorrow. *Come on, now, how about shutting up just for a minute? A joke's a joke.* Hello. Hear me all right? Why, you see, the way things came out today, it looks a little bit like I'd have to go on to Chicago for a while. Looks like a pretty big thing, and it won't mean a very long time, I don't believe. Looks as if I'd be going out there next week, I guess."

"Jack, no!" she said. "Oh, don't do that! You can't do that. You can't leave me alone like this. I've got to see you, dearest, I've got to. You've got to come back, or I've got to come there to you. I can't go through this. Jack, I can't, I——"

"Look, we better say good-night now," he said. "No

49

use trying to make out what you say, when you talk all over yourself like that. And there's so much racket here—*Hey, can the harmony, will you? God, it's terrible. Want me to be thrown out of here?* You go get a good night's sleep, and I'll write you all about it tomorrow."

"Listen!" she said. "Jack, don't go 'way! Help me, darling. Say something to help me through tonight. Say you love me, for God's sake say you still love me. Say it. Say it."

"Ah, I can't talk," he said. "This is fierce. I'll write you first thing in the morning. 'Bye. Thanks for calling up."

"Jack!" she said. "Jack, don't go. Jack, wait a minute. I've got to talk to you. I'll talk quietly. I won't cry. I'll talk so you can hear me. Please, dear, please——"

"All through with Detroit?" said the operator.

"No!" she said. "No, no, no! Get him, get him back again right away! Get him back. No, never mind. Never mind it now. Never——"

The Wonderful Old Gentleman

The Wonderful Old Gentleman

If the Bains had striven for years, they could have been no more successful in making their living-room into a small but admirably complete museum of objects suggesting strain, discomfort, or the tomb. Yet they had never even tried for the effect. Some of the articles that the room contained were wedding-presents; some had been put in from time to time as substitutes as their predecessors succumbed to age and wear; a few had been brought along by the Old Gentleman when he had come to make his home with the Bains some five years before.

It was curious how perfectly they all fitted into the general scheme. It was as if they had all been selected by a single enthusiast to whom time was but little object, so long as he could achieve the eventual result of transforming the Bain living-room into a home chamber of horrors, modified a bit for family use.

It was a high-ceilinged room, with heavy, dark old woodwork, that brought long and unavoidable thoughts of silver handles and weaving worms. The paper was the color of stale mustard. Its design, once a dashing affair of a darker tone splashed with twinkling gold, had faded into lines and smears that resolved themselves, before the eyes of the sensitive, into hordes of battered heads and tortured profiles, some eyeless, some with clotted gashes for mouths.

The furniture was dark and cumbersome and subject to painful creakings—sudden, sharp creaks that seemed to be wrung from its brave silence only when it could bear no more. A close, earthy smell came from its dulled tapestry cushions, and try as Mrs. Bain might, furry gray dust accumulated in the crevices.

The center-table was upheld by the perpetually strained arms of three carved figures, insistently female to the waist, then trailing discreetly off into a confusion of scrolls and scales. Upon it rested a row of blameless books, kept in place at the ends by the straining shoulder-muscles of two bronze-colored plaster elephants, forever pushing at their tedious toil.

On the heavily carved mantel was a gayly colored figure of a curly-headed peasant boy, ingeniously made so that he sat on the shelf and dangled one leg over. He was in the eternal act of removing a thorn from his chubby foot, his round face realistically wrinkled with the cruel pain. Just above him hung a steel-engraving of a chariot-race, the dust flying, the chariots careening wildly, the drivers ferociously lashing their maddened horses, the horses themselves caught by the artist the moment before their hearts burst, and they dropped in their traces.

The opposite wall was devoted to the religious in art; a steel-engraving of the Crucifixion, lavish of ghastly detail; a sepia-print of the martyrdom of Saint Sebastian, the cords cutting deep into the arms writhing from the stake, arrows bristling in the thick, soft-looking body; a water-color copy of a "Mother of Sorrows," the agonized eyes raised to a cold heaven, great, bitter tears forever on the wan cheeks, paler for the grave-like draperies that wrapped the head.

Beneath the windows hung a painting in oil of two lost sheep, huddled hopelessly together in the midst of a wild blizzard. This was one of the Old Gentleman's contributions to the room. Mrs. Bain was wont to observe of it that the frame was worth she didn't know how much.

The wall-space beside the door was reserved for a bit of modern art that had once caught Mr. Bain's eye in a stationer's window—a colored print, showing a railroad-crossing, with a train flying relentlessly toward it, and a low, red automobile trying to dash across the track before the iron terror shattered it into eternity. Nervous visitors who were given chairs facing this scene usually made opportunity to change their seats before they could give their whole minds to the conversation.

The ornaments, placed with careful casualness on the table and the upright piano, included a small gilt lion of Lucerne, a little, chipped, plaster Laocoön, and a savage china kitten eternally about to pounce upon a plump and helpless china mouse. This last had been one of the Old Gentleman's own wedding-gifts. Mrs. Bain explained, in tones low with awe, that it was very old.

The ash-receivers, of Japanese manufacture, were in the form of grotesque heads, tufted with bits of gray human hair, and given bulging, dead, glassy eyes and mouths stretched into great gapes, into which those who had the heart for it might flick their ashes. Thus the smallest details of the room kept loyally to the spirit of the thing, and carried on the effect.

But the three people now sitting in the Bains' living-room were not in the least oppressed by the decorative scheme. Two of them, Mr. and Mrs. Bain, not only had had twenty-eight years of the room to accustom them to it, but had been stanch admirers of it from the first. And no surroundings, however morbid, could close in on the aristocratic calm of Mrs. Bain's sister, Mrs. Whittaker.

She graciously patronized the very chair she now sat in, smiled kindly on the glass of cider she held in her hand. The Bains were poor, and Mrs. Whittaker had, as it is ingenuously called, married well, and none of them ever lost sight of these facts.

But Mrs. Whittaker's attitude of kindly tolerance was not confined to her less fortunate relatives. It extended to friends of her youth, working people, the arts, politics, the United States in general, and God, Who had always supplied her with the best of service. She could have given Him an excellent reference at any time.

The three people sat with a comfortable look of spending the evening. There was an air of expectancy about them, a not unpleasant little nervousness, as of those who wait for a curtain to rise. Mrs. Bain had brought in cider in the best tumblers, and had served some of her nut cookies in the plate painted by hand with clusters of cherries—the plate she had used for sandwiches when, several years ago, her card club had met at her house.

She had thought it over a little tonight, before she lifted out the cherry-plate, then quickly decided and resolutely heaped it with cookies. After all, it was an occasion—informal, perhaps, but still an occasion. The Old Gentleman was dying upstairs. At five o'clock that afternoon the doctor had said that it would be a surprise to him if the Old Gentleman lasted till the middle of the night—a big surprise, he had augmented.

There was no need for them to gather at the Old Gentleman's bedside. He would not have known any of them. In fact, he had not known them for almost a year, addressing them by wrong names and asking them grave, courteous questions about the health of husbands or wives or children who belonged to other branches of the family. But he was quite unconscious now.

Miss Chester, the nurse who had been with him since "this last stroke," as Mrs. Bain importantly called it, was entirely competent to attend and watch him. She had promised to call them if, in her tactful words, she saw any signs.

So the Old Gentleman's daughters and son-in-law waited in the warm living-room, and sipped their cider, and conversed in low, polite tones.

Mrs. Bain cried a little in pauses in the conversation. She had always cried easily and often. Yet, in spite of her years of practice, she did not do it well. Her eyelids grew pink and sticky, and her nose gave her no little trouble, necessitating almost constant sniffling. She sniffled loudly and conscientiously, and frequently removed her pince-nez to wipe her eyes with a crumpled handkerchief, gray with damp.

Mrs. Whittaker, too, bore a handkerchief, but she appeared to be holding it in waiting. She was dressed, in compliment to the occasion, in her black crêpe de Chine, and she had left her lapis-lazuli pin, her olivine bracelet, and her topaz and amethyst rings at home in her bureau drawer, retaining only her lorgnette on its gold chain, in case there should be any reading to be done.

Mrs. Whittaker's dress was always studiously suited to its occasion; thus, her bearing had always that calm that only the correctly attired may enjoy. She was an authority on where to place monograms on linen, how to announce engagements, and what to say in letters of condolence. The word "lady" figured largely in her conversation. Blood, she often predicted, would tell.

Mrs. Bain wore a rumpled white shirt waist and the old blue skirt she saved for "around the kitchen." There had been time to change, after she had telephoned the doctor's verdict to her sister, but she had not been quite sure whether it was the thing to do. She had thought that Mrs. Whittaker might expect her to display a little distraught untidiness at a time like this; might even go in for it in a mild way herself.

Now Mrs. Bain looked at her sister's elaborately

curled, painstakingly brown coiffure, and nervously patted her own straggling hair, gray at the front, with strands of almost lime-color in the little twist at the back. Her eyelids grew wet and sticky again, and she hung her glasses over one forefinger while she applied the damp handkerchief. After all, she reminded herself and the others, it was her poor father.

Oh, but it was really the best thing, Mrs. Whittaker explained in her gentle, patient voice.

"You wouldn't want to see father go on like this," she pointed out. Mr. Bain echoed her, as if struck with the idea. Mrs. Bain had nothing to reply to them. No, she wouldn't want to see the Old Gentleman go on like this.

Five years before, Mrs. Whittaker had decided that the Old Gentleman was getting too old to live alone, with only old Annie to cook for him and look after him. It was only a question of a little time before it "wouldn't have looked right," his living alone, when he had his children to take care of him. Mrs. Whittaker always stopped things before they got to the stage where they didn't look right. So he had come to live with the Bains.

Some of his furniture had been sold; a few things, such as his silver, his tall clock, and the Persian rug he had bought at the World's Fair, Mrs. Whittaker had found room for in her own house; and some he brought with him to the Bains'.

Mrs. Whittaker's house was much larger than her sister's, and she had three servants and no children. But, as she told her friends, she had held back and let Allie and Lewis have the Old Gentleman.

"You see," she explained, dropping her voice to the tones reserved for not very pretty subjects, "Allie and Lewis are—well, they haven't a great deal."

So it was gathered that the Old Gentleman would do big things for the Bains when he came to live with them. Not exactly by paying board—it is a little too much to ask your father to pay for his food and lodging, as if he were a stranger. But, as Mrs. Whittaker suggested, he could do a great deal in the way of buying needed things for the house and keeping everything going.

And the Old Gentleman did contribute to the Bain household. He bought an electric heater and an electric fan, new curtains, stormwindows, and light-fixtures, for his bedroom; and had a very nice little bathroom for his personal use made out of the small guest-room adjoining it.

He shopped for days until he found a coffee-cup large enough for his taste; he bought several large ash-trays, and a dozen extra-size bath-towels, that Mrs. Bain marked with his initials. And every Christmas and birthday he gave Mrs. Bain a round, new, shining ten-dollar gold piece. Of course, he presented gold pieces to Mrs. Whittaker, too, on like appropriate occasions. The Old Gentleman prided himself always on his fair-mindedness. He often said that he was not one to show any favoritism.

Mrs. Whittaker was Cordelia-like to her father during his declining years. She came to see him several times a month, bringing him jelly or potted hyacinths. Sometimes she sent her car and chauffeur for him, so that he might take an easy drive through the town, and Mrs. Bain might be afforded a chance to drop her cooking and accompany him. When she was away on trips with her husband, she almost never neglected to send him picture post-cards of various points of interest.

The Old Gentleman appreciated her affection, and took pride in her. He enjoyed being told that she was like him.

"That Hattie," he used to tell Mrs. Bain, "she's a fine woman—a fine woman."

As soon as she had heard that the Old Gentleman was dying Mrs. Whittaker had come right over, stopping only to change her dress and have her dinner. Her husband was away in the woods with some men, fishing. She explained to the Bains that there was no use in disturbing him—it would have been impossible for him to get back that night. As soon as—well, if anything happened she would telegraph him, and he could return in time for the funeral.

Mrs. Bain was sorry that he was away. She liked her ruddy, jovial, loud-voiced brother-in-law.

"It's too bad that Clint couldn't be here," she said, as she had said several times before. "He's so fond of cider," she added.

"Father," said Mrs. Whittaker, "was always very fond of Clint." Already the Old Gentleman had slipped into the past tense.

"Everybody likes Clint," Mr. Bain stated.

He was included in the "everybody." The last time he had failed in business, Clint had given him the clerical position he had since held over at the brush works. It was pretty generally understood that this had been brought about through Mrs. Whittaker's intervention, but still they were Clint's brush works, and it was Clint who paid him his salary. And forty dollars a week is indubitably forty dollars a week.

"I hope he'll be sure and be here in time for the funeral," said Mrs. Bain. "It will be Wednesday morning, I suppose, Hat?"

Mrs. Whittaker nodded.

"Or perhaps around two o'clock Wednesday afternoon," she amended. "I always think that's a nice time. Father has his frock coat, Allie?"

"Oh, yes," Mrs. Bain said eagerly. "And it's all clean and lovely. He has everything. Hattie, I noticed the other day at Mr. Newton's funeral they had more of a blue necktie on him, so I suppose they're wearing them—Mollie Newton always has everything just so. But I don't know——"

"I think," said Mrs. Whittaker firmly, "that there is nothing lovelier than black for an old gentleman."

"Poor Old Gentleman," said Mr. Bain, shaking his head. "He would have been eighty-five if he just could have lived till next September. Well, I suppose it's all for the best."

He took a small draft of cider and another cooky.

"A wonderful, wonderful life," summarized Mrs. Whittaker. "And a wonderful, wonderful old gentleman."

"Well, I should say so," said Mrs. Bain. "Why, up to the last he was just as interested in everything! It was, 'Allie, how much do you have to give for your eggs now?' and 'Allie, why don't you change your butcher?—this one's robbing you,' and 'Allie, who was that you were talking to on the telephone?' all day long! Everybody used to speak of it."

"And he used to come to the table right up to this stroke," Mr. Bain related, chuckling reminiscently. "My, he used to raise Cain when Allie didn't cut up his meat fast enough to suit him. Always had a temper, *I'll* tell you, the Old Gentleman did. Wouldn't stand for us having anybody in to meals—he didn't like that worth a cent. Eighty-four years old, and sitting right up there at the table with us!"

They vied in telling instances of the Old Gentleman's

intelligence and liveliness, as parents cap one another's anecdotes of precocious children.

"It's only the past year that he had to be helped up-and down-stairs," said Mrs. Bain. "Walked up-stairs all by himself, and more than eighty years old!"

Mrs. Whittaker was amused.

"I remember you said that once when Clint was here," she remarked, "and Clint said, 'Well, if you can't walk up-stairs by the time you're eighty, when are you going to learn?'"

Mrs. Bain smiled politely, because her brother-in-law had said it. Otherwise she would have been shocked and wounded.

"Yes, sir," said Mr. Bain. "Wonderful."

"The only thing I could have wished," Mrs. Bain said, after a pause—"I could have wished he'd been a little different about Paul. Somehow I've never felt quite right since Paul went into the navy."

Mrs. Whittaker's voice fell into the key used for the subject that has been gone over and over and over again.

"Now, Allie," she said, "you know yourself that was the best thing that could have happened. Father told you that himself, often and often. Paul was young, and he wanted to have all his young friends running in and out of the house, banging doors and making all sorts of racket, and it would have been a terrible nuisance for father. You must realize that father was more than eighty years old, Allie."

"Yes, I know," Mrs. Bain said. Her eyes went to the photograph of her son in his seaman's uniform, and she sighed.

"And besides," Mrs. Whittaker pointed out triumphantly "now that Miss Chester's here in his room, there wouldn't have been any room for Paul. So you see!"

There was rather a long pause. Then Mrs. Bain edged toward the other thing that had been weighing upon her.

"Hattie," she said, "I suppose—I suppose we'd ought to let Matt know?"

"I shouldn't," said Mrs. Whittaker composedly. She always took great pains with her "shall's" and "will's." "I only hope that he doesn't see it in the papers in time to come on for the funeral. If you want to have your brother turn up drunk at the services, Allie, *I* don't."

"But I thought he'd straightened up," said Mr. Bain. "Thought he was all right since he got married."

"Yes, I know, I know, Lewis," Mrs. Whittaker said wearily. "I've heard all about that. All I say is, *I* know what Matt is."

"John Loomis was telling me," reported Mr. Bain, "he was going through Akron, and he stopped off to see Matt. Said they had a nice little place, and he seemed to be getting along fine. Said she seemed like a crackerjack housekeeper."

Mrs. Whittaker smiled.

"Yes," she said, "John Loomis and Matt were always two of a kind—you couldn't believe a word either of them said. Probably she did seem to be a good housekeeper. I've no doubt she acted the part very well. Matt never made any bones of the fact that she was on the stage once, for almost a year. Excuse me from having that woman come to father's funeral. If you want to know what *I* think, *I* think that Matt marrying a woman like that had a good deal to do with hastening father's death."

The Bains sat in awe.

"And after all father did for Matt, too," added Mrs. Whittaker, her voice shaken.

"Well, I should think so," Mr. Bain was glad to agree. "I remember how the Old Gentleman used to try and help Matt get along. He'd go down, like it was to Mr. Fuller, that time Matt was working at the bank, and he'd explain to him, 'Now, Mr. Fuller,' he'd say, 'I don't know whether you know it, but this son of mine has always been what you might call the black sheep of the family. He's been kind of a drinker,' he'd say, 'and he's got himself into trouble a couple of times, and if you'd just keep an eye on him, so's to see he keeps straight, it'd be a favor to me.'

"Mr. Fuller told me about it himself. Said it was wonderful the way the Old Gentleman came right out and talked just as frankly to him. Said *he'd* never had any idea Matt was that way—wanted to hear all about it."

Mrs. Whittaker nodded sadly.

"Oh, I know," she said. "Time and again father would do that. And then, as like as not, Matt would get one of his sulky fits, and not turn up at his work."

"And when Matt would be out of work," Mrs. Bain said, "the way father'd hand him out his car-fare, and I don't know what all! When Matt was a grown man, going on thirty years old, father would take him down to Newins & Malley's and buy him a whole new outfit—pick out everything himself. He always used to say Matt was the kind that would get cheated out of his eye-teeth if he went into a store alone."

"My, father hated to see anybody make a fool of themselves about money," Mrs. Whittaker commented. "Remember how he always used to say, 'Anybody can make money, but it takes a wise man to keep it'?"

"I suppose he must be a pretty rich man," Mr. Bain said, abruptly restoring the Old Gentleman to the present.

"Oh—rich!" Mrs. Whittaker's smile was at its kindliest. "But he managed his affairs very well, father did, right up to the last. Everything is in splendid shape, Clint says."

"He showed you the will, didn't he, Hat?" asked Mrs. Bain, forming bits of her sleeve into little plaits between her thin, hard fingers.

"Yes," said her sister. "Yes, he did. He showed me the will. A little over a year ago, I think it was, wasn't it?

You know, just before he started to fail, that time."

She took a small bite of cooky.

"*Awfully* good," she said. She broke into a little bubbly laugh, the laugh she used at teas and wedding receptions and fairly formal dinners. "You know," she went on, as one sharing a good story, "he's gone and left all that old money to me. 'Why, Father!' I said, as soon as I'd read that part. But it seems he'd gotten some sort of idea in his head that Clint and I would be able to take care of it better than anybody else, and you know what father was, once he made up that mind of his. You can just imagine how *I* felt. I couldn't say a thing."

She laughed again, shaking her head in amused bewilderment.

"Oh, and Allie," she said, "he's left you all the furniture he brought here with him, and all the things he bought since he came. And Lewis is to have his set of Thackeray. And that money he lent Lewis, to try and tide him over in the hardware business that time— that's to be regarded as a gift."

She sat back and looked at them, smiling.

"Lewis paid back most all of that money father lent him that time," Mrs. Bain said. "There was only about two hundred dollars more, and then he would have had it all paid up."

"That's to be regarded as a gift," insisted Mrs. Whittaker. She leaned over and patted her brother-in-law's arm. "Father always liked you, Lewis," she said softly.

"Poor Old Gentleman," murmured Mr. Bain.

"Did it—did it say anything about Matt?" asked Mrs. Bain.

"Oh, Allie!" Mrs. Whittaker gently reproved her. "When you think of all the money father spent and spent on Matt, it seems to me he did more than enough—more than enough. And then, when Matt went way off there to live, and married that woman, and never a word about it—father hearing it all through strangers—well, I don't think any of us realized how it hurt father. He never said much about it, but I don't think he ever got over it. I'm always so thankful that poor dear mother didn't live to see how Matt turned out."

"Poor mother," said Mrs. Bain shakily, and brought the grayish handkerchief into action once more. "I can hear her now, just as plain. 'Now, children,' she used to say, 'do for goodness' sake let's all try and keep your father in a good humor.' If I've heard her say it once, I've heard her say it a hundred times. Remember, Hat?"

"Do I remember!" said Mrs. Whittaker. "And do you remember how they used to play whist, and how furious father used to get when he lost?"

"Yes," Mrs. Bain cried excitedly, "and how mother used to have to cheat, so as to be sure and not win from him? She got so she used to be able to do it just as well!"

They laughed softly, filled with memories of the dead days. A pleasant, thoughtful silence fell around them.

Mrs. Bain patted a yawn to extinction, and looked at the clock.

"Ten minutes to eleven," she said. "Goodness, I had no idea it was anywhere near so late. I wish——" She stopped just in time, crimson at what her wish would have been.

"You see, Lew and I have got in the way of going to bed early," she explained. "Father slept so light, we couldn't have people in like we used to before he came here, to play a little bridge or anything, on account of disturbing him. And if we wanted to go to the movies or anywhere, he'd go on so about being left alone that we just kind of gave up going."

"Oh, the Old Gentleman always let you know what he wanted," said Mr. Bain, smiling. "He was a wonder, *I'll* tell you. Nearly eighty-five years old!"

"Think of it," said Mrs. Whittaker.

A door clicked open above them, and feet ran quickly and not lightly down the stairs. Miss Chester burst into the room.

"Oh, Mrs. Bain!" she cried. "Oh, the poor old gentleman! Oh, he's gone! I noticed him kind of stirring and whimpering a little, and he seemed to be trying to make motions at his warm milk, like as if he wanted some. So I put the cup up to his mouth, and he sort of fell over, and just like that, he was gone, and the milk all over him."

Mrs. Bain instantly collapsed into passionate weeping. Her husband put his arm tenderly about her, and murmured a series of "Now-now's."

Mrs. Whittaker rose, set her cider-glass carefully on the table, shook out her handkerchief, and moved toward the door.

"A lovely death," she pronounced. "A wonderful, wonderful life, and now a beautiful, peaceful death. Oh, it's the best thing, Allie; it's the best thing."

"Oh, it is, Mrs. Bain; it's the best thing," Miss Chester said earnestly. "It's really a blessing. That's what it is."

Among them they got Mrs. Bain up the stairs.

The Mantle of Whistler

The Mantle
of Whistler

_T_he hostess, all smiles and sparkles and small,
abortive dance-steps, led the young man with the side-
burns across the room to where sat the girl who had twice
been told she looked like Clara Bow.

"There she is!" she cried. "Here's the girl we've been
looking for! Miss French, let me make you acquainted with
Mr. Bartlett."

"Pleased to meet up with you social," said Mr.
Bartlett.

"Pardon my wet glove," said Miss French.

"Oh, you two!" said the hostess. "I've just been dying to get you two together. I knew you'd get on just like nothing at all. Didn't I tell you he had a marvelous line, Alice? What'd I tell you, Jack—didn't I say over and over again she was a scream? And she's always like this. You wait till you know her as well as I do! Goodness, I just wish I could stay here and listen to you."

However, frustrated in her desire, she smiled heartily, waved her hand like a dear little baby shaking bye-bye, and schottisched across the floor to resume the burdens of hospitality.

"Hey, where have you been all my life?" said the young man who had a marvelous line.

"Don't be an Airedale," said the girl who was always like this.

"Any objection if I sit down?" he said.

"Go right ahead," she said. "Sit down and take a load off your feet."

"I'll do that little thing for you," he said. "Sit down before I fall down, what? Some party, isn't it? What a party this turned out to be!"

"And how!" she said.

" 'And how' is right," he said. " 'S wonderful."

" 'S marvelous," she said.

" 'S awful nice," he said.

" 'S Paradise," she said.

"Right there with the comeback, aren't you?" he said. "What a girl you turned out to be! Some girl, aren't you?"

"Oh, don't be an Airedale," she said.

"Just a real good girl," he said. "Some little looker, too. Where did you get those big, blue eyes from, anyway? Don't you know I'm the guy that always falls for big, blue eyes?"

"You would," she said. "You're just the tripe."

"Hey, listen, listen," he said. "Lay off for a minute, will you? Come on, now, get regular. Aren't you going to tell me where you got those big, blue eyes?"

"Oh, don't be ridic," she said. "They are not big! Are they?"

"Are they big!" he said. "You don't know they're big, do you? Oh, no, nobody ever told you that before. And you don't know what you do to me, when you look up like that, do you? Yes, you don't!"

"I wouldn't know about that," she said.

"Ah, stop that, will you?" he said. "Go ahead, now, come clean. Tell me where you got those big, blue eyes."

"What's your idea in bringing that up?" she said.

"And your hair's pretty cute, too," he said. "I suppose you don't know you've got pretty cute hair. You wouldn't know about that, would you?"

"Even if that was good, I wouldn't like it," she said.

"Come on, now," he said. "Don't you know that hair of yours is pretty cute?"

" 'S wonderful," she said. " 'S marvelous."

"That you should care for me?" he said.

"Oh, don't be an Airedale," she said.

"I could care for you in a big way," he said. "What those big, blue eyes of yours do to me is nobody's business. Know that?"

"Oh, I wouldn't know about that," she said.

"Hey, listen," he said, "what are you trying to do— run me ragged? Don't you ever stop kidding? When are you going to tell me where you got your big, blue eyes?"

"Oh, pull yourself together," she said.

"I'd have to have a care with a girl like you," he said. "Watch my step, that's what I'd have to do."

"Don't be sil," she said.

"You know what?" he said. "I could get a girl like you on the brain."

"The what?" she said.

"Ah, come on, come on," he said. "Lay off that stuff, will you? Tell me where you've been keeping yourself, anyhow. Got any more like you around the house?"

" 'S all there is," she said. " 'R' isn't any more."

"That's Oke with me," he said. "One like you's enough. What those eyes of yours do to me is plenty! Know it?"

"I wouldn't know about that," she said.

"That dress of yours slays me," he said. "Where'd you get the catsy dress? Hm?"

"Don't be an Airedale," she said.

"Hey, where'd you get that expression, anyway?" he said.

"It's a gift," she said.

" 'Gift' is right," he said. "It's a honey."

"You ain't heard nothin' yet," she said.

"You slay me," he said. "I'm telling you. Where do you get all your stuff from?"

"What's your idea in bringing that up?" she said.

The hostess, with enhanced sparkles, romped over to them.

"Well, for heaven's sakes!" she cried. "Aren't you two even going to look at anybody else? What do you think of her, Jack? Isn't she cute?"

"Is she cute!" he said.

"Isn't he marvelous, Alice?" asked the hostess.

"You'd be surprised," she said.

The hostess cocked her head, like a darling, mischievous terrier puppy, and sparkled whimsically at them.

"Oh, you two!" she said. "Didn't I tell you you'd get on just like nothing at all?"

"And how!" said the girl.

" 'And how' is right!" said the young man.

"You two!" cooed the hostess. "I could listen to you all night."

A Telephone Call

A Telephone Call

Please, God, let him telephone me now. Dear God, let him call me now. I won't ask anything else of You, truly I won't. It isn't very much to ask. It would be so little to You, God, such a little, little thing. Only let him telephone now. Please, God. Please, please, please.

If I didn't think about it, maybe the telephone might ring. Sometimes it does that. If I could think of something else. If I could think of something else. Maybe if I counted five hundred by fives, it might ring by that time. I'll count slowly. I won't cheat. And if it rings when I get to three hundred, I won't stop; I won't answer it until I get to five hundred. Five, ten, fifteen, twenty, twenty-five, thirty, thirty-five, forty, forty-five, fifty. . . . Oh, please ring. Please.

This is the last time I'll look at the clock. I will not look at it again. It's ten minutes past seven. He said he would telephone at five o'clock. "I'll call you at five, darling." I think that's where he said "darling." I'm almost sure he said it there. I know he called me "darling" twice, and the other time was when he said good-bye. "Good-bye, darling." He was busy, and he can't say much in the office, but he called me "darling" twice. He couldn't have minded my calling him up. I know you shouldn't keep telephoning them—I know they don't like that. When you do that, they know you are thinking about them and wanting them, and that makes them hate you. But I hadn't talked to him in three days—not in three days. And all I did was ask him how he was; it was just the way anybody might have called him up. He couldn't have minded that. He couldn't have thought I was bothering him. "No, of course you're not," he said. And he said he'd telephone me. He didn't have to say that. I didn't ask him to, truly I didn't. I'm sure I didn't. I don't think he would say he'd telephone me, and then just never do it. Please don't let him do that, God. Please don't.

"I'll call you at five, darling." "Good-bye, darling." He was busy, and he was in a hurry, and there were people around him, but he called me "darling" twice. That's mine, that's mine. I have that, even if I never see him again. Oh, but that's so little. That isn't enough. Nothing's enough, if I never see him again. Please let me see him again, God. Please, I want him so much. I want him so much. I'll be good, God. I will try to be better, I will, if You will let me see him again. If You will let him telephone me. Oh, let him telephone me now.

Ah, don't let my prayer seem too little to You, God. You sit up there, so white and old, with all the angels about You and the stars slipping by. And I come to You with a prayer about a telephone call. Ah, don't laugh, God. You see, You don't know how it feels. You're so safe, there on Your throne, with the blue swirling under You. Nothing can touch You; no one can twist Your heart in his hands. This is suffering, God, this is bad, bad suffering. Won't You help me? For Your Son's sake, help me. You said You would do whatever was asked of You in His name. Oh, God, in the name of Thine only beloved Son, Jesus Christ, our Lord, let him telephone me now.

I must stop this. I mustn't be this way. Look. Suppose a young man says he'll call a girl up, and then something happens, and he doesn't. That isn't so terrible, is it? Why, it's going on all over the world, right this minute. Oh, what do I care what's going on all over the world? Why can't that telephone ring? Why can't it, why can't it? Couldn't you ring? Ah, please, couldn't you? You damned, ugly, shiny thing. It would hurt you to ring, wouldn't it? Oh, that would hurt you. Damn you, I'll pull your filthy roots out of the wall, I'll smash your smug black face in little bits. Damn you to hell.

No, no, no. I must stop. I must think about something else. This is what I'll do. I'll put the clock in the other room. Then I can't look at it. If I do have to look at it, then I'll have to walk into the bedroom, and that will be something to do. Maybe, before I look at it again, he will call me. I'll be so sweet to him, if he calls me. If he says he can't see me tonight, I'll say, "Why, that's all right, dear. Why, of course it's all right." I'll be the way I was when I first met him. Then maybe he'll like me again. I was always sweet, at first. Oh, it's so easy to be sweet to people before you love them.

I think he must still like me a little. He couldn't have called me "darling" twice today, if he didn't still like me a little. It isn't all gone, if he still likes me a little; even if it's only a little, little bit. You see, God, if You would just let him telephone me, I wouldn't have to ask You anything more. I would be sweet to him, I would be gay, I would be just the way I used to be, and then he would love me again. And then I would never have to ask You for anything more. Don't You see, God? So won't You please let him telephone me? Won't You please, please, please?

Are You punishing me, God, because I've been bad? Are You angry with me because I did that? Oh, but, God, there are so many bad people—You could not be hard only to me. And it wasn't very bad; it couldn't have been bad. We didn't hurt anybody, God. Things are only bad when they hurt people. We didn't hurt one single soul; You know that. You know it wasn't bad, don't You, God? So won't You let him telephone me now?

If he doesn't telephone me, I'll know God is angry with me. I'll count five hundred by fives, and if he hasn't called me then, I will know God isn't going to help me, ever again. That will be the sign. Five, ten, fifteen, twenty, twenty-five, thirty, thirty-five, forty, forty-five, fifty, fifty-five. . . . It was bad. I knew it was bad. All right, God, send me to hell. You think You're frightening me with Your hell, don't You? You think Your hell is worse than mine.

I mustn't. I mustn't do this. Suppose he's a little late calling me up—that's nothing to get hysterical about. Maybe he isn't going to call—maybe he's coming straight up here without telephoning. He'll be cross if he sees I have been crying. They don't like you to cry. He doesn't cry. I wish to God I could make him cry. I wish I could make him cry and tread the floor and feel his heart heavy and big and festering in him. I wish I could hurt him like hell.

He doesn't wish that about me. I don't think he even

knows how he makes me feel. I wish he could know, without my telling him. They don't like you to tell them they've made you cry. They don't like you to tell them you're unhappy because of them. If you do, they think you're possessive and exacting. And then they hate you. They hate you whenever you say anything you really think. You always have to keep playing little games. Oh, I thought we didn't have to; I thought this was so big I could say whatever I meant. I guess you can't, ever. I guess there isn't ever anything big enough for that. Oh, if he would just telephone, I wouldn't tell him I had been sad about him. They hate sad people. I would be so sweet and so gay, he couldn't help but like me. If he would only telephone. If he would only telephone.

Maybe that's what he is doing. Maybe he is coming up here without calling me up. Maybe he's on his way now. Something might have happened to him. No, nothing could ever happen to him. I can't picture anything happening to him. I never picture him run over. I never see him lying still and long and dead. I wish he were dead. That's a terrible wish. That's a lovely wish. If he were dead, he would be mine. If he were dead, I would never think of now and the last few weeks. I would remember only the lovely times. It would be all beautiful. I wish he were dead. I wish he were dead, dead, dead.

This is silly. It's silly to go wishing people were dead

just because they don't call you up the very minute they said they would. Maybe the clock's fast; I don't know whether it's right. Maybe he's hardly late at all. Anything could have made him a little late. Maybe he had to stay at his office. Maybe he went home, to call me up from there, and somebody came in. He doesn't like to telephone me in front of people. Maybe he's worried, just a little, little bit, about keeping me waiting. He might even hope that I would call him up. I could do that. I could telephone him.

I mustn't. I mustn't, I mustn't. Oh, God, please don't let me telephone him. Please keep me from doing that. I know, God, just as well as You do, that if he were worried about me, he'd telephone no matter where he was or how many people there were around him. Please make me know that, God. I don't ask You to make it easy for me—You can't do that, for all that You could make a world. Only let me know it, God. Don't let me go on hoping. Don't let me say comforting things to myself. Please don't let me hope, dear God. Please don't.

I won't telephone him. I'll never telephone him again as long as I live. He'll rot in hell, before I'll call him up. You don't have to give me strength, God; I have it myself. If he wanted me, he could get me. He knows where I am. He knows I'm waiting here. He's so sure of me, so sure. I wonder why they hate you, as soon as they are sure of you. I should think it would be so sweet to be sure.

It would be so easy to telephone him. Then I'd know. Maybe it wouldn't be a foolish thing to do. Maybe he wouldn't mind. Maybe he'd like it. Maybe he has been trying to get me. Sometimes people try and try to get you on the telephone, and they say the number doesn't answer. I'm not just saying that to help myself; that really happens. You know that really happens, God. Oh, God, keep me away from that telephone. Keep me away. Let me still have just a little bit of pride. I think I'm going to need it, God. I think it will be all I'll have.

Oh, what does pride matter, when I can't stand it if I don't talk to him? Pride like that is such a silly, shabby little thing. The real pride, the big pride, is in having no pride. I'm not saying that just because I want to call him. I am not. That's true, I know that's true. I will be big. I will be beyond little prides.

Please, God, keep me from telephoning him. Please, God.

I don't see what pride has to do with it. This is such a little thing, for me to be bringing in pride, for me to be making such a fuss about. I may have misunderstood him. Maybe he said for me to call him up, at five. "Call me at five, darling." He could have said that, perfectly well. It's so possible that I didn't hear him right. "Call me at five, darling." I'm almost sure that's what he said. God, don't let me talk this way to myself. Make me know, please make me know.

I'll think about something else. I'll just sit quietly. If I could sit still. If I could sit still. Maybe I could read. Oh, all the books are about people who love each other, truly and sweetly. What do they want to write about that for? Don't they know it isn't true? Don't they know it's a lie, it's a God damned lie? What do they have to tell about that for, when they know how it hurts? Damn them, damn them, damn them.

I won't. I'll be quiet. This is nothing to get excited about. Look. Suppose he were someone I didn't know very well. Suppose he were another girl. Then I'd just telephone and say, "Well, for goodness' sake, what happened to you?" That's what I'd do, and I'd never even think about it. Why can't I be casual and natural, just because I love him? I can be. Honestly, I can be. I'll call him up, and be so easy and pleasant. You see if I won't, God. Oh, don't let me call him. Don't, don't, don't.

God, aren't You really going to let him call me? Are You sure, God? Couldn't You please relent? Couldn't You? I don't even ask You to let him telephone me now, God; only let him do it in a little while. I'll count five hundred by fives. I'll do it so slowly and so fairly. If he hasn't telephoned then, I'll call him. I will. Oh, please, dear God, dear kind God, my blessed Father in Heaven, let him call before then. Please, God. Please.

Five, ten, fifteen, twenty, twenty-five, thirty, thirty-five. . . .

You Were Perfectly Fine

You Were Perfectly Fine

The pale young man eased himself carefully into the low chair, and rolled his head to the side, so that the cool chintz comforted his cheek and temple.

"Oh, dear," he said. "Oh, dear, oh, dear, oh, dear. Oh."

The clear-eyed girl, sitting light and erect on the couch, smiled brightly at him.

"Not feeling so well today?" she said.

"Oh, I'm great," he said. "Corking, I am. Know what

time I got up? Four o'clock this afternoon, sharp. I kept trying to make it, and every time I took my head off the pillow, it would roll under the bed. This isn't my head I've got on now. I think this is something that used to belong to Walt Whitman. Oh, dear, oh, dear, oh, dear."

"Do you think maybe a drink would make you feel better?" she said.

"The hair of the mastiff that bit me?" he said. "Oh, no, thank you. Please never speak of anything like that again. I'm through. I'm all, all through. Look at that hand; steady as a humming-bird. Tell me, was I very terrible last night?"

"Oh, goodness," she said, "everybody was feeling pretty high. You were all right."

"Yeah," he said. "I must have been dandy. Is everybody sore at me?"

"Good heavens, no," she said. "Everyone thought you were terribly funny. Of course, Jim Pierson was a little stuffy, there for a minute at dinner. But people sort of held him back in his chair, and got him calmed down. I don't think anybody at the other tables noticed it at all. Hardly anybody."

"He was going to sock me?" he said. "Oh, Lord. What did I do to him?"

"Why, you didn't do a thing," she said. "You were perfectly fine. But you know how silly Jim gets, when he thinks anybody is making too much fuss over Elinor."

"Was I making a pass at Elinor?" he said. "Did I do that?"

"Of course you didn't," she said. "You were only fooling, that's all. She thought you were awfully amusing. She was having a marvelous time. She only got a little tiny bit annoyed just once, when you poured the clam-juice down her back."

"My God," he said. "Clam-juice down that back. And every vertebra a little Cabot. Dear God. What'll I ever do?"

"Oh, she'll be all right," she said. "Just send her some flowers, or something. Don't worry about it. It isn't anything."

"No, I won't worry," he said. "I haven't got a care in the world. I'm sitting pretty. Oh, dear, oh, dear. Did I do any other fascinating tricks at dinner?"

"You were fine," she said. "Don't be so foolish about it. Everybody was crazy about you. The maître d'hôtel was a little worried because you wouldn't stop singing, but he really didn't mind. All he said was, he was afraid they'd close the place again, if there was so much noise. But he didn't care a bit, himself. I think he loved seeing you have such a good time. Oh, you were just singing away, there, for about an hour. It wasn't so terribly loud, at all."

"So I sang," he said. "That must have been a treat. I sang."

"Don't you remember?" she said. "You just sang one

song after another. Everybody in the place was listening. They loved it. Only you kept insisting that you wanted to sing some song about some kind of fusiliers or other, and everybody kept shushing you, and you'd keep trying to start it again. You were wonderful. We were all trying to make you stop singing for a minute, and eat something, but you wouldn't hear of it. My, you were funny."

"Didn't I eat any dinner?" he said.

"Oh, not a thing," she said. "Every time the waiter would offer you something, you'd give it right back to him, because you said that he was your long-lost brother, changed in the cradle by a gypsy band, and that anything you had was his. You had him simply roaring at you."

"I bet I did," he said. "I bet I was comical. Society's Pet, I must have been. And what happened then, after my overwhelming success with the waiter?"

"Why, nothing much," she said. "You took a sort of dislike to some old man with white hair, sitting across the room, because you didn't like his necktie and you wanted to tell him about it. But we got you out, before he got really mad."

"Oh, we got out," he said. "Did I walk?"

"Walk! Of course you did," she said. "You were absolutely all right. There was that nasty stretch of ice on the sidewalk, and you did sit down awfully hard, you poor dear. But good heavens, that might have happened to anybody."

"Oh, surely," he said. "Mrs. Hoover or anybody. So I fell down on the sidewalk. That would explain what's the matter with my—Yes. I see. And then what, if you don't mind?"

"Ah, now, Peter!" she said. "You can't sit there and say you don't remember what happened after that! I did think that maybe you were just a little tight at dinner—oh, you were perfectly all right, and all that, but I did know you were feeling pretty gay. But you were so serious, from the time you fell down—I never knew you to be that way. Don't you know, how you told me I had never seen your real self before? Oh, Peter, I just couldn't bear it, if you didn't remember that lovely long ride we took together in the taxi! Please, you do remember that, don't you? I think it would simply kill me, if you didn't."

"Oh, yes," he said. "Riding in the taxi. Oh, yes, sure. Pretty long ride, hmm?"

"Round and round and round the park," she said. "Oh, and the trees were shining so in the moonlight. And you said you never knew before that you really had a soul."

"Yes," he said. "I said that. That was me."

"You said such lovely, lovely things," she said. "And I'd never known, all this time, how you had been feeling about me, and I'd never dared to let you see how I felt about you. And then last night—oh, Peter dear, I think that taxi ride was the most important thing that ever happened to us in our lives."

"Yes," he said. "I guess it must have been."

"And we're going to be so happy," she said. "Oh, I just want to tell everybody! But I don't know—I think maybe it would be sweeter to keep it all to ourselves."

"I think it would be," he said.

"Isn't it lovely?" she said.

"Yes," he said. "Great."

"Lovely!" she said.

"Look here," he said, "do you mind if I have a drink? I mean, just medicinally, you know. I'm off the stuff for life, so help me. But I think I feel a collapse coming on."

"Oh, I think it would do you good," she said. "You poor boy, it's a shame you feel so awful. I'll go make you a highball."

"Honestly," he said, "I don't see how you could ever want to speak to me again, after I made such a fool of myself, last night. I think I'd better go join a monastery in Thibet."

"You crazy idiot!" she said. "As if I could ever let you go away now! Stop talking like that. You were perfectly fine."

She jumped up from the couch, kissed him quickly on the forehead, and ran out of the room.

The pale young man looked after her and shook his head long and slowly, then dropped it in his damp and trembling hands.

"Oh, dear," he said. "Oh, dear, oh, dear, oh, dear."

Little Curtis

Little Curtis

$\mathcal{M}$rs. Matson paused in the vestibule of G. Fosdick's Sons' Department Store. She transferred a small parcel from her right hand to the crook of her left arm, gripped her shopping-bag firmly by its German-silver frame, opened it with a capable click, and drew from its orderly interior a little black-bound book and a neatly sharpened pencil.

Shoppers passing in and out jostled her as she stood there, but they neither shared in Mrs. Matson's attention nor hurried her movements. She made no answer to the "Oh, I *beg* your pardons" that bubbled from the lips of the more tender-hearted among them. Calm, sure, gloriously aloof, Mrs. Matson stood, opened her book, poised her pencil, and wrote in delicate, prettily slanting characters: "4 crêpe-paper candy-baskets, $.28."

The dollar-sign was gratifying decorative, the decimal point clear and deep, the 2 daintily curled, the 8 admirably balanced. Mrs. Matson looked approvingly at her handiwork. Still unhurried, she closed the book, replaced it and the pencil in the bag, tested the snap to see that it was indisputably shut, and took the parcel once more in her right hand. Then, with a comfortable air of duty well done, she passed impressively, and with a strong push, from G. Fosdick's Sons' Department Store by means of a portal which bore a placard with the request, "Please Use Other Door."

Slowly Mrs. Matson made her way down Maple Street. The morning sunshine that flooded the town's main thoroughfare caused her neither to squint nor to lower her face. She held her head high, looking about her as one who says, "Our good people, we are pleased with you."

She stopped occasionally by a shop-window, to inspect thoroughly the premature autumn costumes there displayed. But her heart was unfluttered by the envy which attacked the lesser women around her. Though her long black coat, of that vintage when coats were puffed of sleeve and cut sharply in at the waist, was stained and shiny, and her hat had the general air of indecision and lack of spirit that comes with age, and her elderly black gloves were worn in patches of rough gray, Mrs. Matson had no yearnings for the fresh, trim costumes set temptingly before her. Snug in her was the thought of the rows of recent garments, each one in its flowered cretonne casing, occupying the varnished hangers along the poles of her bedroom closet.

She had her unalterable ideas about such people as gave or threw away garments that might still be worn, for warmth and modesty, if not for style. She found it distinctly lower-class to wear one's new clothes "for every day"; there was an unpleasant suggestion of extravagance and riotous living in the practice. The working classes, who, as Mrs. Matson often explained to her friends, went and bought themselves silk shirts and phonographs the minute they got a little money, did such things.

No morbid thought of her possible sudden demise before the clothes in her closet could be worn or enjoyed irked her. Life's uncertainty was not for those of her position. Mrs. Matsons pass away between seventy and eighty; sometimes later, never before.

A blind Negress, a tray of pencils hung about her neck, a cane monotonously tapping the pavement before her, came down the street. Mrs. Matson swerved sharply to the curb to avoid her, wasting a withering glance upon her. It was Mrs. Matson's immediate opinion that the woman could see as well as she could. She never gave to the poor on the streets, and was distressed if she saw others do so. She frequently remarked that these beggars all had big bank-accounts.

She crossed to the car-tracks to await the trolley that would bear her home, her calm upset by her sight of the Negress. "Probably owns an apartment-house," she told herself, and shot an angry glance after the blind woman.

However, her poise was restored by the act of tendering her fare to the courteous conductor. Mrs. Matson rather enjoyed small and legitimate disbursements to those who were appropriately grateful. She gave him her nickel with the manner of one presenting a park to a city, and swept into the car to a desirable seat.

Settled, with the parcel securely wedged between her hip and the window, against loss or robbery, Mrs. Matson again produced the book and pencil. "Car-fare, $.05," she wrote. Again the exquisite handwriting, the neat figures, gave her a flow of satisfaction.

Mrs. Matson, regally without acknowledgment, accepted the conductor's aid in alighting from the car at her corner. She trod the sun-splashed pavement, bowing now and again to neighbors knitting on their porches or bend-ing solicitously over their iris-beds. Slow, stately bows she gave, unaccompanied by smile or word of greeting. After all, she was Mrs. Albert Matson; she had been Miss Laura Whitmore, of the Drop Forge and Tool Works Whitmores. One does not lose sight of such things.

She always enjoyed the first view of her house as she walked toward it. It amplified in her her sense of security and permanence. There it stood, in its tidy, treeless lawns, square and solid and serviceable. You thought of steel-engravings and rows of Scott's novels behind glass, and Sunday dinner in the middle of the day, when you looked at it. You knew immediately that within it no one ever banged a door, no one clattered up- and down-stairs, no one spilled crumbs or dropped ashes or left the light burning in the bathroom.

Expectancy pervaded Mrs. Matson as she approached her home. She spoke of it always as her home. "You must come to see me in my home some time," she graciously commanded new acquaintances. There was a large, institutional sound to it that you didn't get in the word "house."

She liked to think of its cool, high-ceilinged rooms, of its busy maids, of little Curtis waiting to deliver her his respectful kiss. She had adopted him almost a year ago, when he was four. She had, she told her friends, never once regretted it.

In her absence her friends had been wont to comment

sadly upon what a shame it was that the Albert Matsons had no child—and with all the Matson and Whitmore money, too. Neither of them, the friends pointed out, could live forever; it would all have to go to the Henry Matsons' children. And they were but quoting Mrs. Albert Matson's own words when they observed that those children would be just the kind that would run right through it.

Mr. and Mrs. Matson held a joint view of the devastation that would result if their nephews and nieces were ever turned loose among the Matson and Whitmore money. As is frequent in such instances, their worry led them to pay the other Matson family the compliment of the credit for schemes and desires that had never edged into their thoughts.

The Albert Matsons saw their relatives as waiting, with a sort of stalking patience, for the prayed-for moment of their death. For years they conjured up ever more lurid pictures of the Matson children going through their money like Sherman to the sea; for years they carried about with them the notion that their demise was being eagerly awaited, was being made, indeed, the starting-point of bacchanalian plans.

The Albert Matsons were as one in everything, as in this. Their thoughts, their manners, their opinions, their very locutions were phenomena of similarity. People even pointed out that Mr. and Mrs. Matson looked alike. It was regarded as the world's misfortune that so obviously Heaven-made a match was without offspring. And of course—you always had to come back to it, it bulked so before you—there was all that Matson and Whitmore money.

No one, though, ever directly condoled with Mrs. Matson upon her childlessness. In her presence one didn't speak of things like having children. She accepted the fact of babies when they were shown to her; she fastidiously disregarded their mode of arrival.

She had told none of her friends of her decision to adopt a little boy. No one knew about it until the papers were signed and he was established in the Matson house. Mrs. Matson had got him, she explained, "at the best place in New York." No one was surprised at that. Mrs. Matson always went to the best places when she shopped in New York. You thought of her selecting a child as she selected all her other belongings: a good one, one that would last.

She stopped abruptly now, as she came to her gate, a sudden frown creasing her brow. Two little boys, too absorbed to hear her steps, were playing in the hot sun by the hedge—two little boys much alike in age, size, and attire, compact, pink-and-white, good little boys, their cheeks flushed with interest, the backs of their necks warm and damp. They played an interminable, mysterious game with pebbles and twigs and a small tin trolley-car.

Mrs. Matson entered the yard.

"Curtis!" she said.

Both little boys looked up, startled. One of them rose and hung his head before her frown.

"And who," said Mrs. Matson deeply, "who told Georgie he could come here?"

No answer. Georgie, still squatting on his heels, looked inquiringly from her to Curtis. He was interested and unalarmed.

"Was it you, Curtis?" asked Mrs. Matson.

Curtis nodded. You could scarcely tell that he did, his head hung so low.

"Yes, mother dear!" said Mrs. Matson.

"Yes, mother dear," whispered Curtis.

"And how many times," Mrs. Matson inquired, "have I told you that you were not to play with Georgie? How many times, Curtis?"

Curtis murmured vaguely. He wished that Georgie would please go.

"You don't know?" said Mrs. Matson incredulously. "You don't know? After all mother does for you, you don't know how many times she has told you not to play with Georgie? Don't you remember what mother told you she'd have to do if you ever played with Georgie again?"

A pause. Then the nod.

"Yes, mother dear!" said Mrs. Matson.

"Yes, mother dear," said Curtis.

"Well!" Mrs. Matson said. She turned to the enthralled Georgie. "You'll have to go home now, Georgie—go right straight home. And you're not to come here any more, do you understand me? Curtis is not allowed to play with you—not ever."

Georgie rose.

" 'Bye," he said philosophically, and walked away, his farewell unanswered.

Mrs. Matson gazed upon Curtis. Grief disarranged her features.

"Playing!" she said, her voice broken with emotion. "Playing with a furnaceman's child! After all mother does for you!"

She took him by a limp arm and led him, unresisting, along the walk to the house; led him past the maid that opened the door, up the stairs to his little blue bedroom. She put him in it and closed the door.

Then she went to her own room, placed her package carefully on the table, removed her gloves, and laid them, with her bag, in an orderly drawer. She entered her closet, hung up her coat, then stooped for one of the felt slippers that were set scrupulously, in the first dancing position, on the floor beneath her nightgown. It was a lavender slipper, with scallops and a staid rosette; it had a light, flexible leather sole, across which was stamped its name, "Kumfy-Toes."

Mrs. Matson grasped it firmly by the heel and flicked it back and forth. Carrying it, she went to the little boy's room. She began to speak as she turned the door-knob.

"And before mother had time to take her hat off, too," she said. The door closed behind her.

She came out again presently. A scale of shrieks followed her.

"That will do!" she announced, looking back from the door. The shrieks faded obediently to sobs. "That's quite enough of that, thank you. Mother's had just about plenty for one morning. And today, too, with the ladies coming this afternoon, and all mother has to attend to! Oh, I'd be ashamed, Curtis, if I were you—that's what I'd be."

She closed the door, and retired, to remove her hat.

The ladies came in mid-afternoon. There were three of them. Mrs. Kerley, gray and brittle and painstaking, always thoughtful about sending birthday-cards and carrying glass jars of soup to the sick. Mrs. Swan, her visiting sister-in-law, younger, and given to daisied hats and crocheted lace collars, with her transient's air of bright, determined interest in her hostess's acquaintances and activities. And Mrs. Cook. Only she did not count very much. She was extremely deaf, and so pretty well out of things.

She had visited innumerable specialists, spent un-
counted money, endured agonizing treatments, in her en-
deavors to be able to hear what went on about her and to
have a part in it. They had finally fitted her out with a long,
coiling, corrugated speaking-tube, rather like a larger in-
testine. One end of this she placed in her better ear, and
the other she extended to those who would hold speech
with her. But the shining black mouthpiece seemed to
embarrass people and intimidate them; they could think of
nothing better to call into it than "Getting colder out," or
"You keeping pretty well?" To hear such remarks as these
she had gone through years of suffering.

Mrs. Matson, in her last spring's blue taffeta, assigned
her guests to seats about the living-room. It was an afternoon set apart for fancywork and conversation. Later there
would be tea, and two triangular sandwiches apiece made
from the chopped remnants of last night's chicken, and a
cake which was a high favorite with Mrs. Matson, for its
formula required but one egg. She had gone, in person, to
the kitchen to supervise its making. She was not entirely
convinced that her cook was wasteful of materials, but she
felt that the woman would bear watching.

The crêpe-paper baskets, fairly well filled with disks
of peppermint creams, were to enliven the corners of the
tea-table. Mrs. Matson trusted her guests not to regard
them as favors and take them home.

The conversation dealt, and favorably, with the weather. Mrs. Kerley and Mrs. Swan vied with each other in paying compliments to the day.

"So clear," said Mrs. Kerley.

"Not a cloud in the sky," augmented Mrs. Swan. "Not a one."

"The air was just lovely this morning," reported Mrs. Kerley. "I said to myself, 'Well, this is a beautiful day if there ever *was* one.' "

"There's something so balmy about it," said Mrs. Swan.

Mrs. Cook spoke suddenly and overloudly, in the untrustworthy voice of the deaf.

"Phew, this is a scorcher!" she said. "Something terrible out."

The conversation went immediately to literature. It developed that Mrs. Kerley had been reading a lovely book. Its name and that of its author escaped her at the moment, but her enjoyment of it was so keen that she had lingered over it till 'way past ten o'clock the night before. Particularly did she commend its descriptions of some of those Italian places; they were, she affirmed, just like a picture. The book had been drawn to her attention by the young woman at the Little Booke Nooke. It was, on her authority, one of the new ones.

Mrs. Matson frowned at her embroidery. Words

flowed readily from her lips. She seemed to have spoken on the subject before.

"I haven't any use for all these new books," she said. "I wouldn't give them house-room. I don't see why a person wants to sit down and write any such stuff. I often think, I don't believe they know what they're writing about themselves half the time. I don't know who they think wants to read those kind of things. I'm sure *I* don't."

She paused to let her statements sink deep.

"Mr. Matson," she continued—she always spoke of her husband thus; it conveyed an aristocratic sense of aloofness, did away with any suggestion of carnal intimacy between them—"Mr. Matson isn't any hand for these new books, either. He always says, if he could find another book like *David Harum*, he'd read it in a minute. I wish," she added longingly, "I had a dollar for every time I've heard him say that."

Mrs. Kerley smiled. Mrs. Swan threw a rippling little laugh into the pause.

"Well, it's true, you know, it really is true," Mrs. Kerley told Mrs. Swan.

"Oh, it is," Mrs. Swan hastened to reassure her.

"I don't know what we're coming to, *I'm* sure," announced Mrs. Matson.

She sewed, her thread twanging through the tight-stretched circle of linen in her embroidery-hoop.

115

The stoppage of conversation weighed upon Mrs. Swan. She lifted her head and looked out the window.

"My, what a lovely lawn you have!" she said. "I couldn't help noticing it, first thing. We've been living in New York, you know."

"I often say I don't see what people want to shut themselves up in a place like that for," Mrs. Matson said. "You know, you exist, in New York—we live, out here."

Mrs. Swan laughed a bit nervously. Mrs. Kerley nodded. "That's right," she said. "That's pretty good."

Mrs. Matson herself thought it worthy of repetition. She picked up Mrs. Cook's speaking-tube.

"I was just saying to Mrs. Swan," she cried, and called her epigram into the mouthpiece.

"Live where?" asked Mrs. Cook.

Mrs. Matson smiled at her patiently. "New York. You know, that's where I got my little adopted boy."

"Oh, yes," said Mrs. Swan. "Carrie told me. Now, wasn't that lovely of you!"

Mrs. Matson shrugged. "Yes," she said, "I went right to the best place for him. Miss Codman's nursery—it's absolutely reliable. You can get awfully nice children there. There's quite a long waiting-list, they tell me."

"Goodness, just think how it must seem to him to be up here," said Mrs. Swan, "with this big house, and that lovely, smooth lawn, and everything."

Mrs. Matson laughed slightly. "Oh—well," she said. "I hope he appreciates it," remarked Mrs. Swan.

"I think he will," Mrs. Matson said capably. "Of course," she conceded, "he's pretty young right now."

"So lovely," murmured Mrs. Swan. "So sweet to get them young like this and have them grow up."

"Yes, I think that's the nicest way," agreed Mrs. Matson. "And, you know, I really enjoy training him. Naturally, now that we have him here with us, we want him to act like a little gentleman."

"Just think of it," cried Mrs. Swan, "a child like that having all this! And will you have him go to school later on?"

"Oh, yes," Mrs. Matson replied. "Yes, we want him to be educated. You take a child going to some nice little school near here, say, where he'll meet only the best children, and he'll make friends that it will be a pretty good thing for him to know some day."

Mrs. Swan waxed arch. "I suppose you've got it all settled what he's going to be when he grows up," she said.

"Why, certainly," said Mrs. Matson. "He's to go right straight into Mr. Matson's business. My husband," she informed Mrs. Swan, "is the Matson Adding Machines."

"Oh-h-h," said Mrs. Swan on a descending scale.

"I think Curtis will do very well in school," prophesied Mrs. Matson. "He's not at all stupid—picks up everything. Mr. Matson is anxious to have him brought up to be a good, sensible business man—he says that's what this country needs, you know. So I've been trying to teach him the value of money. I've bought him a little bank. I don't think you can begin too early. Because probably some day Curtis is going to have—well——"

Mrs. Matson drifted into light, anecdotal mood.

"Oh, it's funny the way children are," she remarked. "The other day Mrs. Newman brought her little Amy down to play with Curtis, and when I went up to look at them, there he was, trying to give her his brand-new flannel rabbit. So I just took him into my room, and I sat him down, and I said to him, 'Now, Curtis,' I said, 'you must realize that mother had to pay almost two dollars for that rabbit—nearly two hundred pennies,' I said. 'It's very nice to be generous, but you must learn that it isn't a good idea to give things away to people. Now you go in to Amy,' I said, 'and you tell her you're sorry, but she'll have to give that rabbit right back to you.' "

"And did he do it?" asked Mrs. Swan.

"Why, I told him to," Mrs. Matson said.

"Isn't it splendid?" Mrs. Swan asked of the company at large. "Really, when you think of it. A child like that, just suddenly having everything all at once. And probably coming of poor people, too. Are his parents—living?"

"Oh, no, no," Mrs. Matson said briskly. "I couldn't

be bothered with anything like that. Of course, I found out all about them. They were really quite nice, clean people—the father was a college man. Curtis really comes of a very nice family, for an orphan."

"Do you think you'll ever tell him that you aren't— that he isn't—tell him about it?" inquired Mrs. Kerley.

"Dear me, yes, just as soon as he's a little older," Mrs. Matson answered. "I think it's so much nicer for him to know. He'll appreciate everything so much more."

"Does the little thing remember his father and mother at all?" Mrs. Swan asked.

"I really don't know if he does or not," said Mrs. Matson. "Why?"

"Tea," announced the maid, appearing abruptly at the door.

"Tea is served, Mrs. Matson," said Mrs. Matson, her voice lifted.

"Tea is served, Mrs. Matson," echoed the maid.

"*I* don't know what I'm going to do with her," Mrs. Matson told her guests when the girl had disappeared. "Here last night she had company in the kitchen till nearly eleven o'clock at night. The trouble with me is I'm too good to servants. The only way to do is to treat them like cattle."

"They don't appreciate anything else," said Mrs. Kerley.

Mrs. Matson placed her embroidery in her sweet-grass work-basket, and rose.

"Well, shall we go have a cup of tea?" she said.

"Why, how lovely!" cried Mrs. Swan.

Mrs. Cook, who had been knitting doggedly, was informed, via the speaking-tube, of the readiness of tea. She dropped her work instantly, and led the way to the dining-room.

The talk, at the tea-table, was of stitches and patterns. Praise, benignly accepted by Mrs. Matson, was spread by Mrs. Swan and Mrs. Kerley upon the sandwiches, the cake, the baskets, the table-linen, the china, and the design of the silver.

A watch was glanced at, and there arose cries of surprise at the afternoon's flight. There was an assembling of workbags, a fluttering exodus to the hall to put on hats. Mrs. Matson watched her guests.

"Well, it's been just too lovely," Mrs. Swan declared, clasping her hand. "I can't *tell* you how much I've enjoyed it, hearing about the dear little boy, and all. I *hope* you're going to let me see him some time."

"Why, you can see him now, if you'd like," said Mrs. Matson. She went to the foot of the stairs and sang, *"Cur-*tis, *Cur*-tis."

Curtis appeared in the hall above, clean in the gray percale sailor-suit that had been selected in the thrifty expectation of his "growing into it." He looked down at them, caught sight of Mrs. Cook's speaking-tube, and watched it intently, his eyes wide open.

"Come down and see the ladies, Curtis," commanded Mrs. Matson.

Curtis came down, his warm hand squeaking along the bannister. He placed his right foot upon a step, brought his left foot carefully down to it, then started his right one off again. Eventually he reached them.

"Can't you say how-do-you-do to the ladies?" asked Mrs. Matson.

He gave each guest, in turn, a small, flaccid hand.

Mrs. Swan squatted suddenly before him, so that her face was level with his.

"My, what a nice boy!" she cried. "I just love little boys like you, do you know it? Ooh, I could just eat you up! I could!"

She squeezed his arms. Curtis, in alarm, drew his head back from her face.

"And what's *your* name?" she asked him. "Let's see if you can tell me what your name is. I just *bet* you can't!"

He looked at her.

"Can't you tell the lady your name, Curtis?" demanded Mrs. Matson.

"Curtis," he told the lady.

"Why, what a *pretty* name!" she cried. She looked up

at Mrs. Matson. "Was that his real name?" she asked.

"No," Mrs. Matson said, "they had him called something else. But I named him as soon as I got him. My mother was a Curtis."

Thus might one say, "My name was Guelph before I married."

Mrs. Cook spoke sharply. "Lucky!" she said. "Pretty lucky, that young one!"

"Well, I should say so," echoed Mrs. Swan. "Aren't you a pretty lucky little boy? Aren't you, aren't you, aren't you?" She rubbed her nose against his.

"Yes, Mrs. Swan." Mrs. Matson pronounced and frowned at Curtis.

He murmured something.

"Ooh—*you!*" said Mrs. Swan. She rose from her squatting posture. "I'd like to *steal* you, in your little sailor-suit, and all!"

"Mother bought that suit for you, didn't she?" asked Mrs. Matson of Curtis. "Mother bought him all his nice things."

"Oh, he calls you mother? Now, isn't that sweet!" cried Mrs. Swan.

"Yes, I think it's nice," said Mrs. Matson.

There was a brisk, sure step on the porch; a key turned in the lock. Mr. Matson was among them.

"Well," said Mrs. Matson upon seeing her mate. It

was her invariable evening greeting to him.

"Ah," said Mr. Matson. It was his to her.

Mrs. Kerley cooed. Mrs. Swan blinked vivaciously. Mrs. Cook applied her speaking-tube to her ear in the anticipation of hearing something good.

"I don't think you've met Mrs. Swan, Albert," remarked Mrs. Matson. He bowed.

"Oh, I've heard so much about Mr. Matson," cried Mrs. Swan.

Again he bowed.

"We've been making friends with your dear little boy," Mrs. Swan said. She pinched Curtis's cheek. "You sweetie, you!"

"Well, Curtis," said Mr. Matson, "haven't you got a good evening for me?"

Curtis gave his hand to his present father with a weak smile of politeness. He looked modestly down.

"That's more like it," summarized Mr. Matson. His parental duties accomplished, he turned to fulfill his social obligations. Boldly he caught up Mrs. Cook's speaking-tube. Curtis watched.

"Getting cooler out," roared Mr. Matson. "I thought it would."

Mrs. Cook nodded. "That's good!" she shouted.

Mr. Matson pressed forward to open the door for her. He was of generous proportions, and the hall was narrow.

One of the buttons-of-leisure on his coat-sleeve caught in Mrs. Cook's speaking-tube. It fell, with a startling crash, to the floor, and writhed about.

Curtis's control went. Peal upon peal of high, helpless laughter came from him. He laughed on, against Mrs. Matson's cry of "Curtis!" against Mr. Matson's frown. He doubled over, his hands on his little brown knees, and laughed mad laughter.

"Curtis!" bellowed Mr. Matson. The laughter died. Curtis straightened himself, and one last little moan of enjoyment escaped him.

Mr. Matson pointed with a magnificent gesture. "Upstairs!" he boomed.

Curtis turned and climbed the stairs. He looked small beside the banister.

"Well, of all the—" said Mrs. Matson. "I never knew him to do a thing like that since he's been here. I never heard him do such a thing!"

"That young man," pronounced Mr. Matson, "needs a good talking to."

"He needs more than that," his spouse said.

Mr. Matson stooped with a faint creaking, retrieved the speaking-tube, and presented it to Mrs. Cook. "Not at all," he said in anticipation of the thanks which she left unspoken. He bowed.

"Pardon me," he ordered, and mounted the stairs.

Mrs. Matson moved to the door in the wake of her guests. She was bewildered and, it seemed, grieved.

"I never," she affirmed, "never knew that child to go on that way."

"Oh, children," Mrs. Kerley assured her, "they're funny sometimes—especially a little boy like that. You can't expect so much. My goodness, you'll fix all that! I always say I don't know any child that's getting any better bringing up than that young one—just as if he was your own."

Peace returned to the breast of Mrs. Matson. "Oh— goodness!" she said. There was almost a coyness in her smile as she closed the door on the departing.

The Last

Tea

The Last Tea

The young man in the chocolate-brown suit sat down at the table, where the girl with the artificial camellia had been sitting for forty minutes.

"Guess I must be late," he said. "Sorry you been waiting."

"Oh, goodness!" she said. "I just got here myself, just about a second ago. I simply went ahead and ordered because I was dying for a cup of tea. I was late, myself. I haven't been here more than a minute."

"That's good," he said. "Hey, hey, easy on the sugar—one lump is fair enough. And take away those cakes. Terrible! Do I feel terrible!"

"Ah," she said, "you do? Ah. Whadda matter?"

"Oh, I'm ruined," he said. "I'm in terrible shape."

"Ah, the poor boy," she said. "Was it feelin' mizzable? Ah, and it came way up here to meet me! You shouldn't have done that—I'd have understood. Ah, just think of it coming all the way up here when it's so sick!"

"Oh, that's all right," he said. "I might as well be here as any place else. Any place is like any other place, the way I feel today. Oh, I'm all shot."

"Why, that's just awful," she said. "Why, you poor sick thing. Goodness, I hope it isn't influenza. They say there's a lot of it around."

"Influenza!" he said. "I wish that was all I had. Oh, I'm poisoned. I'm through. I'm off the stuff for life. Know what time I got to bed? Twenty minutes past five, A.M., this morning. What a night! What an evening!"

"I thought," she said, "that you were going to stay at the office and work late. You said you'd be working every night this week."

"Yeah, I know," he said. "But it gave me the heebs, thinking about going down there and sitting at that desk. I went up to May's—she was throwing a party. Say, there was somebody there said they knew you."

"Honestly?" she said. "Man or woman?"

"Jane," he said. "Name's Carol McCall. Say, why haven't I been told about her before? That's what I call a girl. What a looker she is!"

"Oh, really?" she said. "That's funny—I never heard of anyone that thought that. I've heard people say she was sort of nice-looking, if she wouldn't make up so much. But I never heard of anyone that thought she was pretty."

"Pretty is right," he said. "What a couple of eyes she's got on her!"

"Really?" she said. "I never noticed them particularly. But I haven't seen her for a long time—sometimes people change, or something."

"She says she used to go to school with you," he said.

"Well, we went to the same school," she said. "I simply happened to go to public school because it happened to be right near us, and mother hated to have me crossing streets. But she was three or four classes ahead of me. She's ages older than I am."

"She's three or four classes ahead of them all," he said. "Dance! Can she step! 'Burn your clothes, baby,' I kept telling her. I must have been fried pretty."

"I was out dancing myself, last night," she said. "Wally Dillon and I. He's just been pestering me to go out with him. He's the most wonderful dancer. Goodness! I didn't get home till I don't know what time. I must look just simply a wreck. Don't I?"

"You look all right," he said.

"Wally's crazy," she said. "The things he says! For some crazy reason or other, he's got it into his head that I've got beautiful eyes, and, well, he just kept talking about them till I didn't know where to look, I was so embarrassed. I got so red, I thought everybody in the place would be looking at me. I got just as red as a brick. Beautiful eyes! Isn't he crazy?"

"He's all right," he said. "Say, this little McCall girl, she's had all kinds of offers to go into moving pictures. 'Why don't you go ahead and go?' I told her. But she says she doesn't feel like it."

"There was a man up at the lake, two summers ago," she said. "He was a director or something with one of the big moving-picture people—oh, he had all kinds of influence!—and he used to keep insisting and insisting that I ought to be in the movies. Said I ought to be doing sort of Garbo parts. I used to just laugh at him. Imagine!"

"She's had about a million offers," he said. "I told her to go ahead and go. She keeps getting these offers all the time."

"Oh, really?" she said. "Oh, listen, I knew I had something to ask you. Did you call me up last night, by any chance?"

"Me?" he said. "No, I didn't call you."

"While I was out, mother said this man's voice kept calling up," she said. "I thought maybe it might be you, by some chance. I wonder who it could have been. Oh—I guess I know who it was. Yes, that's who it was!"

"No, I didn't call you," he said. "I couldn't have seen a telephone, last night. What a head I had on me, this morning! I called Carol up, around ten, and she said she was feeling great. Can that girl hold her liquor!"

"It's a funny thing about me," she said. "It just makes me feel sort of sick to see a girl drink. It's just something in me, I guess. I don't mind a man so much, but it makes me feel perfectly terrible to see a girl get intoxicated. It's just the way I am, I suppose."

"Does she carry it!" he said. "And then feels great the next day. There's a girl! Hey, what are you doing there? I don't want any more tea, thanks. I'm not one of these tea boys. And these tea rooms give me the heebs. Look at all those old dames, will you? Enough to give you the heebs."

"Of course, if you'd rather be some place, drinking, with I don't know what kinds of people," she said, "I'm sure I don't see how I can help that. Goodness, there are enough people that are glad enough to take me to tea. I don't know how many people keep calling me up and pestering me to take me to tea. Plenty of people!"

"All right, all right, I'm here, aren't I?" he said. "Keep your hair on."

"I could name them all day," she said.

"All right," he said. "What's there to crab about?"

"Goodness, it isn't any of my business what you do," she said. "But I hate to see you wasting your time with people that aren't nearly good enough for you. That's all."

"No need worrying over me," he said. "I'll be all right. Listen. You don't have to worry."

"It's just I don't like to see you wasting your time," she said, "staying up all night and then feeling terribly the next day. Ah, I was forgetting he was so sick. Ah, I was mean, wasn't I, scolding him when he was so mizzable. Poor boy. How's he feel now?"

"Oh, I'm all right," he said. "I feel fine. You want anything else? How about getting a check? I got to make a telephone call before six."

"Oh, really?" she said. "Calling up Carol?"

"She said she might be in around now," he said.

"Seeing her tonight?" she said.

"She's going to let me know when I call up," he said. "She's probably got about a million dates. Why?"

"I was just wondering," she said. "Goodness, I've got to fly! I'm having dinner with Wally, and he's so crazy, he's probably there now. He's called me up about a hundred times today."

"Wait till I pay the check," he said, "and I'll put you on a bus."

"Oh, don't bother," she said. "It's right at the corner.

I've got to fly. I suppose you want to stay and call up your friend from here?"

"It's an idea," he said. "Sure you'll be all right?"

"Oh, sure," she said. Busily she gathered her gloves and purse, and left her chair. He rose, not quite fully, as she stopped beside him.

"When'll I see you again?" she said.

"I'll call you up," he said. "I'm all tied up, down at the office and everything. Tell you what I'll do, I'll give you a ring."

"Honestly, I have more dates!" she said. "It's terrible. I don't know when I'll have a minute. But you call up, will you?"

"I'll do that," he said. "Take care of yourself."

"You take care of yourself," she said. "Hope you'll feel all right."

"Oh, I'm fine," he said. "Just beginning to come back to life."

"Be sure and let me know how you feel," she said, "Will you? Sure, now? Well, good-bye. Oh, have a good time tonight!"

"Thanks," he said. "Hope you have a good time, too."

"Oh, I will," she said. "I expect to. I've got to rush! Oh, I nearly forgot! Thanks ever so much for the tea. It was lovely."

"Be your age, will you?" he said.

"It was," she said. "Well. Now don't forget to call me up, will you? Sure? Well, good-bye."

"Olive oil," he said.

She walked on down the little lane between the blue-painted tables.

Big Blonde

Big Blonde

azel Morse was a large, fair woman of the type that incites some men when they use the word "blonde" to click their tongues and wag their heads roguishly. She prided herself upon her small feet and suffered for her vanity, boxing them in snub-toed, high-heeled slippers of the shortest bearable size. The curious things about her were her hands, strange terminations to the flabby white arms splattered with pale tan spots—long, quivering hands with deep and convex nails. She should not have disfigured them with little jewels.

She was not a woman given to recollections. At her middle thirties, her old days were a blurred and flickering sequence, an imperfect film, dealing with the actions of strangers.

In her twenties, after the deferred death of a hazy widowed mother, she had been employed as a model in a wholesale dress establishment—it was still the day of the big woman, and she was then prettily colored and erect and high-breasted. Her job was not onerous, and she met numbers of men and spent numbers of evenings with them, laughing at their jokes and telling them she loved their neckties. Men liked her, and she took it for granted that the liking of many men was a desirable thing. Popularity seemed to her to be worth all the work that had to be put into its achievement. Men liked you because you were fun, and when they liked you they took you out, and there you were. So, and successfully, she was fun. She was a good sport. Men like a good sport.

No other form of diversion, simpler or more complicated, drew her attention. She never pondered if she might not be better occupied doing something else. Her ideas, or, better, her acceptances, ran right along with those of the other substantially built blondes in whom she found her friends.

When she had been working in the dress establishment some years she met Herbie Morse. He was thin, quick, attractive, with shifting lines about his shiny, brown eyes and a habit of fiercely biting at the skin around his finger nails. He drank largely; she found that entertaining. Her habitual greeting to him was an allusion to his state of the previous night.

"Oh, what a peach you had," she used to say, through her easy laugh. "I thought I'd die, the way you kept asking the waiter to dance with you."

She liked him immediately upon their meeting. She was enormously amused at his fast, slurred sentences, his interpolations of apt phrases from vaudeville acts and comic strips; she thrilled at the feel of his lean arm tucked firm beneath the sleeve of her coat; she wanted to touch the wet, flat surface of his hair. He was as promptly drawn to her. They were married six weeks after they had met.

She was delighted at the idea of being a bride; coquetted with it, played upon it. Other offers of marriage she had had, and not a few of them, but it happened that they were all from stout, serious men who had visited the dress establishment as buyers; men from Des Moines and Houston and Chicago and, in her phrase, even funnier places. There was always something immensely comic to her in the thought of living elsewhere than New York. She could not regard as serious proposals that she share a western residence.

She wanted to be married. She was nearing thirty

now, and she did not take the years well. She spread and softened, and her darkening hair turned her to inexpert dabblings with peroxide. There were times when she had little flashes of fear about her job. And she had had a couple of thousand evenings of being a good sport among her male acquaintances. She had come to be more conscientious than spontaneous about it.

Herbie earned enough, and they took a little apartment far uptown. There was a Mission-furnished diningroom with a hanging central light globed in liver-colored glass; in the living-room were an "over-stuffed suite," a Boston fern and a reproduction of the Henner "Magdalene" with the red hair and the blue draperies; the bedroom was in gray enamel and old rose, with Herbie's photograph on Hazel's dressing-table and Hazel's likeness on Herbie's chest of drawers.

She cooked—and she was a good cook—and marketed and chatted with the delivery boys and the colored laundress. She loved the flat, she loved her life, she loved Herbie. In the first months of their marriage, she gave him all the passion she was ever to know.

She had not realized how tired she was. It was a delight, a new game, a holiday, to give up being a good sport. If her head ached or her arches throbbed, she complained piteously, babyishly. If her mood was quiet, she did not talk. If tears came to her eyes, she let them fall.

She fell readily into the habit of tears during the first year of her marriage. Even in her good sport days, she had been known to weep lavishly and disinterestedly on occasion. Her behavior at the theater was a standing joke. She could weep at anything in a play—tiny garments, love both unrequited and mutual, seduction, purity, faithful servitors, wedlock, the triangle.

"There goes Haze," her friends would say, watching her. "She's off again."

Wedded and relaxed, she poured her tears freely. To her who had laughed so much, crying was delicious. All sorrows became her sorrows; she was Tenderness. She would cry long and softly over newspaper accounts of kidnaped babies, deserted wives, unemployed men, strayed cats, heroic dogs. Even when the paper was no longer before her, her mind revolved upon these things and the drops slipped rhythmically over her plump cheeks.

"Honestly," she would say to Herbie, "all the sadness there is in the world when you stop to think about it!"

"Yeah," Herbie would say.

She missed nobody. The old crowd, the people who had brought her and Herbie together, dropped from their lives, lingeringly at first. When she thought of this at all, it was only to consider it fitting. This was marriage. This was peace.

143

But the thing was that Herbie was not amused.

For a time, he had enjoyed being alone with her. He found the voluntary isolation novel and sweet. Then it palled with a ferocious suddenness. It was as if one night, sitting with her in the steam-heated living-room, he would ask no more; and the next night he was through and done with the whole thing.

He became annoyed by her misty melancholies. At first, when he came home to find her softly tired and moody, he kissed her neck and patted her shoulder and begged her to tell her Herbie what was wrong. She loved that. But time slid by, and he found that there was never anything really, personally, the matter.

"Ah, for God's sake," he would say, "Crabbing again. All right, sit here and crab your head off. I'm going out."

And he would slam out of the flat and come back late and drunk.

She was completely bewildered by what happened to their marriage. First they were lovers; and then, it seemed without transition, they were enemies. She never understood it.

There were longer and longer intervals between his leaving his office and his arrival at the apartment. She went through agonies of picturing him run over and bleeding, dead and covered with a sheet. Then she lost her fears for his safety and grew sullen and wounded. When a person wanted to be with a person, he came as soon as possible. She desperately wanted him to want to be with her; her own hours only marked the time till he would come. It was often nearly nine o'clock before he came home to dinner. Always he had had many drinks, and their effect would die in him, leaving him loud and querulous and bristling for affronts.

He was too nervous, he said, to sit and do nothing for an evening. He boasted, probably not in all truth, that he had never read a book in his life.

"What am I expected to do—sit around this dump on my tail all night?" he would ask, rhetorically. And again he would slam out.

She did not know what to do. She could not manage him. She could not meet him.

She fought him furiously. A terrific domesticity had come upon her, and she would bite and scratch to guard it. She wanted what she called "a nice home." She wanted a sober, tender husband, prompt at dinner, punctual at work. She wanted sweet, comforting evenings. The idea of intimacy with other men was terrible to her; the thought that Herbie might be seeking entertainment in other women set her frantic.

It seemed to her that almost everything she read— novels from the drug-store lending library, magazine stories, women's pages in the papers—dealt with wives who lost their husbands' love. She could bear those, at that, better than accounts of neat, companionable marriage and living happily ever after.

She was frightened. Several times when Herbie came home in the evening, he found her determinedly dressed— she had had to alter those of her clothes that were not new, to make them fasten—and rouged.

"Let's go wild tonight, what do you say?" she would hail him. "A person's got lots of time to hang around and do nothing when they're dead."

So they would go out, to chop houses and the less expensive cabarets. But it turned out badly. She could no longer find amusement in watching Herbie drink. She could not laugh at his whimsicalities, she was so tensely counting his indulgences. And she was unable to keep back her remonstrances—"Ah, come on, Herb, you've had enough, haven't you? You'll feel something terrible in the morning."

He would be immediately enraged. All right, crab; crab, crab, crab, crab, that was all she ever did. What a lousy sport *she* was! There would be scenes, and one or the other of them would rise and stalk out in fury.

She could not recall the definite day that she started drinking, herself. There was nothing separate about her days. Like drops upon a window-pane, they ran together and trickled away. She had been married six months; then a year; then three years.

She had never needed to drink, formerly. She could sit for most of a night at a table where the others were imbibing earnestly and never droop in looks or spirits, nor be bored by the doings of those about her. If she took a cocktail, it was so unusual as to cause twenty minutes or so of jocular comment. But now anguish was in her. Frequently, after a quarrel, Herbie would stay out for the night, and she could not learn from him where the time had been spent. Her heart felt tight and sore in her breast, and her mind turned like an electric fan.

She hated the taste of liquor. Gin, plain or in mixtures, made her promptly sick. After experiment, she found that Scotch whisky was best for her. She took it without water, because that was the quickest way to its effect.

Herbie pressed it on her. He was glad to see her drink. They both felt it might restore her high spirits, and their good times together might again be possible.

" 'Atta girl," he would approve her. "Let's see you get boiled, baby."

But it brought them no nearer. When she drank with him, there would be a little while of gayety and then, strangely without beginning, they would be in a wild quarrel. They would wake in the morning not sure what it had all been about, foggy as to what had been said and done, but each deeply injured and bitterly resentful. There would be days of vengeful silence.

There had been a time when they had made up their quarrels, usually in bed. There would be kisses and little names and assurances of fresh starts. . . . "Oh, it's going to be great now, Herb. We'll have swell times. I was a crab. I guess I must have been tired. But everything's going to be swell. You'll see."

Now there were no gentle reconciliations. They resumed friendly relations only in the brief magnanimity caused by liquor, before more liquor drew them into new battles. The scenes became more violent. There were shouted invectives and pushes, and sometimes sharp slaps. Once she had a black eye. Herbie was horrified next day at sight of it. He did not go to work; he followed her about, suggesting remedies and heaping dark blame on himself. But after they had had a few drinks—"to pull themselves together"—she made so many wistful references to her bruise that he shouted at her and rushed out and was gone for two days.

Each time he left the place in a rage, he threatened never to come back. She did not believe him, nor did she consider separation. Somewhere in her head or her heart was the lazy, nebulous hope that things would change and she and Herbie settle suddenly into soothing married life. Here were her home, her furniture, her husband, her station. She summoned no alternatives.

She could no longer bustle and potter. She had no

more vicarious tears; the hot drops she shed were for
herself. She walked ceaselessly about the rooms, her
thoughts running mechanically round and round Herbie.
In those days began the hatred of being alone that she was
never to overcome. You could be by yourself when things
were all right, but when you were blue you got the howling
horrors.

She commenced drinking alone, little, short drinks all
through the day. It was only with Herbie that alcohol made
her nervous and quick in offense. Alone, it blurred sharp
things for her. She lived in a haze of it. Her life took on a
dream-like quality. Nothing was astonishing.

A Mrs. Martin moved into the flat across the hall. She
was a great blonde woman of forty, a promise in looks of
what Mrs. Morse was to be. They made acquaintance,
quickly became inseparable. Mrs. Morse spent her days in
the opposite apartment. They drank together, to brace
themselves after the drinks of the nights before.

She never confided her troubles about Herbie to Mrs.
Martin. The subject was too bewildering to her to find
comfort in talk. She let it be assumed that her husband's
business kept him much away. It was not regarded as
important; husbands, as such, played but shadowy parts in
Mrs. Martin's circle.

Mrs. Martin had no visible spouse; you were left to
decide for yourself whether he was or was not dead. She

had an admirer, Joe, who came to see her almost nightly. Often he brought several friends with him—"The Boys," they were called. The Boys were big, red, good-humored men, perhaps forty-five, perhaps fifty. Mrs. Morse was glad of invitations to join the parties—Herbie was scarcely ever at home at night now. If he did come home, she did not visit Mrs. Martin. An evening alone with Herbie meant inevitably a quarrel, yet she would stay with him. There was always her thin and wordless idea that, maybe, this night, things would begin to be all right.

The Boys brought plenty of liquor along with them whenever they came to Mrs. Martin's. Drinking with them, Mrs. Morse became lively and good-natured and audacious. She was quickly popular. When she had drunk enough to cloud her most recent battle with Herbie, she was excited by their approbation. Crab, was she? Rotten sport, was she? Well, there were some that thought different.

Ed was one of The Boys. He lived in Utica—had "his own business" there, was the awed report—but he came to New York almost every week. He was married. He showed Mrs. Morse the then current photographs of Junior and Sister, and she praised them abundantly and sincerely. Soon it was accepted by the others that Ed was her particular friend.

He staked her when they all played poker; sat next her

and occasionally rubbed his knee against hers during the game. She was rather lucky. Frequently she went home with a twenty-dollar bill or a ten-dollar bill or a handful of crumpled dollars. She was glad of them. Herbie was getting, in her words, something awful about money. To ask him for it brought an instant row.

"What the hell do you do with it?" he would say. "Shoot it all on Scotch?"

"I try to run this house half-way decent," she would retort. "Never thought of that, did you? Oh, no, his lordship couldn't be bothered with that."

Again, she could not find a definite day, to fix the beginning of Ed's proprietorship. It became his custom to kiss her on the mouth when he came in, as well as for farewell, and he gave her little quick kisses of approval all through the evening. She liked this rather more than she disliked It. She never thought of his kisses when she was not with him.

He would run his hand lingeringly over her back and shoulders.

"Some dizzy blonde, eh?" he would say. "Some doll."

One afternoon she came home from Mrs. Martin's to find Herbie in the bedroom. He had been away for several nights, evidently on a prolonged drinking bout. His face was gray, his hands jerked as if they were on wires. On the bed were two old suitcases, packed high. Only her photograph remained on his bureau, and the wide doors of his closet disclosed nothing but coat-hangers.

"I'm blowing," he said. "I'm through with the whole works. I got a job in Detroit."

She sat down on the edge of the bed. She had drunk much the night before, and the four Scotches she had had with Mrs. Martin had only increased her fogginess.

"Good job?" she said.

"Oh, yeah," he said. "Looks all right."

He closed a suitcase with difficulty, swearing at it in whispers.

"There's some dough in the bank," he said. "The bank book's in your top drawer. You can have the furniture and stuff."

He looked at her, and his forehead twitched.

"God damn it, I'm through, I'm telling you," he cried. "I'm through."

"All right, all right," she said. "I heard you, didn't I?"

She saw him as if he were at one end of a cañon and she at the other. Her head was beginning to ache bumpingly, and her voice had a dreary, tiresome tone. She could not have raised it.

"Like a drink before you go?" she asked.

Again he looked at her, and a corner of his mouth jerked up.

"Cockeyed again for a change, aren't you?" he said. "That's nice. Sure, get a couple of shots, will you?"

She went to the pantry, mixed him a stiff highball, poured herself a couple of inches of whisky and drank it. Then she gave herself another portion and brought the glasses into the bedroom. He had strapped both suitcases and had put on his hat and overcoat.

He took his highball.

"Well," he said, and he gave a sudden, uncertain laugh. "Here's mud in your eye."

"Mud in your eye," she said.

They drank. He put down his glass and took up the heavy suitcases.

"Got to get a train around six," he said.

She followed him down the hall. There was a song, a song that Mrs. Martin played doggedly on the phonograph, running loudly through her mind. She had never liked the thing.

"Night and daytime,
Always playtime.
Ain't we got fun?"

At the door he put down the bags and faced her.

"Well," he said. "Well, take care of yourself. You'll be all right, will you?"

"Oh, sure," she said.

He opened the door, then came back to her, holding out his hand.

" 'Bye, Haze," he said. "Good luck to you."

She took his hand and shook it.

"Pardon my wet glove," she said.

When the door had closed behind him, she went back to the pantry.

She was flushed and lively when she went in to Mrs. Martin's that evening. The Boys were there, Ed among them. He was glad to be in town, frisky and loud and full of jokes. But she spoke quietly to him for a minute.

"Herbie blew today," she said. "Going to live out west."

"That so?" he said. He looked at her and played with the fountain pen clipped to his waistcoat pocket.

"Think he's gone for good, do you?" he asked.

"Yeah," she said. "I know he is. I know. Yeah."

"You going to live on across the hall just the same?" he said. "Know what you're going to do?"

"Gee, I don't know," she said. "I don't give much of a damn."

"Oh, come on, that's no way to talk," he told her. "What you need—you need a little snifter. How about it?"

"Yeah," she said. "Just straight."

She won forty-three dollars at poker. When the game broke up, Ed took her back to her apartment.

"Got a little kiss for me?" he asked.

He wrapped her in his big arms and kissed her vio-
lently. She was entirely passive. He held her away and
looked at her.

"Little tight, honey?" he asked, anxiously. "Not
going to be sick, are you?"

"Me?" she said. "I'm swell."

II

When Ed left in the morning, he took her photograph with
him. He said he wanted her picture to look at, up in Utica.
"You can have that one on the bureau," she said.

She put Herbie's picture in a drawer, out of her sight.
When she could look at it, she meant to tear it up. She was
fairly successful in keeping her mind from racing around
him. Whisky slowed it for her. She was almost peaceful, in
her mist.

She accepted her relationship with Ed without question or enthusiasm. When he was away, she seldom
thought definitely of him. He was good to her; he gave her
frequent presents and a regular allowance. She was even
able to save. She did not plan ahead of any day, but her
wants were few, and you might as well put money in the
bank as have it lying around.

When the lease of her apartment neared its end, it was
Ed who suggested moving. His friendship with Mrs. Mar-

155

tin and Joe had become strained over a dispute at poker; a feud was impending.

"Let's get the hell out of here," Ed said. "What I want you to have is a place near the Grand Central. Make it easier for me."

So she took a little flat in the Forties. A colored maid came in every day to clean and to make coffee for her—she was "through with that housekeeping stuff," she said, and Ed, twenty years married to a passionately domestic woman, admired this romantic uselessness and felt doubly a man of the world in abetting it.

The coffee was all she had until she went out to dinner, but alcohol kept her fat. Prohibition she regarded only as a basis for jokes. You could always get all you wanted. She was never noticeably drunk and seldom nearly sober. It required a larger daily allowance to keep her misty-minded. Too little, and she was achingly melancholy.

Ed brought her to Jimmy's. He was proud, with the pride of the transient who would be mistaken for a native, in his knowledge of small, recent restaurants occupying the lower floors of shabby brownstone houses; places where, upon mentioning the name of an habitué friend, might be obtained strange whisky and fresh gin in many of their ramifications. Jimmy's place was the favorite of his acquaintances.

There, through Ed, Mrs. Morse met many men and
women, formed quick friendships. The men often took her
out when Ed was in Utica. He was proud of her popularity.

She fell into the habit of going to Jimmy's alone when
she had no engagement. She was certain to meet some
people she knew, and join them. It was a club for her
friends, both men and women.

The women at Jimmy's looked remarkably alike, and
this was curious, for, through feuds, removals and opportunities of more profitable contacts, the personnel of the
group changed constantly. Yet always the newcomers resembled those whom they replaced. They were all big
women and stout, broad of shoulder and abundantly
breasted, with faces thickly clothed in soft, high-colored
flesh. They laughed loud and often, showing opaque and
lusterless teeth like squares of crockery. There was about
them the health of the big, yet a slight, unwholesome
suggestion of stubborn preservation. They might have
been thirty-six or forty-five or anywhere between.

They composed their titles of their own first names
with their husbands' surnames—Mrs. Florence Miller,
Mrs. Vera Riley, Mrs. Lilian Block. This gave at the same
time the solidity of marriage and the glamour of freedom.
Yet only one or two were actually divorced. Most of them
never referred to their dimmed spouses; some, a shorter
time separate, described them in terms of great biological

interest. Several were mothers, each of an only child—a boy at school somewhere, or a girl being cared for by a grandmother. Often, well on towards morning, there would be displays of kodak portraits and of tears.

They were comfortable women, cordial and friendly and irrepressibly matronly. Theirs was the quality of ease. Become fatalistic, especially about money matters, they were unworried. Whenever their funds dropped alarmingly, a new donor appeared; this had always happened. The aim of each was to have one man, permanently, to pay all her bills, in return for which she would have immediately given up other admirers and probably would have become exceedingly fond of him; for the affections of all of them were, by now, unexacting, tranquil, and easily arranged. This end, however, grew increasingly difficult yearly. Mrs. Morse was regarded as fortunate.

Ed had a good year, increased her allowance and gave her a sealskin coat. But she had to be careful of her moods with him. He insisted upon gayety. He would not listen to admissions of aches or weariness.

"Hey, listen," he would say, "I got worries of my own, and plenty. Nobody wants to hear other people's troubles, sweetie. What you got to do, you got to be a sport and forget it. See? Well, slip us a little smile, then. That's my girl."

She never had enough interest to quarrel with him as

she had with Herbie, but she wanted the privilege of occasional admitted sadness. It was strange. The other women she saw did not have to fight their moods. There was Mrs. Florence Miller who got regular crying jags, and the men sought only to cheer and comfort her. The others spent whole evenings in grieved recitals of worries and ills; their escorts paid them deep sympathy. But she was instantly undesirable when she was low in spirits. Once, at Jimmy's, when she could not make herself lively, Ed had walked out and left her.

"Why the hell don't you stay home and not go spoiling everybody's evening?" he had roared.

Even her slightest acquaintances seemed irritated if she were not conspicuously lighthearted.

"What's the matter with you, anyway?" they would say. "Be your age, why don't you? Have a little drink and snap out of it."

When her relationship with Ed had continued nearly three years, he moved to Florida to live. He hated leaving her; he gave her a large check and some shares of a sound stock, and his pale eyes were wet when he said good-bye. She did not miss him. He came to New York infrequently, perhaps two or three times a year, and hurried directly from the train to see her. She was always pleased to have him come and never sorry to see him go.

Charley, an acquaintance of Ed's that she had met at

Jimmy's, had long admired her. He had always made opportunities of touching her and leaning close to talk to her. He asked repeatedly of all their friends if they had ever heard such a fine laugh as she had. After Ed left, Charley became the main figure in her life. She classified him and spoke of him as "not so bad." There was nearly a year of Charley; then she divided her time between him and Sydney, another frequenter of Jimmy's; then Charley slipped away altogether.

Sydney was a little, brightly dressed, clever Jew. She was perhaps nearest contentment with him. He amused her always; her laughter was not forced.

He admired her completely. Her softness and size delighted him. And he thought she was great, he often told her, because she kept gay and lively when she was drunk.

"Once I had a gal," he said, "used to try and throw herself out of the window every time she got a can on. Jee-*zuss*," he added, feelingly.

Then Sydney married a rich and watchful bride, and then there was Billy. No—after Sydney came Fred, then Billy. In her haze, she never recalled how men entered her life and left it. There were no surprises. She had no thrill at their advent, nor woe at their departure. She seemed to be always able to attract men. There was never another as rich as Ed, but they were all generous to her, in their means.

160

Once she had news of Herbie. She met Mrs. Martin
dining at Jimmy's, and the old friendship was vigorously
renewed. The still admiring Joe, while on a business trip,
had seen Herbie. He had settled in Chicago, he looked fine,
he was living with some woman—seemed to be crazy
about her. Mrs. Morse had been drinking vastly that day.
She took the news with mild interest, as one hearing of the
sex peccadilloes of somebody whose name is, after a moment's groping, familiar.

"Must be damn near seven years since I saw him,"
she commented. "Gee. Seven years."

More and more, her days lost their individuality. She
never knew dates, nor was sure of the day of the week.

"My God, was that a year ago!" she would exclaim,
when an event was recalled in conversation.

She was tired so much of the time. Tired and blue.
Almost everything could give her the blues. Those old
horses she saw on Sixth Avenue—struggling and slipping
along the car-tracks, or standing at the curb, their heads
dropped level with their worn knees. The tightly stored
tears would squeeze from her eyes as she teetered past on
her aching feet in the stubby, champagne-colored slippers.

The thought of death came and stayed with her and
lent her a sort of drowsy cheer. It would be nice, nice and
restful, to be dead.

There was no settled, shocked moment when she first

thought of killing herself; it seemed to her as if the idea had always been with her. She pounced upon all the accounts of suicides in the newspapers. There was an epidemic of self-killings—or maybe it was just that she searched for the stories of them so eagerly that she found many. To read of them roused reassurance in her; she felt a cozy solidarity with the big company of the voluntary dead.

She slept, aided by whisky, till deep into the afternoons, then lay abed, a bottle and glass at her hand, until it was time to dress to go out for dinner. She was beginning to feel towards alcohol a little puzzled distrust, as toward an old friend who has refused a simple favor. Whisky could still soothe her for most of the time, but there were sudden, inexplicable moments when the cloud fell treacherously away from her, and she was sawn by the sorrow and bewilderment and nuisance of all living. She played voluptuously with the thought of cool, sleepy retreat. She had never been troubled by religious belief and no vision of an after-life intimidated her. She dreamed by day of never again putting on tight shoes, of never having to laugh and listen and admire, of never more being a good sport. Never.

But how would you do it? It made her sick to think of jumping from heights. She could not stand a gun. At the theater, if one of the actors drew a revolver, she crammed her fingers into her ears and could not even look at the stage until after the shot had been fired. There was no gas in her flat. She looked long at the bright blue veins in her slim wrists—a cut with a razor blade, and there you'd be. But it would hurt, hurt like hell, and there would be blood to see. Poison—something tasteless and quick and painless—was the thing. But they wouldn't sell it to you in drugstores, because of the law.

She had few other thoughts.

There was a new man now—Art. He was short and fat and exacting and hard on her patience when he was drunk. But there had been only occasionals for some time before him, and she was glad of a little stability. Too, Art must be away for weeks at a stretch, selling silks, and that was restful. She was convincingly gay with him, though the effort shook her.

"The best sport in the world," he would murmur, deep in her neck. "The best sport in the world."

One night, when he had taken her to Jimmy's, she went into the dressing-room with Mrs. Florence Miller. There, while designing curly mouths on their faces with lip-rouge, they compared experiences of insomnia.

"Honestly," Mrs. Morse said, "I wouldn't close an eye if I didn't go to bed full of Scotch. I lie there and toss and turn and toss and turn. Blue! Does a person get blue lying awake that way!"

"Say, listen, Hazel," Mrs. Miller said, impressively, "I'm telling you I'd be awake for a year if I didn't take veronal. That stuff makes you sleep like a fool."

"Isn't it poison, or something?" Mrs. Morse asked.

"Oh, you take too much and you're out for the count," said Mrs. Miller. "I just take five grains—they come in tablets. I'd be scared to fool around with it. But five grains, and you cork off pretty."

"Can you get it anywhere?" Mrs. Morse felt superbly Machiavellian.

"Get all you want in Jersey," said Mrs. Miller. "They won't give it to you here without you have a doctor's prescription. Finished? We'd better go back and see what the boys are doing."

That night, Art left Mrs. Morse at the door of her apartment; his mother was in town. Mrs. Morse was still sober, and it happened that there was no whisky left in her cupboard. She lay in bed, looking up at the black ceiling.

She rose early, for her, and went to New Jersey. She had never taken the tube, and did not understand it. So she went to the Pennsylvania Station and bought a railroad ticket to Newark. She thought of nothing in particular on the trip out. She looked at the uninspired hats of the women about her and gazed through the smeared window at the flat, gritty scene.

In Newark, in the first drug-store she came to, she

asked for a tin of talcum powder, a nailbrush and a box of veronal tablets. The powder and the brush were to make the hypnotic seem also a casual need. The clerk was entirely unconcerned. "We only keep them in bottles," he said, and wrapped up for her a little glass vial containing ten white tablets, stacked one on another.

She went to another drug-store and bought a face-cloth, an orange-wood stick and a bottle of veronal tablets. The clerk was also uninterested.

"Well, I guess I got enough to kill an ox," she thought, and went back to the station.

At home, she put the little vials in the drawer of her dressing-table and stood looking at them with a dreamy tenderness.

"There they are, God bless them," she said, and she kissed her finger-tip and touched each bottle.

The colored maid was busy in the living-room.

"Hey, Nettie," Mrs. Morse called. "Be an angel, will you? Run around to Jimmy's and get me a quart of Scotch."

She hummed while she awaited the girl's return.

During the next few days, whisky ministered to her as tenderly as it had done when she first turned to its aid. Alone, she was soothed and vague, at Jimmy's she was the gayest of the groups. Art was delighted with her.

Then, one night, she had an appointment to meet Art

at Jimmy's for an early dinner. He was to leave afterward on a business excursion, to be away for a week. Mrs. Morse had been drinking all the afternoon; while she dressed to go out, she felt herself rising pleasurably from drowsiness to high spirits. But as she came out into the street the effects of the whisky deserted her completely, and she was filled with a slow, grinding wretchedness so horrible that she stood swaying on the pavement, unable for a moment to move forward. It was a gray night with spurts of mean, thin snow, and the streets shone with dark ice. As she slowly crossed Sixth Avenue, consciously dragging one foot past the other, a big, scarred horse pulling a rickety express-wagon crashed to his knees before her. The driver swore and screamed and lashed the beast insanely, bringing the whip back over his shoulder for every blow, while the horse struggled to get a footing on the slippery asphalt. A group gathered and watched with interest.

Art was waiting, when Mrs. Morse reached Jimmy's.

"What's the matter with you, for God's sake?" was his greeting to her.

"I saw a horse," she said. "Gee, I—a person feels sorry for horses. I—it isn't just horses. Everything's kind of terrible, isn't it? I can't help getting sunk."

"Ah, sunk, me eye," he said. "What's the idea of all the bellyaching? What have you got to be sunk about?"

"I can't help it," she said.

"Ah, help it, me eye," he said. "Pull yourself together, will you? Come on and sit down, and take that face off you."

She drank industriously and she tried hard, but she could not overcome her melancholy. Others joined them and commented on her gloom, and she could do no more for them than smile weakly. She made little dabs at her eyes with her handkerchief, trying to time her movements so they would be unnoticed, but several times Art caught her and scowled and shifted impatiently in his chair.

When it was time for him to go to his train, she said she would leave, too, and go home.

"And not a bad idea, either," he said. "See if you can't sleep yourself out of it. I'll see you Thursday. For God's sake, try and cheer up by then, will you?"

"Yeah," she said. "I will."

In her bedroom, she undressed with a tense speed wholly unlike her usual slow uncertainty. She put on her nightgown, took off her hair-net and passed the comb quickly through her dry, vari-colored hair. Then she took the two little vials from the drawer and carried them into the bathroom. The splintering misery had gone from her, and she felt the quick excitement of one who is about to receive an anticipated gift.

She uncorked the vials, filled a glass with water and stood before the mirror, a tablet between her fingers. Suddenly she bowed graciously to her reflection, and raised the glass to it.

"Well, here's mud in your eye," she said.

The tablets were unpleasant to take, dry and powdery and sticking obstinately halfway down her throat. It took her a long time to swallow all twenty of them. She stood watching her reflection with deep, impersonal interest, studying the movements of the gulping throat. Once more she spoke aloud.

"For God's sake, try and cheer up by Thursday, will you?" she said. "Well, you know what he can do. He and the whole lot of them."

She had no idea how quickly to expect effect from the veronal. When she had taken the last tablet, she stood uncertainly, wondering, still with a courteous, vicarious interest, if death would strike her down then and there. She felt in no way strange, save for a slight stirring of sickness from the effort of swallowing the tablets, nor did her reflected face look at all different. It would not be immediate, then; it might even take an hour or so.

She stretched her arms high and gave a vast yawn.

"Guess I'll go to bed," she said. "Gee, I'm nearly dead."

That struck her as comic, and she turned out the bathroom light and went in and laid herself down in her bed, chuckling softly all the time.

"Gee, I'm nearly dead," she quoted. "That's a hot one!"

III

Nettie, the colored maid, came in late the next afternoon to clean the apartment, and found Mrs. Morse in her bed. But then, that was not unusual. Usually, though, the sounds of cleaning waked her, and she did not like to wake up. Nettie, an agreeable girl, had learned to move softly about her work.

But when she had done the living-room and stolen in to tidy the little square bedroom, she could not avoid a tiny clatter as she arranged the objects on the dressing-table. Instinctively, she glanced over her shoulder at the sleeper, and without warning a sickly uneasiness crept over her. She came to the bed and stared down at the woman lying there.

Mrs. Morse lay on her back, one flabby, white arm flung up, the wrist against her forehead. Her stiff hair hung untenderly along her face. The bed covers were pushed down, exposing a deep square of soft neck and a pink nightgown, its fabric worn uneven by many launderings; her great breasts, freed from their tight confiner, sagged beneath her arm-pits. Now and then she made knotted, snoring sounds, and from the corner of her opened mouth to the blurred turn of her jaw ran a lane of crusted spittle.

"Mis' Morse," Nettie called. "Oh, Mis' Morse! It's terrible late."

Mrs. Morse made no move.

"Mis' Morse," said Nettie. "Look, Mis' Morse. How'm I goin' get this bed made?"

Panic sprang upon the girl. She shook the woman's hot shoulder.

"Ah, wake up, will yuh?" she whined. "Ah, please wake up."

Suddenly the girl turned and ran out in the hall to the elevator door, keeping her thumb firm on the black, shiny button until the elderly car and its Negro attendant stood before her. She poured a jumble of words over the boy, and led him back to the apartment. He tiptoed creakingly in to the bedside; first gingerly, then so lustily that he left marks in the soft flesh, he prodded the unconscious woman.

"Hey, there!" he cried, and listened intently, as for an echo.

"Jeez. Out like a light," he commented.

At his interest in the spectacle, Nettie's panic left her. Importance was big in both of them. They talked in quick, unfinished whispers, and it was the boy's suggestion that he fetch the young doctor who lived on the ground floor. Nettie hurried along with him. They looked forward to the limelit moment of breaking their news of something untoward, something pleasurably unpleasant. Mrs. Morse had become the medium of drama. With no ill wish to her, they hoped that her state was serious, that she would not let them down by being awake and normal on their return. A little fear of this determined them to make the most, to the doctor, of her present condition. "Matter of life and death," returned to Nettie from her thin store of reading. She considered startling the doctor with the phrase.

The doctor was in and none too pleased at interruption. He wore a yellow and blue striped dressing-gown, and he was lying on his sofa, laughing with a dark girl, her face scaly with inexpensive powder, who perched on the arm. Half-emptied highball glasses stood beside them, and her coat and hat were neatly hung up with the comfortable implication of a long stay.

Always something, the doctor grumbled. Couldn't let anybody alone after a hard day. But he put some bottles and instruments into a case, changed his dressing-gown for his coat and started out with the Negroes.

"Snap it up there, big boy," the girl called after him. "Don't be all night."

The doctor strode loudly into Mrs. Morse's flat and on to the bedroom, Nettie and the boy right behind him. Mrs. Morse had not moved; her sleep was as deep, but soundless, now. The doctor looked sharply at her, then plunged his thumbs into the lidded pits above her eyeballs and threw his weight upon them. A high, sickened cry broke from Nettie.

"Look like he tryin' to push her right on th'ough the bed," said the boy. He chuckled.

Mrs. Morse gave no sign under the pressure. Abruptly the doctor abandoned it, and with one quick movement swept the covers down to the foot of the bed. With another he flung her nightgown back and lifted the thick, white legs, cross-hatched with blocks of tiny, iris-colored veins. He pinched them repeatedly, with long, cruel nips, back of the knees. She did not awaken.

"What's she been drinking?" he asked Nettie, over his shoulder.

With the certain celerity of one who knows just where to lay hands on a thing, Nettie went into the bathroom, bound for the cupboard where Mrs. Morse kept her whisky. But she stopped at the sight of the two vials, with their red and white labels, lying before the mirror. She brought them to the doctor.

"Oh, for the Lord Almighty's sweet sake!" he said. He dropped Mrs. Morse's legs, and pushed them impatiently across the bed. "What did she want to go taking that trip for? Rotten yellow trick, that's what a thing like that is. Now we'll have to pump her out, and all that stuff. Nuisance, a thing like that is; that's what it amounts to. Here, George, take me down in the elevator. You wait here, maid. She won't do anything."

"She won' die on me, will she?" cried Nettie.

"No," said the doctor. "God, no. You couldn't kill her with an axe."

IV

After two days, Mrs. Morse came back to consciousness, dazed at first, then with a comprehension that brought with it the slow, saturating wretchedness.

"Oh, Lord, oh, Lord," she moaned, and tears for herself and for life striped her cheeks.

Nettie came in at the sound. For two days she had done the ugly, incessant tasks in the nursing of the unconscious, for two nights she had caught broken bits of sleep on the living-room couch. She looked coldly at the big, blown woman in the bed.

"What you been tryin' to do, Mis' Morse?" she said. "What kine o' work is that, takin' all that stuff?"

"Oh, Lord," moaned Mrs. Morse, again, and she tried to cover her eyes with her arms. But the joints felt stiff and brittle, and she cried out at their ache.

"Tha's no way to ack, takin' them pills," said Nettie. "You can thank you' stars you heah at all. How you feel now?"

"Oh, I feel great," said Mrs. Morse. "Swell, I feel."

Her hot, painful tears fell as if they would never stop.

"Tha's no way to take on, cryin' like that," Nettie said. "After what you done. The doctor, he says he could have you arrested, doin' a thing like that. He was fit to be tied, here."

"Why couldn't he let me alone?" wailed Mrs. Morse. "Why the hell couldn't he have?"

"Tha's terr'ble, Mis' Morse, swearin' an' talkin' like that," said Nettie, "after what people done for you. Here I ain' had no sleep at all for two nights, an' I had to give up goin' out to my other ladies!"

"Oh, I'm sorry, Nettie," she said. "You're a peach. I'm sorry I've given you so much trouble. I couldn't help it. I just got sunk. Didn't you ever feel like doing it? When everything looks just lousy to you?"

"I wouldn't think o' no such thing," declared Nettie. "You got to cheer up. Tha's what you got to do. Everybody's got their troubles."

"Yeah," said Mrs. Morse. "I know."

"Come a pretty picture card for you," Nettie said. "Maybe that will cheer you up."

She handed Mrs. Morse a post-card. Mrs. Morse had to cover one eye with her hand, in order to read the message; her eyes were not yet focusing correctly.

It was from Art. On the back of a view of the Detroit Athletic Club he had written: "Greeting and salutations. Hope you have lost that gloom. Cheer up and don't take any rubber nickles. See you on Thursday."

She dropped the card to the floor. Misery crushed her as if she were between great smooth stones. There passed

174

before her a slow, slow pageant of days spent lying in her
flat, of evenings at Jimmy's being a good sport, making
herself laugh and coo at Art and other Arts; she saw a long
parade of weary horses and shivering beggars and all
beaten, driven, stumbling things. Her feet throbbed as if
she had crammed them into the stubby champagne-colored slippers. Her heart seemed to swell and harden.

"Nettie," she cried, "for heaven's sake pour me a
drink, will you?"

The maid looked doubtful.

"Now you know, Mis' Morse," she said, "you been
near daid. I don' know if the doctor he let you drink
nothin' yet."

"Oh, never mind him," she said. "You get me one,
and bring in the bottle. Take one yourself."

"Well," said Nettie.

She poured them each a drink, deferentially leaving
hers in the bathroom to be taken in solitude, and brought
Mrs. Morse's glass in to her.

Mrs. Morse looked into the liquor and shuddered
back from its odor. Maybe it would help. Maybe, when you
had been knocked cold for a few days, your very first drink
would give you a lift. Maybe whisky would be her friend
again. She prayed without addressing a God, without
knowing a God. Oh, please, please, let her be able to get
drunk, please keep her always drunk.

She lifted the glass.

175

"Thanks, Nettie," she said. "Here's mud in your eye."

The maid giggled. "Tha's the way, Mis' Morse," she said. "You cheer up, now."

"Yeah," said Mrs. Morse. "Sure."

Arrangement in Black and White

Arrangement in Black and White

The woman with the pink velvet poppies wreathed round the assisted gold of her hair traversed the crowded room at an interesting gait combining a skip with a sidle, and clutched the lean arm of her host.

"Now I got you!" she said. "Now you can't get away!"

"Why, hello," said her host. "Well. How are you?"

"Oh, I'm finely," she said. "Just simply finely. Listen. I want you to do me the most terrible favor. Will you? Will you please? Pretty please?"

"What is it?" said her host.

"Listen," she said. "I want to meet Walter Williams. Honestly, I'm just simply crazy about that man. Oh, when he sings! When he sings those spirituals! Well, I said to Burton, 'It's a good thing for you Walter Williams is colored,' I said, 'or you'd have lots of reason to be jealous.' I'd really love to meet him. I'd like to tell him I've heard him sing. Will you be an angel and introduce me to him?"

"Why, certainly," said her host. "I thought you'd meet him. The party's for him. Where is he, anyway?"

"He's over there by the bookcase," she said. "Let's wait till those people get through talking to him. Well, I think you're simply marvelous, giving this perfectly marvelous party for him, and having him meet all these white people, and all. Isn't he terribly grateful?"

"I hope not," said her host.

"I think it's really terribly nice," she said. "I do. I don't see why on earth it isn't perfectly all right to meet· colored people. I haven't any feeling at all about it—not one single bit. Burton—oh, he's just the other way. Well, you know, he comes from Virginia, and you know how they are."

"Did he come tonight?" said her host.

"No, he couldn't," she said. "I'm a regular grass widow tonight. I told him when I left, 'There's no telling what I'll do,' I said. He was just so tired out, he couldn't move. Isn't it a shame?"

"Ah," said her host.

"Wait till I tell him I met Walter Williams!" she said. "He'll just about die. Oh, we have more arguments about colored people. I talk to him like I don't know what, I get so excited. 'Oh, don't be so silly,' I say. But I must say for Burton, he's heaps broader-minded than lots of these Southerners. He's really awfully fond of colored people. Well, he says himself, he wouldn't have white servants. And you know, he had this old colored nurse, this regular old nigger mammy, and he just simply loves her. Why, every time he goes home, he goes out in the kitchen to see her. He does, really, to this day. All he says is, he says he hasn't got a word to say against colored people as long as they keep their place. He's always doing things for them— giving them clothes and I don't know what all. The only thing he says, he says he wouldn't sit down at the table with one for a million dollars. 'Oh,' I say to him, 'you make me sick, talking like that.' I'm just terrible to him. Aren't I terrible?"

"Oh, no, no, no," said her host. "No, no."

"I am," she said. "I know I am. Poor Burton! Now, me, I don't feel that way at all. I haven't the slightest feeling about colored people. Why, I'm just crazy about some of them. They're just like children—just as easy-going, and always singing and laughing and everything. Aren't they the happiest things you ever saw in your life? Honestly, it makes me laugh just to hear them. Oh, I like

them. I really do. Well, now, listen, I have this colored
laundress, I've had her for years, and I'm devoted to her.
She's a real character. And I want to tell you, I think of her
as my friend. That's the way I think of her. As I say to
Burton, 'Well, for Heaven's sakes, we're all human be-
ings!' Aren't we?"

"Yes," said her host. "Yes, indeed."

"Now this Walter Williams," she said. "I think a man
like that's a real artist. I do. I think he deserves an awful
lot of credit. Goodness, I'm so crazy about music or anything, I don't care what color he is. I honestly think if a
person's an artist, nobody ought to have any feeling at all
about meeting them. That's absolutely what I say to Burton. Don't you think I'm right?"

"Yes," said her host. "Oh, yes."

"That's the way I feel," she said. "I just can't understand people being narrow-minded. Why, I absolutely
think it's a privilege to meet a man like Walter Williams.
Now, I do. I haven't any feeling at all. Well, my goodness,
the good Lord made him, just the same as He did any of
us. Didn't He?"

"Surely," said her host. "Yes, indeed."

"That's what I say," she said. "Oh, I get so furious
when people are narrow-minded about colored people. It's
just all I can do not to say something. Of course, I do admit
when you get a bad colored man, they're simply terrible.

But as I say to Burton, there are some bad white people, too, in this world. Aren't there?"

"I guess there are," said her host.

"Why, I'd really be glad to have a man like Walter Williams come to my house and sing for us, some time," she said. "Of course, I couldn't ask him on account of Burton, but I wouldn't have any feeling about it at all. Oh, can't he sing! Isn't it marvelous, the way they all have music in them? It just seems to be right *in* them. Come on, let's us go on over and talk to him. Listen, what shall I do when I'm introduced? Ought I to shake hands? Or what?"

"Why, do whatever you want," said her host.

"I guess maybe I'd better," she said. "I wouldn't for the world have him think I had any feeling. I think I'd better shake hands, just the way I would with anybody else. That's just exactly what I'll do."

They reached the tall young Negro, standing by the bookcase. The host performed introductions; the Negro bowed.

"How do you do?" he said.

The woman with the pink velvet poppies extended her hand at the length of her arm and held it so for all the world to see, until the Negro took it, shook it, and gave it back to her.

"Oh, how do you do, Mr. Williams," she said. "Well, how do you do. I've just been saying, I've enjoyed your singing so awfully much. I've been to your concerts, and we have you on the phonograph and everything. Oh, I just enjoy it!"

She spoke with great distinctness, moving her lips meticulously, as if in parlance with the deaf.

"I'm so glad," he said.

"I'm just simply crazy about that 'Walter Boy' thing you sing," she said. "Honestly, I can't get it out of my head. I have my husband nearly crazy, the way I go around humming it all the time. Oh, he looks just as black as the ace of—Er. Well, tell me, where on earth do you ever get all those songs of yours? How do you ever get hold of them?"

"Why," he said, "there are so many different——"

"I should think you'd love singing them," she said. "It must be more fun. All those darling old spirituals— oh, I just love them! Well, what are you doing, now? Are you still keeping up your singing? Why don't you have another concert, some time?"

"I'm having one the sixteenth of this month," he said.

"Well, I'll be there," she said. "I'll be there, if I possibly can. You can count on me. Goodness, here comes a whole raft of people to talk to you. You're just a regular guest of honor! Oh, who's that girl in white? I've seen her some place."

"That's Katherine Burke," said her host.

"Good Heavens," she said, "is that Katherine Burke? Why, she looks entirely different off the stage. I thought she was much better-looking. I had no idea she was so terribly dark. Why, she looks almost like—Oh, I think she's a wonderful actress! Don't you think she's a wonder actress, Mr. Williams? Oh, I think she's marvelous. Don't you?"

"Yes, I do," he said.

"Oh, I do, too," she said. "Just wonderful. Well, goodness, we must give someone else a chance to talk to the guest of honor. Now, don't forget, Mr. Williams, I'm going to be at that concert if I possibly can. I'll be there applauding like everything. And if I can't come, I'm going to tell everybody I know to go, anyway. Don't you forget!"

"I won't," he said. "Thank you so much."

The host took her arm and piloted her into the next room.

"Oh, my dear," she said. "I nearly died! Honestly, I give you my word, I nearly passed away. Did you hear that terrible break I made? I was just going to say Katherine Burke looked almost like a nigger. I just caught myself in time. Oh, do you think he noticed?"

"I don't believe so," said her host.

"Well, thank goodness," she said, "because I wouldn't have embarrassed him for anything. Why, he's awfully nice. Just as nice as he can be. Nice manners, and everything. You know, so many colored people, you give them an inch, and they walk all over you. But he doesn't try any of that. Well, he's got more sense, I suppose. He's really nice. Don't you think so?"

"Yes," said her host.

"I liked him," she said. "I haven't any feeling at all because he's a colored man. I felt just as natural as I would with anybody. Talked to him just as naturally, and everything. But honestly, I could hardly keep a straight face. I kept thinking of Burton. Oh, wait till I tell Burton I called him 'Mister'!"

Dialogue at Three in the Morning

Dialogue at Three in the Morning

"Plain water in mine," said the woman in the petunia-colored hat. "Or never mind about the water. Hell with it. Just straight Scotch. What I care? Just straight. That's me. Never gave anybody any trouble in my life. All right, they can say what they like about me, but I know—I know—I never gave anybody any trouble in my life. You can tell them that from me, see? What I care?"

"Listen," said the man with the ice-blue hair. And he leaned across the table toward her, and frowned heavily at the designs he drew with the plated knife. "Listen. I just want you to get this thing clear——"

"Yeah," she said. "Get things clear. That's good. That gives me a big laugh. That's laughable, a thing like that is. Say, if there's anybody around here that's going to get things clear, I'm going to be the one around here that's going to get things clear. What you do, you go back to Jeannette, see, and you tell her I know what she's saying about me. I don't want to get you into this, but you tell her that from me. You can keep out of it. You don't have to tell her you told me. You don't even have to tell her you saw me. Say, if you're ashamed to tell people you know me, that's all right with me, see? I'm not going to give anybody any trouble. If you're ashamed to tell your friends you're a friend of mine, what I care? I guess I'll be able to stand that, all right. I've stood a lot of things."

"Ah, listen," he said. "Listen. Will you please listen just a minute?"

"Yeah, listen," she said. "That's fine. Listen. Well, I'm through with this listening stuff. You can tell them all from me, see, I'm going to be the one that's going to do the talking from now on. You can tell Jeannette that. What I care? You can run right to her and blab that. Says I look fat in my red dress, does she? That's a nice thing to have anybody say about you. Makes you feel great, that does. You can tell Miss Jeannette she's got a lot to do to make cracks about a person's red dress. That's pretty laughable, that is. Say, when I ask her to pay for anything I wear, then it will be time for her to crack. Her or anybody else. I make my own living, thank God, and I don't have to ask anybody for anything. You can tell them all that. You or anybody else."

"Will you do me a favor?" he said. "Will you do me one little favor? Will you? Will you listen just——"

"Yeah, favors," she said. "Nobody's got to do me any favors. I make my own living, and I don't have to ask any favors off of anybody. I never gave anybody any trouble in my life. And if they don't like it, they know what they can do. Tiffany's window, see? The whole lot of them. Oh, did I break that glass? Oh, isn't that terrible. All right—if it's broken it's broken. Isn't it? Hell with it. Hell with them all."

"If you'd listen," he said. "There isn't anything for you to get sore about. Just listen——"

"Who's sore?" she said. "I'm not sore. I'm all right. You don't have to worry about me. You or Jeannette or anybody else. Sore. Say, if a person's not going to get sore about a thing like that, what kind of a thing is a person expected to get sore about? After all I've done for her. Trouble with me is, I'm too kind-hearted. That's what everybody always told me. 'Trouble with you is, you're too kind-hearted,' they said. And now look what she goes around and says about me. And you let her say a thing like that to you, and you're ashamed to say you're a friend of mine. All right, you don't have to. You can go back to Jeannette and stay there. The whole lot of you."

"Now listen, sweetheart," he said. "Haven't I always been your friend? Haven't I? Well now, wouldn't you listen to your friend just for a——"

"Friends," she said. "Friends. Fine lot of friends I got. Go around cutting your throat. That's what you get for being kind-hearted. Just a big kind-hearted slob. That's me. Oh, hell with the water. I'll drink it straight. I make my own living, and go around not giving anybody any trouble, and then the whole lot of them turn on me. After the way I was brought up, and the home we used to have, and all, and they go around making cracks about me. Work all day long, and don't ask anything off of anybody. And here I am with a weak heart, besides. I'd just as soon I was dead. What've I got to live for, anyway? Kindly answer me that one question. What've I got to live for?"

Tears striped her cheeks.

The man with the ice-blue hair reached across the Scotch-soaked tablecloth and took her hand.

"Ah, listen," he said. "Listen."

From the unknown, a waiter appeared. He chirped and fluttered about them. Presently, you felt, he would cover them with leaves. . . .

Horsie

Horsie

$\mathcal{W}$hen young Mrs. Gerald Cruger came home from the hospital, Miss Wilmarth came along with her and the baby. Miss Wilmarth was an admirable trained nurse, sure and calm and tireless, with a real taste for the arranging of flowers in bowls and vases. She had never known a patient to receive so many flowers, or such uncommon ones; yellow violets and strange lilies and little white orchids poised like a bevy of delicate moths along green branches. Care and thought must have been put into their

selection that they, like all the other fragile and costly
things she kept about her, should be so right for young
Mrs. Cruger. No one who knew her could have caught up
the telephone and lightly bidden the florist to deliver her
one of his five-dollar assortments of tulips, stock, and
daffodils. Camilla Cruger was no complement to garden
blooms.

Sometimes, when she opened the shiny boxes and
carefully grouped the cards, there would come a curious
expression upon Miss Wilmarth's face. Playing over
shorter features, it might almost have been one of wistful-
ness. Upon Miss Wilmarth, it served to perfect the strange
resemblance that she bore through her years; her face was
truly complete with that look of friendly melancholy pecu-
liar to the gentle horse. It was not, of course, Miss Wilmarth's fault that she looked like a horse. Indeed, there
was nowhere to attach any blame. But the resemblance
remained.

She was tall, pronounced of bone, and erect of car-
riage; it was somehow impossible to speculate upon her
appearance undressed. Her long face was innocent, indeed
ignorant, of cosmetics, and its color stayed steady. Confusion, heat, or haste caused her neck to flush crimson. Her
mild hair was pinned with loops of nicked black wire into
a narrow knot, practical to support her little high cap, like
a charlotte russe from a bake-shop. She had big, trust-

worthy hands, scrubbed and dry, with nails cut short and
so deeply cleaned with some small sharp instrument that
the ends stood away from the spatulate finger-tips. Gerald
Cruger, who nightly sat opposite her at his own dinner
table, tried not to see her hands. It irritated him to be
reminded by their sight that they must feel like straw
matting and smell of white soap. For him, women who
were not softly lovely were simply not women.

He tried, too, so far as it was possible to his beautiful
manners, to keep his eyes from her face. Not that it was
unpleasant—a kind face, certainly. But, as he told
Camilla, once he looked he stayed fascinated, awaiting the
toss and the whinny.

"I love horses, myself," he said to Camilla, who lay all
white and languid on her apricot satin chaise-lounge. "I'm
a fool for a horse. Ah, what a noble animal, darling! All I
say is, nobody has any business to go around looking like
a horse and behaving as if it were all right. You don't catch
horses going around looking like people, do you?"

He did not dislike Miss Wilmarth; he only resented
her. He had no bad wish in the world for her, but he waited
with longing the day she would leave. She was so skilled
and rhythmic in her work that she disrupted the household
but little. Nevertheless, her presence was an onus. There
was that thing of dining with her every evening. It was a
chore for him, certainly, and one that did not ease with

repetition, but there was no choice. Everyone had always heard of trained nurses' bristling insistence that they be not treated as servants; Miss Wilmarth could not be asked to dine with the maids. He would not have dinner out; be away from *Camilla?* It was too much to expect the maids to institute a second dinner service or to carry trays, other than Camilla's, up and down the stairs. There were only three servants and they had work enough.

"Those children," Camilla's mother was wont to say, chuckling. "Those two kids. The independence of them! Struggling along on cheese and kisses. Why, they hardly let me pay for the trained nurse. And it was all we could do, last Christmas, to make Camilla take the Packard and the chauffeur."

So Gerald dined each night with Miss Wilmarth. The small dread of his hour with her struck suddenly at him in the afternoon. He would forget it for stretches of minutes, only to be smitten sharper as the time drew near. On his way home from his office, he found grim entertainment in rehearsing his table talk, and plotting desperate innovations to it.

Cruger's Compulsory Conversations: Lesson I, a Dinner with a Miss Wilmarth, a Trained Nurse. Good evening, Miss Wilmarth. Well! And how were the patients all day? That's good, that's fine. Well! The baby gained two ounces, did she? That's fine. Yes, that's right, she will be

before we know it. That's right. Well! Mrs. Cruger seems
to be getting stronger every day, doesn't she? That's good,
that's fine. That's right, up and about before we know it.
Yes, she certainly will. Well! Any visitors today? That's
good. Didn't stay too long, did they? That's fine. Well! No,
no, no, Miss Wilmarth—*you* go ahead. I wasn't going to
say anything at all, really. No, really. Well! Well! I see
where they found those two aviators after all. Yes, they
certainly do run risks. That's right. Yes. Well! I see where
they've been having a regular old-fashioned blizzard out
west. Yes, we certainly have had a mild winter. That's
right. Well! I see where they held up that jeweler's shop
right in broad daylight on Fifth Avenue. Yes, I certainly
don't know what we're coming to. That's right. Well! I see
the cat. Do you see the cat? The cat is on the mat. It
certainly is. Well! Pardon me, Miss Wilmarth, but must
you look so much like a horse? Do you like to look like a
horse, Miss Wilmarth? That's good, Miss Wilmarth, that's
fine. You certainly do, Miss Wilmarth. That's right. Well!
Will you for God's sake finish your oats, Miss Wilmarth,
and let me get out of this?

Every evening he reached the dining-room before
Miss Wilmarth and stared gloomily at silver and candle-
flame until she was upon him. No sound of football her-
alded her coming, for her ample canvas oxfords were soled
with rubber; there would be a protest of parquet, a trem-

bling of ornaments, a creak, a rustle, and the authoritative smell of stiff linen; and there she would be, set for her ritual of evening cheer.

"Well, Mary," she would cry to the waitress, "you know what they say—better late than never!"

But no smile would mellow Mary's lips, no light her eyes. Mary, in converse with the cook, habitually referred to Miss Wilmarth as "that one." She wished no truck with Miss Wilmarth or any of the others of her guild; always in and out of a person's pantry.

Once or twice Gerald saw a strange expression upon Miss Wilmarth's face as she witnessed the failure of her adage with the maid. He could not quite classify it. Though he did not know, it was the look she sometimes had when she opened the shiny white boxes and lifted the exquisite, scentless blossoms that were sent to Camilla. Anyway, whatever it was, it increased her equine resemblance to such a point that he thought of proffering her an apple.

But she always had her big smile turned toward him when she sat down. Then she would look at the thick watch strapped to her wrist and give a little squeal that brought the edges of his teeth together.

"Mercy!" she would say. "My good mercy! Why, I had no more idea it was so late. Well, you musn't blame me, Mr. Cruger. Don't you scold *me*. You'll just have to blame that daughter of yours. She's the one that keeps us all busy."

"She certainly is," he would say. "That's right."

He would think, and with small pleasure, of the infant Diane, pink and undistinguished and angry, among the ruffles and *choux* of her bassinet. It was her doing that Camilla had stayed so long away from him in the odorous limbo of the hospital, her doing that Camilla lay all day upon her apricot satin chaise-lounge. "We must take our time," the doctor said, "just ta-a-ake our ti-yem." Yes; well, that would all be because of young Diane. It was because of her, indeed, that night upon night he must face Miss Wilmarth and comb up conversation. All right, young Diane, there you are and nothing to do about it. But you'll be an only child, young woman, that's what you'll be.

Always Miss Wilmarth followed her opening pleasantry about the baby with a companion piece. Gerald had come to know it so well he could have said it in duet with her.

"You wait," she would say. "Just you wait. You're the one that's going to be kept busy when the beaux start coming around. You'll see. That young lady's going to be a heartbreaker if ever I saw one."

"I guess that's right," Gerald would say, and he would essay a small laugh and fail at it. It made him uncomfortable, somehow embarrassed him to hear Miss Wilmarth banter of swains and conquest. It was unseemly, as rouge would have been unseemly on her long mouth and perfume on her flat bosom.

He would hurry her over to her own ground. "Well!" he would say. "Well! And how were the patients all day?"

But that, even with the baby's weight and the list of the day's visitors, seldom lasted past the soup.

"Doesn't that woman ever go out?" he asked Camilla. "Doesn't our Horsie ever rate a night off?"

"Where would she want to go?" Camilla said. Her low, lazy words had always the trick of seeming a little weary of their subject.

"Well," Gerald said, "she might take herself a moonlight canter around the park."

"Oh, she doubtless gets a thrill out of dining with you," Camilla said. "You're a man, they tell me, and she can't have seen many. Poor old horse. She's not a bad soul."

"Yes," he said, "and what a round of pleasure it is, having dinner every night with Not a Bad Soul."

"What makes you think," Camilla said, "that I am caught up in any whirl of gayety, lying here?"

"Oh, darling," he said. "Oh, my poor darling. I didn't mean it, honestly I didn't. Oh, *Lord*, I didn't mean it. How could I complain, after all you've been through, and I haven't done a thing? Please, sweet, please. Ah, Camilla, say you know I didn't mean it."

"After all," Camilla said, "you just have her at dinner. I have her around all day."

"Sweetheart, please," he said. "Oh, poor angel."

He dropped to his knees by the chaise-longue and crushed her limp, fragrant hand against his mouth. Then he remembered about being very, very gentle. He ran little apologetic kisses up and down her fingers and murmured of gardenias and lilies and thus exhausted his knowledge of white flowers.

Her visitors said that Camilla looked lovelier than ever, but they were mistaken. She was only as lovely as she had always been. They spoke in hushed voices of the new look in her eyes since her motherhood; but it was the same far brightness that had always lain there. They said how white she was and how apart from other people; they forgot that she had always been pale as moonlight and had always worn a delicate disdain, as light as the lace that covered her breast. Her doctor cautioned tenderly against hurry, besought her to take recovery slowly—Camilla, who had never done anything quickly in her life. Her friends gathered, adoring, about the apricot satin chaise-longue where Camilla lay and moved her hands as if they hung heavy from her wrists; they had been wont before to gather and adore at the white satin sofa in the drawing-room where Camilla reclined, her hands like heavy lilies in a languid breeze. Every night, when Gerald crossed the threshold of her fragrant room, his heart leaped and his words caught in his throat; but those things had always befallen him at the sight of her. Motherhood had not brought perfection to Camilla's loveliness. She had had that before.

Gerald came home early enough, each evening, to have a while with her before dinner. He made his cocktails in her room, and watched her as she slowly drank one. Miss Wilmarth was in and out, touching flowers, patting pillows. Sometimes she brought Diane in on display, and those would be minutes of real discomfort for Gerald. He could not bear to watch her with the baby in her arms, so acute was his vicarious embarrassment at her behavior. She would bring her long head down close to Diane's tiny, stern face and toss it back again high on her rangy neck, all the while that strange words, in a strange high voice, came from her.

"Well, her wuzza booful dirl. Ess, her wuzza. Her wuzza, wuzza, wuzza. Ess, her *wuzz.*" She would bring the baby over to him. "See, Daddy. Isn't us a gate, bid dirl? Isn't us booful? Say 'nigh-nigh,' Daddy. Us doe teepy-bye, now. Say 'nigh-nigh.' "

Oh, God.

Then she would bring the baby to Camilla. "Say 'nigh-nigh,' " she would cry. " 'Nigh-nigh,' Mummy."

"If that brat ever calls you 'Mummy,' " he told Camilla once, fiercely, "I'll turn her out in the snow."

Camilla would look at the baby, amusement in her slow glance. "Good night, useless," she would say. She would hold out a finger, for Diane's pink hand to curl around. And Gerald's heart would quicken, and his eyes sting and shine.

Once he tore his gaze from Camilla to look at Miss Wilmarth, surprised by the sudden cessation of her falsetto. She was no longer lowering her head and tossing it back. She was standing quite still, looking at him over the baby; she looked away quickly, but not before he had seen that curious expression on her face again. It puzzled him, made him vaguely uneasy. That night, she made no further exhortations to Diane's parents to utter the phrase "nigh-nigh." In silence she carried the baby out of the room and back to the nursery.

One evening, Gerald brought two men home with him; lean, easily dressed young men, good at golf and squash rackets, his companions through his college and in his clubs. They had cocktails in Camilla's room, grouped about the chaise-longue. Miss Wilmarth, standing in the nursery adjoining, testing the temperature of the baby's milk against her wrist, could hear them all talking lightly and swiftly, tossing their sentences into the air to hang there unfinished. Now and again she could distinguish Camilla's lazy voice; the others stopped immediately when she spoke, and when she was done there were long peals of laughter. Miss Wilmarth pictured her lying there, in golden chiffon and deep lace, her light figure turned always a little away from those about her, so that she must move her head and speak her slow words over her shoulder to them. The trained nurse's face was astoundingly equine as she looked at the wall that separated them.

They stayed in Camilla's room a long time, and there was always more laughter. The door from the nursery into the hall was open, and presently she heard the door of Camilla's room being opened, too. She had been able to hear only voices before, but now she could distinguish Gerald's words as he called back from the threshold; they had no meaning to her.

"Only wait, fellers," he said. "Wait till you see Spark Plug."

He came to the nursery door. He held a cocktail shaker in one hand and a filled glass in the other.

"Oh, Miss Wilmarth," he said. "Oh, good evening, Miss Wilmarth. Why, I didn't know this door was open—I mean, I hope we haven't been disturbing you."

"Oh, not the least little bit," she said. "Goodness."

"Well!" he said. "I—we were wondering if you wouldn't have a little cocktail. Won't you please?" He held out the glass to her.

"Mercy," she said, taking it. "Why, thank you ever so much. Thank you, Mr. Cruger."

"And, oh, Miss Wilmarth," he said, "would you tell Mary there'll be two more to dinner? And ask her not to have it before half an hour or so, will you? Would you mind?"

"Not the least little bit," she said. "Of course I will."

"Thank you," he said. "Well! Thank you, Miss Wilmarth. Well! See you at dinner."

"Thank *you*," she said. "I'm the one that ought to thank *you*. For the lovely little cocktail."

"Oh," he said, and failed at an easy laugh. He went back into Camilla's room and closed the door behind him.

Miss Wilmarth set her cocktail upon a table, and went down to inform Mary of the impending guests. She felt light and quick, and she told Mary gayly, awaiting a flash of gayety in response. But Mary received the news impassively, made a grunt but no words, and slammed out through the swinging doors into the kitchen. Miss Wilmarth stood looking after her. Somehow servants never seemed to— She should have become used to it

Even though the dinner hour was delayed, Miss Wilmarth was a little late. The three young men were standing in the dining-room, talking all at once and laughing all together. They stopped their noise when Miss Wilmarth entered, and Gerald moved forward to perform introductions. He looked at her, and then looked away. Prickling embarrassment tormented him. He introduced the young men, with his eyes away from her.

Miss Wilmarth had dressed for dinner. She had discarded her linen uniform and put on a frock of dark blue taffeta, cut down to a point at the neck and given sleeves that left bare the angles of her elbows. Small, stiff ruffles occurred about the hips, and the skirt was short for its year. It revealed that Miss Wilmarth had clothed her ankles in roughened gray silk and her feet in black, casket-shaped slippers, upon which little bows quivered as if in lonely terror at the expanse before them. She had been busied with her hair; it was crimped and loosened, and ends that had escaped the tongs were already sliding from their pins. All the length of her nose and chin was heavily powdered; not with a perfumed dust, tinted to praise her skin, but with coarse, bright white talcum.

Gerald presented his guests; Miss Wilmarth, Mr. Minot; Miss Wilmarth, Mr. Forster. One of the young men, it turned out, was Freddy, and one, Tommy. Miss Wilmarth said she was pleased to meet each of them. Each of them asked her how she did.

She sat down at the candle-lit table with the three beautiful young men. Her usual evening vivacity was gone from her. In silence she unfolded her napkin and took up her soup spoon. Her neck glowed crimson, and her face, even with its powder, looked more than ever as if it should have been resting over the top rail of a paddock fence.

"Well!" Gerald said.

"Well!" Mr. Minot said.

"Getting much warmer out, isn't it?" Mr. Forster said. "Notice it?"

"It is, at that," Gerald said. "Well. We're about due for warm weather."

"Yes, we ought to expect it now," Mr. Minot said. "Any day now."

"Oh, it'll be here," Mr. Forster said. "It'll come."

"I love spring," said Miss Wilmarth. "I just love it."

Gerald looked deep into his soup plate. The two young men looked at her.

"Darn good time of year," Mr. Minot said. "Certainly is."

"And how it is!" Mr. Forster said.

They ate their soup.

There was champagne all through dinner. Miss Wilmarth watched Mary fill her glass, none too full. The wine looked gay and pretty. She looked about the table before she took her first sip. She remembered Camilla's voice and the men's laughter.

"Well," she cried. "Here's a health, everybody!"

The guests looked at her. Gerald reached for his glass and gazed at it as intently as if he beheld a champagne goblet for the first time. They all murmured and drank.

"Well!" Mr. Minot said. "Your patients seem to be getting along pretty well, Miss Witmark. Don't they?"

"I should say they do," she said. "And they're pretty

nice patients, too. Aren't they, Mr. Cruger?"

"They certainly are," Gerald said. "That's right."

"They certainly are," Mr. Minot said. "That's what they are. Well. You must meet all sorts of people in your work, I suppose. Must be pretty interesting."

"Oh, sometimes it is," Miss Wilmarth said. "It depends on the people." Her words fell from her lips clear and separate, sterile as if each had been freshly swabbed with boracic acid solution. In her ears rang Camilla's light, insolent drawl.

"That's right," Mr. Forster said. "Everything depends on the people, doesn't it? Always does, wherever you go. No matter what you do. Still, it must be wonderfully interesting work. Wonderfully."

"Wonderful the way this country's come right up in medicine," Mr. Minot said. "They tell me we have the greatest doctors in the world, right here. As good as any in Vienna. Or Harley Street."

"I see," Gerald said, "where they think they've found a new cure for spinal meningitis."

"*Have* they really?" Mr. Minot said.

"Yes, I saw that, too," Mr. Forster said. "Wonderful thing. Wonderfully interesting."

"Oh, say, Gerald," Mr. Minot said, and he went from there into an account, hole by hole, of his most recent performance at golf. Gerald and Mr. Forster listened and questioned him.

The three young men left the topic of golf and came back to it again, and left it and came back. In the intervals, they related to Miss Wilmarth various brief items that had caught their eyes in the newspapers. Miss Wilmarth answered in exclamations, and turned her big smile readily to each of them. There was no laughter during dinner.

It was a short meal, as courses went. After it, Miss Wilmarth bade the guests good-night and received their bows and their "*Good* night, Miss Witmark." She said she was awfully glad to have met them. They murmured.

"Well, good night, then, Mr. Cruger," she said. "See you tomorrow!"

"Good night, Miss Wilmarth," Gerald said.

The three young men went and sat with Camilla. Miss Wilmarth could hear their voices and their laughter as she hung up her dark blue taffeta dress.

Miss Wilmarth stayed with the Crugers for five weeks. Camilla was pronounced well—so well that she could have dined downstairs on the last few nights of Miss Wilmarth's stay, had she been able to support the fardel of dinner at the table with the trained nurse.

"I really couldn't dine opposite that face," she told Gerald. "You go amuse Horsie at dinner, stupid. You must be good at it, by now."

"All right, I will, darling," he said. "But God keep me, when she asks for another lump of sugar, from holding it out to her on my palm."

"Only two more nights," Camilla said, "and then Thursday Nana'll be here, and she'll be gone forever."

" 'Forever,' sweet, is my favorite word in the language," Gerald said.

Nana was the round and competent Scottish woman who had nursed Camilla through her childhood and was scheduled to engineer the unknowing Diane through hers. She was a comfortable woman, easy to have in the house; a servant, and knew it.

Only two more nights. Gerald went down to dinner whistling a good old tune.

"The old gray mare, she ain't what she used to be,
Ain't what she used to be, ain't what she used to
be——"

The final dinners with Miss Wilmarth were like all the others. He arrived first, and stared at the candles until she came.

"Well, Mary," she cried on her entrance, "you know what they say—better late then never."

Mary, to the last, remained unamused.

Gerald was elated all the day of Miss Wilmarth's departure. He had a holiday feeling, a last-day-of-school jubilation with none of its faint regret. He left his office early, stopped at a florist's shop, and went home to Camilla.

Nana was installed in the nursery, but Miss Wilmarth had not yet left. She was in Camilla's room, and he saw her for the second time out of uniform. She wore a long brown coat and a brown rubbed velvet hat of no definite shape. Obviously, she was in the middle of the embarrassments of farewell. The melancholy of her face made it so like a horse's that the hat above it was preposterous.

"Why, there's Mr. Cruger!" she cried.

"Oh, good evening, Miss Wilmarth," he said. "Well! Ah, hello, darling. How are you, sweet? Like these?"

He laid a florist's box in Camilla's lap. In it were strange little yellow roses, with stems and leaves and tiny, soft thorns all of blood red. Miss Wilmarth gave a little squeal at the sight of them.

"Oh, the darlings!" she cried. "Oh, the boofuls!"

"And these are for you, Miss Wilmarth," he said. He made himself face her and hold out to her a square, smaller box.

"Why, Mr. Cruger," she said. "For me, really? Why, really, Mr. Cruger."

She opened the box and found four gardenias, with green foil and pale green ribbon holding them together.

"Oh, now, really, Mr. Cruger," she said. "Why, I never in all my life—Oh, now, you shouldn't have done it. Really, you shouldn't. My good mercy! Well, I never saw anything so lovely in all my life. Did you, Mrs. Cruger?

They're *lovely*. Well, I just don't know how to *begin* to thank you. Why, I just—well, I just adore them."

Gerald made sounds designed to convey the intelligence that he was glad she liked them, that it was nothing, that she was welcome. Her squeaks of thanks made red rise back of his ears.

"They're nice ones," Camilla said. "Put them on, Miss Wilmarth. And these are awfully cunning, Jerry. Sometimes you have your points."

"Oh, I didn't think I'd *wear* them," Miss Wilmarth said. "I thought I'd just take them in the box like this, so they'd keep better. And it's such a nice box—I'd like to have it. I—I'd like to keep it."

She looked down at the flowers. Gerald was in sudden horror that she might bring her head down close to them and toss it back high, crying "wuzza, wuzza, wuzza" at them the while.

"Honestly," she said, "I just can't take my eyes *off* them."

"The woman is mad," Camilla said. "It's the effect of living with us, I suppose. I hope we haven't ruined you for life, Miss Wilmarth."

"Why, Mrs. Cruger," Miss Wilmarth cried. "Now, really! I was just telling Mrs. Cruger, Mr. Cruger, that I've never been on a pleasanter case. I've just had the time of my life, all the time I was here. I don't know when I—honestly, I can't stop looking at my posies, they're so lovely. Well, I just can't thank you for all you've done."

"Well, we ought to thank you, Miss Wilmarth," Gerald said. "We certainly ought."

"I really hate to say 'good-bye,' " Miss Wilmarth said. "I just hate it."

"Oh, don't say it," Camilla said. "I never dream of saying it. And remember, you must come in and see the baby, any time you can."

"Yes, you certainly must," Gerald said. "That's right."

"Oh, I will," Miss Wilmarth said. "Mercy, I just don't dare go take another look at her, or I wouldn't be able to leave, ever. Well, what am I thinking of! Why, the car's been waiting all this time. Mrs. Cruger simply insists on sending me home in the car, Mr. Cruger. Isn't she terrible?"

"Why, not at all," he said. "Why, of course."

"Well, it's only five blocks down and over to Lexington," she said, "or I really couldn't think of troubling you."

"Why, not at all," Gerald said. "Well! Is that where you live, Miss Wilmarth?"

She lived in some place of her own sometimes? She wasn't always disarranging somebody else's household?

"Yes," Miss Wilmarth said. "I have Mother there."

Oh. Now Gerald had never thought of her having a mother. Then there must have been a father, too, some time. And Miss Wilmarth existed becuase two people once had loved and known. It was not a thought to dwell upon.

"My aunt's with us, too," Miss Wilmarth said. "It makes it nice for Mother—you see, Mother doesn't get around very well any more. It's a little bit crowded for the three of us—I sleep on the davenport when I'm home, between cases. But it's so nice for Mother, having my aunt there."

"Oh, yes," Gerald said. "Yes, it certainly must be. Well! Well! May I close your bags for you, Miss Wilmarth?"

"Oh, that's all done," she said. "The suitcase is downstairs. I'll just go get my hat-box. Well, good-by, then, Mrs. Cruger, and take care of yourself. And thank you a thousand times."

"Good luck, Miss Wilmarth," Camilla said. "Come see the baby."

Miss Wilmarth looked at Camilla and at Gerald standing beside her, touching one long white hand. She left the room to fetch her hat-box.

"I'll take it down for you, Miss Wilmarth," Gerald called after her.

He bent and kissed Camilla gently, very, very gently.

"Well, it's nearly over, darling," he said. "Sometimes I am practically convinced that there is a God."

"It was darn decent of you to bring her gardenias," Camilla said. "What made you think of it?"

"I was so crazed at the idea that she was really going," he said, "that I must have lost my head. No one was more surprised than I, buying gardenias for Horsie. Thank the Lord she didn't put them on. I couldn't have stood that sight."

"She's not really at her best in her street clothes," Camilla said. "She seems to lack a certain *chic.*" She stretched her arms slowly above her head and let them sink slowly back. "That was a fascinating glimpse of her home life she gave us. Great fun."

"Oh, I don't suppose she minds," he said. "I'll go down now and back her into the car, and the hell with her."

He bent again over Camilla.

"Oh, you look so lovely, sweet," he said. "So *lovely.*"

Miss Wilmarth was coming down the hall, when Gerald left the room, managing a pasteboard hat-box, the florist's box, and a big leather purse that had known service. He took the boxes from her, against her protests, and followed her down the stairs and out to the motor at the curb. The chauffeur stood at the open door. Gerald was glad of that presence.

"Well, good luck, Miss Wilmarth," he said. "And thank you so much."

"Thank *you,* Mr. Cruger," she said. "I—I can't tell

you how I've enjoyed it all the time I was here. I never had a pleasanter— And the flowers, and everything. I just don't know what to say. I'm the one that ought to thank *you.*"

She held out her hand, in a brown cotton glove. Anyway, worn cotton was easier to the touch than dry, corded flesh. It was the last moment of her. He scarcely minded looking at the long face on the red, red neck.

"Well!" he said. "Well! Got everything? Well, good luck, again, Miss Wilmarth, and don't forget us."

"Oh, I won't," she said. "I—oh, I won't do that."

She turned from him and got quickly into the car, to sit upright against the pale gray cushions. The chauffeur placed her hat-box at her feet and the florist's box on the seat beside her, closed the door smartly, and returned to his wheel. Gerald waved cheerily as the car slid away. Miss Wilmarth did not wave to him.

When she looked back, through the little rear window, he had already disappeared in the house. He must have run across the sidewalk—run, to get back to the fragrant room and the little yellow roses and Camilla. Their little pink baby would lie sleeping in its bed. They would be alone together; they would dine alone together by candlelight; they would be alone together in the night. Every morning and every evening Gerald would drop to his knees beside her to kiss her perfumed hand and call her sweet. Always she would be perfect, in scented chiffon and deep lace. There would be lean, easy young men, to listen to her drawl and give her their laughter. Every day there would be shiny white boxes for her, filled with curious blooms. It was perhaps fortunate that no one looked in the limousine. A beholder must have been startled to learn that a human face could look as much like that of a weary mare as did Miss Wilmarth's.

Presently the car swerved, in a turn of the traffic. The florist's box slipped against Miss Wilmarth's knee. She looked down at it. Then she took it on her lap, raised the lid a little and peeped at the waxy white bouquet. It would have been all fair then for a chance spectator; Miss Wilmarth's strange resemblance was not apparent, as she looked at her flowers. They were her flowers. A man had given them to her. She had been given flowers. They might not fade maybe for days. And she could keep the box.

Here We Are

Here We Are

The young man in the new blue suit finished arranging the glistening luggage in tight corners of the Pullman compartment. The train had leaped at curves and bounced along straightaways, rendering balance a praiseworthy achievement and a sporadic one; and the young man had pushed and hoisted and tucked and shifted the bags with concentrated care.

Nevertheless, eight minutes for the settling of two suitcases and a hat-box is a long time.

He sat down, leaning back against bristled green plush, in the seat opposite the girl in beige. She looked as new as a peeled egg. Her hat, her fur, her frock, her gloves were glossy and stiff with novelty. On the arc of the thin, slippery sole of one beige shoe was gummed a tiny oblong of white paper, printed with the price set and paid for that slipper and its fellow, and the name of the shop that had dispensed them.

She had been staring raptly out of the window, drinking in the big weathered signboards that extolled the phenomena of codfish without bones and screens no rust could corrupt. As the young man sat down, she turned politely from the pane, met his eyes, started a smile and got it about half done, and rested her gaze just above his right shoulder.

"Well!" the young man said.

"Well!" she said.

"Well, here we are," he said.

"Here we are," she said. "Aren't we?"

"I should say we were," he said. "Eeyop. Here we are."

"Well!" she said.

"Well!" he said. "Well. How does it feel to be an old married lady?"

"Oh, it's too soon to ask me that," she said. "At least—I mean. Well, I mean, goodness, we've only been married about three hours, haven't we?"

The young man studied his wrist-watch as if he were just acquiring the knack of reading time.

"We have been married," he said, "exactly two hours and twenty-six minutes."

"My," she said. "It seems like longer."

"No," he said. "It isn't hardly half-past six yet."

"It seems like later," she said. "I guess it's because it starts getting dark so early."

"It does, at that," he said. "The nights are going to be pretty long from now on. I mean. I mean—well, it starts getting dark early."

"I didn't have any idea what time it was," she said. "Everything was so mixed up, I sort of don't know where I am, or what it's all about. Getting back from the church, and then all those people, and then changing all my clothes, and then everybody throwing things, and all. Goodness, I don't see how people do it every day."

"Do what?" he said.

"Get married," she said. "When you think of all the people, all over the world, getting married just as if it was nothing. Chinese people and everybody. Just as if it wasn't anything."

"Well, let's not worry about people all over the world," he said. "Let's don't think about a lot of Chinese. We've got something better to think about. I mean. I mean—well, what do we care about them?"

"I know," she said. "But I just sort of got to thinking of them, all of them, all over everywhere, doing it all the time. At least, I mean—getting married, you know. And it's—well, it's sort of such a big thing to do, it makes you feel queer. You think of them, all of them, all doing it just like it wasn't anything. And how does anybody know what's going to happen next?"

"Let them worry," he said. "We don't have to. We know darn well what's going to happen next. I mean. I mean—well, we know it's going to be great. Well, we know we're going to be happy. Don't we?"

"Oh, of course," she said. "Only you think of all the people, and you have to sort of keep thinking. It makes you feel funny. An awful lot of people that get married, it doesn't turn out so well. And I guess they all must have thought it was going to be great."

"Come on, now," he said. "This is no way to start a honeymoon, with all this thinking going on. Look at us— all married and everything done. I mean. The wedding all done and all."

"Ah, it was nice, wasn't it?" she said. "Did you really like my veil?"

"You looked great," he said. "Just great."

"Oh, I'm terribly glad," she said. "Ellie and Louise looked lovely, didn't they? I'm terribly glad they did finally decide on pink. They looked perfectly lovely."

"Listen," he said. "I want to tell you something. When I was standing up there in that old church waiting for you to come up, and I saw those two bridesmaids, I thought to myself, I thought, 'Well, I never knew Louise could look like that!' Why, she'd have knocked anybody's eye out."

"Oh, really?" she said. "Funny. Of course, everybody thought her dress and hat were lovely, but a lot of people seemed to think she looked sort of tired. People have been saying that a lot, lately. I tell them I think it's awfully mean of them to go around saying that about her. I tell them they've got to remember that Louise isn't so terribly young any more, and they've got to expect her to look like that. Louise can say she's twenty-three all she wants to, but she's a good deal nearer twenty-seven."

"Well, she was certainly a knock-out at the wedding," he said. "Boy!"

"I'm terribly glad you thought so," she said. "I'm glad some one did. How did you think Ellie looked?"

"Why, I honestly didn't get a look at her," he said.

"Oh, really?" she said. "Well, I certainly think that's too bad. I don't suppose I ought to say it about my own sister, but I never saw anybody look as beautiful as Ellie looked today. And always so sweet and unselfish, too. And you didn't even notice her. But you never pay attention to

Ellie, anyway. Don't think I haven't noticed it. It makes me feel just terrible. It makes me feel just awful, that you don't like my own sister."

"I do so like her!" he said. "I'm crazy for Ellie. I think she's a great kid."

"Don't think it makes any difference to Ellie!" she said. "Ellie's got enough people crazy about her. It isn't anything to her whether you like her or not. Don't flatter yourself she cares! Only, the only thing is, it makes it awfully hard for me you don't like her, that's the only thing. I keep thinking, when we come back and get in the apartment and everything, it's going to be awfully hard for me that you won't want my own sister to come and see me. It's going to make it awfully hard for me that you won't ever want my family around. I know how you feel about my family. Don't think I haven't seen it. Only, if you don't ever want to see them, that's your loss. Not theirs. Don't flatter yourself!"

"Oh, now, come on!" he said. "What's all this talk about not wanting your family around? Why, you know how I feel about your family. I think your old woman—I think your mother's swell. And Ellie. And your father. What's all this talk?"

"Well, I've seen it," she said. "Don't think I haven't. Lots of people they get married, and they think it's going to be great and everything, and then it all goes to pieces because people don't like people's families, or something like that. Don't tell me! I've seen it happen."

"Honey," he said, "what is all this? What are you getting all angry about? Hey, look, this is our honeymoon. What are you trying to start a fight for? Ah, I guess you're just feeling sort of nervous."

"Me?" she said. "What have I got to be nervous about? I mean. I mean, goodness, I'm not nervous."

"You know, lots of times," he said, "they say that girls get kind of nervous and yippy on account of thinking about—I mean. I mean—well, it's like you said, things are all so sort of mixed up and everything, right now. But afterwards, it'll be all right. I mean. I mean—well, look, honey, you don't look any too comfortable. Don't you want to take your hat off? And let's don't ever fight, ever. Will we?"

"Ah, I'm sorry I was cross," she said. "I guess I did feel a little bit funny. All mixed up, and then thinking of all those people all over everywhere, and then being sort of 'way off here, all alone with you. It's so sort of different. It's sort of such a big thing. You can't blame a person for thinking, can you? Yes, don't let's ever, ever fight. We won't be like a whole lot of them. We won't fight or be nasty or anything. Will we?"

"You bet your life we won't," he said.

"I guess I will take this darned old hat off," she said.

"It kind of presses. Just put it up on the rack, will you, dear? Do you like it, sweetheart?"

"Looks good on you," he said.

"No, but I mean," she said, "do you really like it?"

"Well, I'll tell you," he said. "I know this is the new style and everything like that, and it's probably great. I don't know anything about things like that. Only I like the kind of a hat like that blue hat you had. Gee, I liked that hat."

"Oh, really?" she said. "Well, that's nice. That's lovely. The first thing you say to me, as soon as you get me off on a train away from my family and everything, is that you don't like my hat. The first thing you say to your wife is you think she has terrible taste in hats. That's nice, isn't it?"

"Now, honey," he said, "I never said anything like that. I only said——"

"What you don't seem to realize," she said, "is this hat cost twenty-two dollars. Twenty-two dollars. And that horrible old blue thing you think you're so crazy about, that cost three ninety-five."

"I don't give a darn what they cost," he said. "I only said—I said I liked that blue hat. I don't know anything about hats. I'll be crazy about this one as soon as I get used to it. Only it's kind of not like your other hats. I don't know about the new styles. What do I know about women's hats?"

"It's too bad," she said, "you didn't marry somebody that would get the kind of hats you'd like. Hats that cost three ninety-five. Why didn't you marry Louise? You always think she looks so beautiful. You'd love her taste in hats. Why didn't you marry her?"

"Ah, now, honey," he said. "For heaven's sakes!"

"Why didn't you marry her?" she said. "All you've done, ever since we got on this train, is talk about her. Here I've sat and sat, and just listened to you saying how wonderful Louise is. I suppose that's nice, getting me all off here alone with you, and then raving about Louise right in front of my face. Why didn't you ask her to marry you? I'm sure she would have jumped at the chance. There aren't so many people asking her to marry them. It's too bad you didn't marry her. I'm sure you'd have been much happier."

"Listen, baby," he said, "while you're talking about things like that, why didn't you marry Joe Brooks? I suppose he could have given you all the twenty-two-dollar hats you wanted, I suppose!"

"Well, I'm not so sure I'm not sorry I didn't," she said. "There! Joe Brooks wouldn't have waited until he got me all off alone and then sneered at my taste in clothes. Joe Brooks wouldn't ever hurt my feelings. Joe Brooks has always been fond of me. There!"

"Yeah," he said. "He's fond of you. He was so fond of you he didn't even send a wedding present. That's how fond of you he was."

"I happen to know for a fact," she said, "that he was away on business, and as soon as he comes back he's going to give me anything I want, for the apartment."

"Listen," he said. "I don't want anything he gives you in our apartment. Anything he gives you, I'll throw right out the window. That's what I think of your friend Joe Brooks. And how do you know where he is and what he's going to do, anyway? Has he been writing to you?"

"I suppose my friends can correspond with me," she said. "I didn't hear there was any law against that."

"Well, I suppose they can't!" he said. "And what do you think of that? I'm not going to have my wife getting a lot of letters from cheap traveling salesmen!"

"Joe Brooks is not a cheap traveling salesman!" she said. "He is not! He gets a wonderful salary."

"Oh, yeah?" he said. "Where did you hear that?"

"He told me so himself," she said.

"Oh, he told you so himself," he said. "I see. He told you so himself."

"You've got a lot of right to talk about Joe Brooks," she said. "You and your friend Louise. All you ever talk about is Louise."

"Oh, for heaven's sakes!" he said. "What do I care about Louise? I just thought she was a friend of yours, that's all. That's why I ever even noticed her."

"Well, you certainly took an awful lot of notice of her

232

today," she said. "On our wedding day! You said yourself when you were standing there in the church you just kept thinking of her. Right up at the altar. Oh, right in the presence of God! And all you thought about was Louise."

"Listen, honey," he said, "I never should have said that. How does anybody know what kind of crazy things come into their heads when they're standing there waiting to get married? I was just telling you that because it was so kind of crazy. I thought it would make you laugh."

"I know," she said. "I've been all sort of mixed up today, too. I told you that. Everything so strange and everything. And me all the time thinking about all those people all over the world, and now us here all alone, and everything. I know you get all mixed up. Only I did think, when you kept talking about how beautiful Louise looked, you did it with malice and forethought."

"I never did anything with malice and forethought!" he said. "I just told you that about Louise because I thought it would make you laugh."

"Well, it didn't," she said.

"No, I know it didn't," he said. "It certainly did not. Ah, baby, and we ought to be laughing, too. Hell, honey lamb, this is our honeymoon. What's the matter?"

"I don't know," she said. "We used to squabble a lot when we were going together and then engaged and everything, but I thought everything would be so different as soon as you were married. And now I feel so sort of strange and everything. I feel so sort of alone."

"Well, you see, sweetheart," he said, "we're not really married yet. I mean. I mean—well, things will be different afterwards. Oh, hell. I mean, we haven't been married very long."

"No," she said.

"Well, we haven't got much longer to wait now," he said. "I mean—well, we'll be in New York in about twenty minutes. Then we can have dinner, and sort of see what we feel like doing. Or I mean. Is there anything special you want to do tonight?"

"What?" she said.

"What I mean to say," he said, "would you like to go to a show or something?"

"Why, whatever you like," she said. "I sort of didn't think people went to theaters and things on their—I mean, I've got a couple of letters I simply must write. Don't let me forget."

"Oh," he said. "You're going to write letters tonight?"

"Well, you see," she said, "I've been perfectly terrible. What with all the excitement and everything, I never did thank poor old Mrs. Sprague for her berry spoon, and I never did a thing about those book ends the McMasters sent. It's just too awful of me. I've got to write them this very night."

"And when you've finished writing your letters," he said, "maybe I could get you a magazine or a bag of peanuts."

"What?" she said.

"I mean," he said, "I wouldn't want you to be bored."

"As if I could be bored with you!" she said. "Silly! Aren't we married? Bored!"

"What I thought," he said, "I thought when we got in, we could go right up to the Biltmore and anyway leave our bags, and maybe have a little dinner in the room, kind of quiet, and then do whatever we wanted. I mean. I mean—well, let's go right up there from the station."

"Oh, yes, let's," she said. "I'm so glad we're going to the Biltmore. I just love it. The twice I've stayed in New York we've always stayed there, Papa and Mamma and Ellie and I, and I was crazy about it. I always sleep so well there. I go right off to sleep the minute I put my head on the pillow."

"Oh, you do?" he said.

"At least, I mean," she said. " 'Way up high it's so quiet."

"We might go to some show or other tomorrow night instead of tonight," he said. "Don't you think that would be better?"

"Yes, I think it might," she said.

He rose, balanced a moment, crossed over and sat down beside her.

"Do you really have to write those letters tonight?" he said.

"Well," she said, "I don't suppose they'd get there any quicker than if I wrote them tomorrow."

There was a silence with things going on in it.

"And we won't ever fight any more, will we?" he said.

"Oh, no," she said. "Not ever! I don't know what made me do like that. It all got so sort of funny, sort of like a nightmare, the way I got thinking of all those people getting married all the time; and so many of them, it goes to pieces on account of fighting and everything. I got all mixed up thinking about them. Oh, I don't want to be like them. But we won't be, will we?"

"Sure we won't," he said.

"We won't go all to pieces," she said. "We won't fight. It'll all be different, now we're married. It'll all be lovely. Reach me down my hat, will you, sweetheart? It's time I was putting it on. Thanks. Ah, I'm so sorry you don't like it."

"I do so like it!" he said.

"You said you didn't," she said. "You said you thought it was perfectly terrible."

"I never said any such thing," he said. "You're crazy."

"All right, I may be crazy," she said. "Thank you

very much. But that's what you said. Not that it matters—it's just a little thing. But it makes you feel pretty funny to think you've gone and married somebody that says you have perfectly terrible taste in hats. And then goes and says you're crazy, beside."

"Now, listen here," he said. "Nobody said any such thing. Why, I love that hat. The more I look at it the better I like it. I think it's great."

"That isn't what you said before," she said.

"Honey," he said. "Stop it, will you? What do you want to start all this for? I love the damned hat. I mean, I love your hat. I love anything you wear. What more do you want me to say?"

"Well, I don't want you to say it like that," she said.

"I said I think it's great," he said. "That's all I said."

"Do you really?" she said. "Do you honestly? Ah, I'm so glad. I'd hate you not to like my hat. It would be—I don't know, it would be sort of such a bad start."

"Well, I'm crazy for it," he said. "Now we've got that settled, for heaven's sakes. Ah, baby. Baby lamb. We're not going to have any bad starts. Look at us—we're on our honeymoon. Pretty soon we'll be regular old married people. I mean. I mean, in a few minutes we'll be getting in to New York, and then we'll be going to the hotel, and then everything will be all right. I mean—well, look at us! Here we are, married! Here we are!"

"Yes, here we are," she said. "Aren't we?"

Too Bad

Too Bad

I

"My dear," Mrs. Marshall said to Mrs. Ames, "I never was so surprised in my life. Never in my life. Why, Grace and I were like that—just like *that.*"

She held up her right hand, the upstanding first and second fingers rigidly close together, in illustration.

Mrs. Ames shook her head sadly, and offered the cinnamon toast.

"Imagine!" said Mrs. Marshall, refusing it though

with a longing eye. "We were going to have dinner with them last Tuesday night, and then I got this letter from Grace from this little place up in Connecticut, saying she was going to be up there she didn't know how long, and she thought, when she came back, she'd probably take just one big room with a kitchenette. Ernest was living at the Athletic Club, she said."

"But what did they do about their apartment?" Mrs. Ames's voice was high with anxiety.

"Why, it seems his sister took it, furnished and all— by the way, remind me, I must go and see her," said Mrs. Marshall. "They wanted to move into town, anyway, and they were looking for a place."

"Doesn't she feel terribly about it—his sister?" asked Mrs. Ames.

"Oh—terribly," Mrs. Marshall dismissed the word as inadequate. "My dear, think how everybody that knew them feels. Think how I feel. I don't know when I've had a thing depress me more. If it had been anybody but the Weldons!"

Mrs. Ames nodded.

"That's what I said," she reported.

"That's what everybody says." Mrs. Marshall quickly took away any undeserved credit. "To think of the Weldons separating! Why, I always used to say to Jim, 'Well, there's one happily married couple, anyway,' I used to say, 'so congenial, and with that nice apartment, and all.' And then, right out of a clear sky, they go and separate. I simply can't understand what on earth made them do it. It just seems too awful!"

Again Mrs. Ames nodded, slowly and sadly.

"Yes, it always seems too bad, a thing like that does," she said. "It's too bad."

II

Mrs. Ernest Weldon wandered about the orderly living-room, giving it some of those little feminine touches. She was not especially good as a touch-giver. The idea was pretty, and appealing to her. Before she was married, she had dreamed of herself as moving softly about her new dwelling, deftly moving a vase here or straightening a flower there, and thus transforming it from a house to a home. Even now, after seven years of marriage, she liked to picture herself in the gracious act.

But, though she conscientiously made a try at it every night as soon as the silk-shaded lamps were lit, she was always a bit bewildered as to how one went about performing those tiny miracles that make all the difference in the world to a room. The living-room, it seemed to her, looked good enough as it was—as good as it would ever look, with that mantelpiece and the same old furniture. Delia, one of the most thoroughly feminine of creatures, had subjected it to a long series of emphatic touches earlier in the day, and none of her handiwork had since been disturbed. But the feat of making all the difference in the world, so Mrs. Weldon had always heard, was not a thing to be left to servants. Touch-giving was a wife's job. And Mrs. Weldon was not one to shirk the business she had entered.

With an almost pitiable air of uncertainty, she strayed over to the mantel, lifted a small Japanese vase, and stood with it in her hand, gazing helplessly around the room. The white-enameled bookcase caught her eye, and gratefully she crossed to it and set the vase upon it, carefully rearranging various ornaments to make room. To relieve the congestion, she took up a framed photograph of Mr. Weldon's sister in evening gown and eye-glasses, again looked all about, and then set it timidly on the piano. She smoothed the piano-cover ingratiatingly, straightened the copies of "A Day in Venice," "To a Wild Rose," and Kreisler's "Caprice Viennois," which stood ever upon the rack, walked over to the tea-table and effected a change of places between the cream-jug and the sugar-bowl.

Then she stepped back, and surveyed her innovations. It was amazing how little difference they made to the room.

Sighing, Mrs. Weldon turned her attention to a bowl of daffodils, slightly past their first freshness. There was nothing to be done there; the omniscient Delia had refreshed them with clear water, had clipped their stems, and removed their more passé sisters. Still Mrs. Weldon bent over them pulling them gently about.

She liked to think of herself as one for whom flowers would thrive, who must always have blossoms about her, if she would be truly happy. When her living-room flowers died, she almost never forgot to stop in at the florist's, the next day, and get a fresh bunch. She told people, in little bursts of confidence, that she loved flowers. There was something almost apologetic in her way of uttering her tender avowal, as if she would beg her listeners not to consider her too bizarre in her taste. It seemed rather as though she expected the hearer to fall back, startled, at her words, crying, "Not really! Well, what *are* we coming to?"

She had other little confessions of affection, too, that she made from time to time; always with a little hesitation, as if understandably delicate about baring her heart, she told her love for color, the country, a good time, a really interesting play, nice materials, well-made clothes, and sunshine. But it was her fondness for flowers that she acknowledged oftenest. She seemed to feel that this, even more than her other predilections, set her apart from the general.

Mrs. Weldon gave the elderly daffodils a final pat, now, and once more surveyed the room, to see if any other repairs suggested themselves. Her lips tightened as the little Japanese vase met her gaze; distinctly, it had been better off in the first place. She set it back, the irritation that the sight of the mantel always gave her welling within her.

She had hated the mantelpiece from the moment they had first come to look at the apartment. There were other things that she had always hated about the place, too—the long, narrow hall, the dark dining-room, the inadequate closets. But Ernest had seemed to like the apartment well enough, so she had said nothing, then or since. After all, what was the use of fussing? Probably there would always be drawbacks, wherever they lived. There were enough in the last place they had had.

So they had taken the apartment on a five-year lease—that was four years and three months still to go. Mrs. Weldon felt suddenly weary. She lay down on the davenport, and pressed her thin hand against her dull brown hair.

Mr. Weldon came down the street, bent almost double in his battle with the wind from the river. His mind went over its nightly dark thoughts on living near Riverside Drive, five blocks from a subway station—two of those blocks loud with savage gales. He did not much like their apartment, even when he reached it. As soon as he had seen that dining-room, he had realized that they must always breakfast by artificial light—a thing he hated. But

Grace had never appeared to notice it, so he had held his peace. It didn't matter much, anyway, he explained to himself. There was pretty sure to be something wrong, everywhere. The dining-room wasn't much worse than that bedroom on the court, in the last place. Grace had never seemed to mind that, either.

Mrs. Weldon opened the door at his ring.

"Well!" she said, cheerily.

They smiled brightly at each other.

"Hel-lo," he said. "Well! You home?"

They kissed, slightly. She watched with polite interest while he hung up his hat and coat, removed the evening papers from his pocket, and handed one to her.

"Bring the papers?" she said, taking it.

She preceded him along the narrow hall to the living-room, where he let himself slowly down into his big chair, with a sound between a sigh and a groan. She sat opposite him, on the davenport. Again they smiled brightly at each other.

"Well, what have you been doing with yourself today?" he inquired.

She had been expecting the question. She had planned, before he came in, how she would tell him all the little events of her day—how the woman in the grocer's shop had had an argument with the cashier, and how Delia had tried out a new salad for lunch, with but moderate success, and how Alice Marshall had come to tea and it was quite true that Norma Matthews was going to have another baby. She had woven them into a lively little narrative, carefully choosing amusing phrases of description; had felt that she was going to tell it well and with spirit, and that he might laugh at the account of the occurrence in the grocer's. But now, as she considered it, it seemed to her a long, dull story. She had not the energy to begin it. And he was already smoothing out his paper.

"Oh, nothing," she said, with a gay little laugh. "Did you have a nice day?"

"Why—"he began. He had had some idea of telling her how he had finally put through that Detroit thing, and how tickled J. G. had seemed to be about it. But his interest waned, even as he started to speak. Besides, she was engrossed in breaking off a loose thread from the silk flowers on one of the pillows beside her.

"Oh, pretty fair," he said.

"Tired?" she asked, anxiously.

"Not so much," he answered. "Why—want to do anything tonight?"

"Why, not unless you do," she said, brightly. "Whatever you say."

"Whatever *you* say," he corrected her, pleasantly.

The subject closed. There was a third exchange of smiles, and then he hid most of himself behind his paper.

Mrs. Weldon, too, turned to the newspaper. But it

was an off night for news—some sort of tariff business, a failure in Wall Street, an impending strike, a four-day-old murder mystery. No one she knew had died or become engaged or married, or had attended any social functions. The fashions depicted on the woman's page were for Miss Fourteen-to-Sixteen. The advertisements ran mostly to bread, and sauces, and foot remedies, and sales of kitchen utensils. She put the paper down.

She wondered how Ernest could get so much enjoyment out of a newspaper. He could occupy himself with one for almost an hour, and then pick up another and go all through the same news with unabated interest. She wished that she could. She wished, even more than that, that she could think of something to say. She glanced around the room for inspiration.

"See my pretty daffy-down-dillies?" she said, finding it. To anyone else, she would have referred to them as daffodils.

Mr. Weldon looked in the direction of the flowers.

"M-m-mm," he said appreciatively, and returned to the news.

She looked at him, and shook her head despondently. He did not see, behind the paper; nor did she see that he was not reading. He was waiting, his hands gripping the printed sheet till their knuckles were blue-white, for her next remark.

It came.

"I love flowers," she said, in one of her little rushes of confidence.

Her husband did not answer. He sighed, his grip relaxed, and he went on reading.

Mrs. Weldon searched the room for another suggestion.

"Ernie," she cooed, "I'm so comfortable. Wouldn't you like to get up and get my handkerchief off the piano for me?"

He rose instantly. "Why, certainly," he said.

The way to ask people to fetch handkerchiefs, he thought as he went back to his chair, was to ask them to do it, and not try to make them think that you were giving them a treat. Either come right out and ask them, would they or wouldn't they, or else get up and get your handkerchief yourself.

"Thank you ever so much," his wife said enthusiastically.

Delia appeared in the doorway. "Dinner," she murmured bashfully, as if it were not quite a nice word for a young woman to use, and vanished.

"Dinner, Ern," cried Mrs. Weldon gayly, getting up.

"Just minute," issued indistinctly from behind the newspaper.

Mrs. Weldon waited. Then her lips compressed, and she went over and playfully took the paper from her husband's hands. She smiled carefully at him, and he smiled back at her.

"You go ahead in," he said, rising. "I'll be right with you. I've just got to wash up."

She looked after him, and something like a volcanic eruption took place within her. You'd think that just one night—just one little night—he might go and wash before dinner was announced. Just one night—it didn't seem much to ask. But she said nothing. God knew it was aggravating, but after all, it wasn't worth the trouble of fussing about.

She was waiting, cheerful and bright, courteously refraining from beginning her soup, when he took his place at the table.

"Oh, tomato soup, eh?" he said.

"Yes," she answered. "You like it, don't you?"

"Who—me?" he said. "Oh, yes, Yes, indeed."

She smiled at him.

"Yes, I thought you liked it," she said.

"You like it, too, don't you?" he inquired.

"Oh, yes," she assured him. "Yes, I like it ever so much. I'm awfully fond of tomato soup."

"Yes," he said, "there's nothing much better than tomato soup on a cold night."

She nodded.

"I think it's nice, too," she confided.

They had had tomato soup for dinner probably three times a month during their married life.

The soup was finished, and Delia brought in the meat.

"Well, that looks pretty good," said Mr. Weldon, carving it. "We haven't had steak for a long time."

"Why, yes, we have, too, Ern," his wife said eagerly. "We had it—let me see, what night were the Baileys here?—we had it Wednesday night—no, Thursday night. Don't you remember?"

"Did we?" he said. "Yes, I guess you're right. It seemed longer, somehow."

Mrs. Weldon smiled politely. She could not think of any way to prolong the discussion.

What did married people talk about, anyway, when they were alone together? She had seen married couples— not dubious ones but people she really knew were husbands and wives—at the theater or in trains, talking together as animatedly as if they were just acquaintances. She always watched them, marvelingly, wondering what on earth they found to say.

She could talk well enough to other people. There never seemed to be enough time for her to finish saying all she wanted to to her friends; she recalled how she had run on to Alice Marshall, only that afternoon. Both men and women found her attractive to listen to, not brilliant, not particularly funny, but still amusing and agreeable. She was never at a loss for something to say, never conscious of groping around for a topic. She had a good memory for bits of fresh gossip, or little stories of some celebrity that she had read or heard somewhere, and a knack of telling them entertainingly. Things people said to her stimulated her to quick replies, and more amusing narratives. They weren't especially scintillating people, either; it was just that they talked to her.

That was the trick of it. If nobody said anything to you, how were you to carry on a conversation from there? Inside, she was always bitter and angry at Ernest for not helping her out.

Ernest, too, seemed to be talkative enough when he was with others. People were always coming up and telling her how much they had enjoyed meeting her husband, and what fun he was. They weren't just being polite. There was no reason why they should go out of their way to say it.

Even when she and Ernest had another couple in to dinner or bridge, they both talked and laughed easily, all evening long. But as soon as the guests said good-night and what an awfully nice evening it had been, and the door had closed behind them, there the Weldons were again, without a word to say to each other. It would have been intimate and amusing to have talked over their guests' clothes and skill at bridge and probable domestic and financial affairs, and she would do it the next day, with great interest, too, to Alice Marshall, or some other one of her friends. But she couldn't do it with Ernest. Just as she started to, she found she simply couldn't make the effort.

So they would put away the card-table and empty the ash-receivers, with many "Oh, I beg your pardon's" and "No, no—I was in your way's," and then Ernest would say, "Well, I guess I'll go along to bed," and she would answer, "All right—I'll be in in a minute," and they would smile cheerfully at each other, and another evening would be over.

She tried to remember what they used to talk about before they were married, when they were engaged. It seemed to her that they never had had much to say to each other. But she hadn't worried about it then; indeed, she had felt the satisfaction of the correct, in their courtship, for she had always heard that true love was inarticulate. Then, besides, there had been always kissing and things, to take up your mind. But it had turned out that true marriage was apparently equally dumb. And you can't depend on kisses and all the rest of it to while away the evenings, after seven years.

You'd think that you would get used to it, in seven years, would realize that that was the way it was, and let it go at that. You don't, though. A thing like that gets on your nerves. It isn't one of those cozy, companionable silences that people occasionally fall into together. It makes you feel as if you must do something about it, as if you weren't performing your duty. You have the feeling a hostess has when her party is going badly, when her guests sit in corners and refuse to mingle. It makes you nervous and self-conscious, and you talk desperately about tomato soup, and say things like "daffy-down-dilly."

Mrs. Weldon cast about in her mind for a subject to offer her husband. There was Alice Marshall's new system of reducing—no, that was pretty dull. There was the case she had read in the morning's paper about the man of eighty-seven who had taken, as his fourth wife, a girl of twenty—he had probably seen that, and as long as he hadn't thought it worth repeating, he wouldn't think it worth hearing. There was the thing the Baileys' little boy had said about Jesus—no, she had told him that the night before.

She looked over at him, desultorily eating his rhubarb pie. She wished he wouldn't put that smeary stuff on his head. Perhaps it was necessary, if his hair really was falling out, but it did seem that he might find some more attractive remedy, if he only had the consideration to look around for one. Anyway, why must his hair fall out? There was something a little disgusting about people with falling hair.

"Like your pie, Ernie?" she asked vivaciously.

"Why, I don't know," he said, thinking it over. "I'm

not so crazy about rhubarb, I don't think. Are you?"

"No, I'm not so awfully crazy about it," she answered. "But then, I'm not really crazy about any kind of pie."

"Aren't you really?" he said, politely surprised. "I like pie pretty well—some kinds of pie."

"Do you?" The polite surprise was hers now.

"Why, yes," he said. "I like a nice huckleberry pie, or a nice lemon meringue pie, or a—" He lost interest in the thing himself, and his voice died away.

He avoided looking at her left hand, which lay on the edge of the table, palm upward. The long, gray-white ends of her nails protruded beyond the tips of her fingers, and the sight made him uncomfortable. Why in God's name must she wear her finger nails that heathenish length, and file them to those horrible points? If there was anything that he hated, it was a woman with pointed finger nails.

They returned to the living-room, and Mr. Weldon again eased himself down into his chair, reaching for the second paper.

"Quite sure there isn't anything you'd like to do tonight?" he asked solicitously. "Like to go to the movies, or anything?"

"Oh, no," she said. "Unless there's something you want to do."

"No, no," he answered. "I just thought maybe you wanted to."

"Not unless you do," she said.

He began on his paper, and she wandered aimlessly about the room. She had forgotten to get a new book from the library, and it had never in her life occurred to her to reread a book that she had once completed. She thought vaguely of playing Canfield, but she did not care enough about it to go to the trouble of getting out the cards, and setting up the table. There was some sewing that she could do, and she thought that she might presently go into the bedroom and fetch the nightgown that she was making for herself. Yes, she would probably do that, in a little while.

Ernest would read industriously, and, along toward the middle of the paper, he would start yawning aloud. Something happened inside Mrs. Weldon when he did this. She would murmur that she had to speak to Delia, and hurry to the kitchen. She would stay there rather a long time, looking vaguely into jars and inquiring half-heartedly about laundry lists, and, when she returned, he would have gone in to get ready for bed.

In a year, three hundred of their evenings were like this. Seven times three hundred is more than two thousand.

Mrs. Weldon went into the bedroom, and brought back her sewing. She sat down, pinned the pink satin to her knee, and began whipping narrow lace along the top of the half-made garment. It was fussy work. The fine thread knotted and drew, and she could not get the light adjusted so that the shadow of her head did not fall on her work. She grew a little sick, from the strain on her eyes.

Mr. Weldon turned a page, and yawned aloud. "Wah-huh-huh-huh-huh," he went on on a descending scale. He yawned again, and this time climbed the scale.

III

"My dear," Mrs. Ames said to Mrs. Marshall, "don't you really think that there must have been some other woman?"

"Oh, I simply couldn't think it was anything like that," said Mrs. Marshall. "Not Ernest Weldon. So devoted—home every night at half-past six, and such good company, and so jolly, and all. I don't see how there *could* have been."

"Sometimes," observed Mrs. Ames, "those awfully jolly men at home are just the kind."

"Yes, I know," Mrs. Marshall said. "But not Ernest Weldon. Why, I used to say to Jim, 'I never saw such a devoted husband in my life,' I said. Oh, not Ernest Weldon."

"I don't suppose," began Mrs. Ames, and hesitated. "I don't suppose," she went on, intently pressing the bit of sodden lemon in her cup with her teaspoon, "that Grace—that there was ever anyone—or anything like that?"

"Oh, Heavens, no," cried Mrs. Marshall. "Grace Weldon just gave her whole life to that man. It was Ernest this and Ernest that every minute. I simply can't understand it. If there was one earthly reason—if they ever fought, or if Ernest drank, or anything like that. But they got along so beautifully together—why, it just seems as if they must have been crazy to go and do a thing like this. Well, I can't begin to tell you how blue it's made me. It seems so awful!"

"Yes," said Mrs. Ames, "it certainly is too bad."

From the Diary of a New York Lady

From the Diary of a New York Lady

DURING DAYS OF PANIC,
FRENZY, AND WORLD CHANGE

*M*onday. Breakfast tray about eleven; didn't want it. The champagne at the Amorys' last night was *too* revolting, but what *can* you do? You can't stay until five o'clock on just *nothing*. They had those *divine* Hungarian musicians in the green coats, and Stewie Hunter took off one of his shoes and led them with it, and it *couldn't* have been funnier. He is *the* wittiest number in the *entire* world; he *couldn't* be more perfect. Ollie Martin brought me home and we both fell asleep in the car—*too* screaming.

Miss Rose came about noon to do my nails, simply *covered* with *the* most divine gossip. The Morrises are going to separate *any minute,* and Freddie Warren *definitely* has ulcers, and Gertie Leonard simply *won't* let Bill Crawford out of her sight even with Jack Leonard *right there in the room,* and it's all *true* about Sheila Phillips and Babs Deering. It *couldn't* have been more thrilling. Miss Rose is *too* marvelous; I really think that a lot of times people like that are a lot more intelligent than a lot of people. Didn't notice until after she had gone that the damn fool had put that *revolting* tangerine-colored polish on my nails; *couldn't* have been more furious. Started to read a book, but too nervous. Called up and found I could get two tickets for the opening of "Run Like a Rabbit" tonight for forty-eight dollars. Told them they had *the* nerve of the world, but what *can* you do? Think Joe said he was dining out, so telephoned some *divine* numbers to get someone to go to the theater with me, but they were all tied up. Finally got Ollie Martin. He *couldn't* have more poise, and what do *I* care if he *is* one? *Can't* decide whether to wear the green crêpe or the red wool. Every time I look at my finger nails, I could *spit. Damn* Miss Rose.

Tuesday. Joe came barging in my room this morning at *practically nine o'clock. Couldn't* have been more furious. Started to fight, but *too* dead. Know he said he wouldn't be home to dinner. Absolutely *cold* all day;

couldn't *move*. Last night *couldn't* have been more per-fect. Ollie and I dined at Thirty-Eight East, absolutely *poisonous* food, and not one *living* soul that you'd be seen *dead* with, and "Run Like a Rabbit" was *the* world's worst. Took Ollie up to the Barlows' party and it *couldn't* have been more attractive—*couldn't* have been more people absolutely *stinking*. They had those Hungarians in the green coats, and Stewie Hunter was leading them with a fork—everybody simply *died*. He had *yards* of green toi-let paper hung around his neck like a lei; he *couldn't* have been in better form. Met a *really new number*, very tall, *too* marvelous, and one of those people that you can *really* talk to them. I told him sometimes I get so *nauseated* I could *yip*, and I felt I absolutely *had* to do something like write or paint. He said why didn't I write or paint. Came home alone; Ollie passed out *stiff*. Called up the new number three times today to get him to come to dinner and go with me to the opening of "Never Say Good Morning," but first he was out and then he was all tied up with his mother. Finally got Ollie Martin. Tried to read a book, but couldn't sit still. *Can't* decide whether to wear the red lace or the pink with the feathers. Feel *too* exhausted, but what *can* you do?

Wednesday. *The* most terrible thing happened *just this minute*. Broke one of my finger nails *right off short*.

Absolutely *the* most horrible thing I ever had happen to
me in my life. Called up Miss Rose to come over and shape
it for me, but she was out for the day. I do have *the* worst
luck in the *entire* world. Now I'll have to go around like
this all day and all night, but what *can* you do? *Damn* Miss
Rose. Last night *too* hectic. "Never Say Good Morning"
too foul, *never* saw more poisonous clothes on the stage.
Took Ollie up to the Ballards' party; *couldn't* have been
better. They had those Hungarians in the green coats and
Stewie Hunter was leading them with a freesia—*too* perfect. He had on Peggy Cooper's ermine coat and Phyllis
Minton's silver turban; *simply* unbelievable. Asked simply
sheaves of *divine* people to come here Friday night; got the
address of those Hungarians in the green coats from Betty
Ballard. She says just engage them until four, and then
whoever gives them another three hundred dollars, they'll
stay till five. *Couldn't* be cheaper. Started home with Ollie,
but had to drop him at his house; he *couldn't* have been
sicker. Called up the new number today to get him to come
to dinner and go to the opening of "Everybody Up" with
me tonight, but he was tied up. Joe's going to be out; he
didn't *condescend* to say *where, of course.* Started to read
the papers, but nothing in them except that Mona Wheatley is in Reno charging *intolerable cruelty.* Called up Jim
Wheatley to see if he had anything to do tonight, but he
was tied up. Finally got Ollie Martin. *Can't* decide whether

to wear the white satin or the black chiffon or the yellow pebble crêpe. Simply *wrecked* to the *core* about my finger nail. Can't *bear* it. *Never* knew *anybody* to have such *unbelievable* things happen to them.

Thursday. Simply *collapsing* on my *feet*. Last night *too* marvelous. "Everybody Up" *too* divine, *couldn't* be filthier, and the new number was there, *too* celestial, only he didn't see me. He was with Florence Keeler in that *loathsome* gold Schiaparelli model of hers that every *shopgirl* has had since *God* knows. He must be out of his *mind;* she wouldn't *look* at a man. Took Ollie to the Watsons' party; *couldn't* have been more thrilling. Everybody simply *blind.* They had those Hungarians in the green coats and Stewie Hunter was leading them with a lamp, and, after the lamp got broken, he and Tommy Thomas did adagio dances—*too* wonderful. Somebody told me Tommy's doctor told him he had to absolutely get *right out of town,* he has *the* world's worst stomach, but you'd *never* know it. Came home alone, couldn't find Ollie *anywhere.* Miss Rose came at noon to shape my nail, *couldn't* have been more fascinating. Sylvia Eaton can't go *out the door* unless she's had a hypodermic, and Doris Mason *knows every single word* about Douggie Mason and that girl up in Harlem, and Evelyn North won't be *induced* to keep away from those three acrobats, and they don't *dare* tell Stuyvie Ray-

mond *what* he's got the matter with him. *Never* knew
anyone that had a more simply *fascinating* life than Miss
Rose. Made her take that *vile* tangerine polish off my nails
and put on dark red. Didn't notice until after she had gone
that it's practically *black* in electric light; *couldn't* be in a
worse state. *Damn* Miss Rose. Joe left a note saying he was
going to dine out, so telephoned the new number to get
him to come to dinner and go with me to that new movie
tonight, but he didn't answer. Sent him three telegrams to
absolutely surely come tomorrow night. Finally got Ollie
Martin for tonight. Looked at the papers, but nothing in
them except that the Harry Motts are throwing a tea with
Hungarian music on Sunday. Think will ask the new number to go to it with me; they must have meant to invite me.
Began to read a book, but too exhausted. *Can't* decide
whether to wear the new blue with the white jacket or save
it till tomorrow night and wear the ivory moire. Simply
heartsick every time I think of my nails. *Couldn't* be
wilder. Could *kill* Miss Rose, but what *can* you do?

Friday. Absolutely *sunk; couldn't* be worse. Last
night *too* divine, movie *simply* deadly. Took Ollie to the
Kingslands' party, *too* unbelievable, everybody absolutely
rolling. They had those Hungarians in the green coats, but
Stewie Hunter wasn't there. He's got a *complete* nervous
breakdown. Worried *sick* for fear he won't be well by

tonight; will absolutely *never* forgive him if he doesn't come. Started home with Ollie, but dropped him at his house because he *couldn't* stop crying. Joe left word with the butler he's going to the country this afternoon for the week-end; *of course* he wouldn't *stoop* to say *what* country. Called up *streams* of marvelous numbers to get someone to come dine and go with me to the opening of "White Man's Folly," and then go somewhere after to dance for a while; can't *bear* to be the first one there at your own party. Everybody was tied up. Finally got Ollie Martin. *Couldn't* feel more depressed; never should have gone *anywhere near* champagne and Scotch together. Started to read a book, but too restless. Called up Anne Lyman to ask about the new baby and *couldn't* remember if it was a boy or girl—*must* get a secretary *next week*. Anne *couldn't* have been more of a help; she said she didn't know whether to name it Patricia or Gloria, so then of course I knew it was a girl *right away*. Suggested calling it Barbara; forgot she already had one. Absolutely *walking the floor* like a *panther* all day. Could *spit* about Stewie Hunter. Can't *face* deciding whether to wear the blue with the white jacket or the purple with the beige roses. Every time I look at those *revolting* black nails, I want to absolutely *yip*. I really have *the* most horrible things happen to me of anybody in the *entire* world. *Damn* Miss Rose.

The Waltz

The Waltz

Why, thank you so much. I'd adore to.

I don't want to dance with him. I don't want to dance
with anybody. And even if I did, it wouldn't be him. He'd
be well down among the last ten. I've seen the way he
dances; it looks like something you do on St. Walpurgis
Night. Just think, not a quarter of an hour ago, here I was
sitting, feeling so sorry for the poor girl he was dancing
with. And now *I'm* going to be the poor girl. Well, well.
Isn't it a small world?

And a peach of a world, too. A true little corker. Its events are so fascinatingly unpredictable, are not they? Here I was, minding my own business, not doing a stitch of harm to any living soul. And then he comes into my life, all smiles and city manners, to sue me for the favor of one memorable mazurka. Why, he scarcely knows my name, let alone what it stands for. It stands for Despair, Bewilderment, Futility, Degradation, and Premeditated Murder, but little does he wot. I don't wot his name, either; I haven't any idea what it is. Jukes, would be my guess from the look in his eyes. How do you do, Mr. Jukes? And how is that dear little brother of yours, with the two heads?

Ah, now why did he have to come around me, with his low requests? Why can't he let me lead my own life? I ask so little—just to be left alone in my quiet corner of the table, to do my evening brooding over all my sorrows. And he must come, with his bows and his scrapes and his may-I-have-this-ones. And I had to go and tell him that I'd adore to dance with him. I cannot understand why I wasn't struck right down dead. Yes, and being struck dead would look like a day in the country, compared to struggling out a dance with this boy. But what could I do? Everyone else at the table had got up to dance, except him and me. There I was, trapped. Trapped like a trap in a trap.

What can you say, when a man asks you to dance with him? I most certainly will *not* dance with you, I'll see you

274

in hell first. Why, thank you, I'd like to awfully, but I'm having labor pains. Oh, yes, *do* let's dance together—it's so nice to meet a man who isn't a scaredy-cat about catching my beri-beri. No. There was nothing for me to do, but say I'd adore to. Well, we might as well get it over with. All right, Cannonball, let's run out on the field. You won the toss; you can lead.

Why, I think it's more of a waltz, really. Isn't it? We might just listen to the music a second. Shall we? Oh, yes, it's a waltz. Mind? Why, I'm simply thrilled. I'd love to waltz with you.

I'd love to waltz with you. I'd love to waltz with you, I'd love to have my tonsils out, I'd love to be in a midnight fire at sea. Well, it's too late now. We're getting under way. *Oh.* Oh, dear. Oh, dear, dear, dear. Oh, this is even worse than I thought it would be. I suppose that's the one dependable law of life—everything is always worse than you thought it was going to be. Oh, if I had had any real grasp of what this dance would be like, I'd have held out for sitting it out. Well, it will probably amount to the same thing in the end. We'll be sitting it out on the floor in a minute, if he keeps this up.

I'm so glad I brought it to his attention that this is a waltz they're playing. Heaven knows what might have happened, if he had thought it was something fast; we'd have blown the sides right out of the building. Why does he

always want to be somewhere that he isn't? Why can't we
stay in one place just long enough to get acclimated? It's
this constant rush, rush, rush, that's the curse of American
life. That's the reason that we're all of us so—*Ow!* For
God's sake, don't *kick*, you idiot; this is only second down.
Oh, my shin. My poor, poor shin, that I've had ever since
I was a little girl!

*Oh, no, no, no. Goodness, no. It didn't hurt the least
little bit. And anyway it was my fault. Really it was.
Truly. Well, you're just being sweet, to say that. It really
was all my fault.*

I wonder what I'd better do—kill him this instant,
with my naked hands, or wait and let him drop in his
traces. Maybe it's best not to make a scene. I guess I'll just
lie low, and watch the pace get him. He can't keep this up
indefinitely—he's only flesh and blood. Die he must, and
die he shall, for what he did to me. I don't want to be of
the over-sensitive type, but you can't tell me that kick was
unpremeditated. Freud says there are no accidents. I've
led no cloistered life, I've known dancing partners who
have spoiled my slippers and torn my dress; but when it
comes to kicking, I am Outraged Womanhood. When you
kick me in the shin, *smile*.

Maybe he didn't do it maliciously. Maybe it's just his
way of showing his high spirits. I suppose I ought to be
glad that one of us is having such a good time. I suppose

I ought to think myself lucky if he brings me back alive. Maybe it's captious to demand of a practically strange man that he leave your shins as he found them. After all, the poor boy's doing the best he can. Probably he grew up in the hill country, and never had no larnin'. I bet they had to throw him on his back to get shoes on him.

Yes, it's lovely, isn't it? It's simply lovely. It's the loveliest waltz. Isn't it? Oh, I think it's lovely, too.

Why, I'm getting positively drawn to the Triple Threat here. He's my hero. He has the heart of a lion, and the sinews of a buffalo. Look at him—never a thought of the consequences, never afraid of his face, hurling himself into every scrimmage, eyes shining, cheeks ablaze. And shall it be said that I hung back? No, a thousand times no. What's it to me if I have to spend the next couple of years in a plaster cast? Come on, Butch, right through them! Who wants to live forever?

Oh. Oh, dear. Oh, he's all right, thank goodness. For a while I thought they'd have to carry him off the field. Ah, I couldn't bear to have anything happen to him. I love him. I love him better than anybody in the world. Look at the spirit he gets into a dreary, commonplace waltz; how effete the other dancers seem, beside him. He is youth and vigor and courage, he is strength and gayety and—*Ow!* Get off my instep, you hulking peasant! What do you think I am, anyway—a gangplank? *Ow!*

No, of course it didn't hurt. Why, it didn't a bit. Honestly. And it was all my fault. You see, that little step of yours—well, it's perfectly lovely, but it's just a tiny bit tricky to follow at first. Oh, did you work it up yourself? You really did? Well, aren't you amazing! Oh, now I think I've got it. Oh, I think it's lovely. I was watching you do it when you were dancing before. It's awfully effective when you look at it.

It's awfully effective when you look at it. I bet I'm awfully effective when you look at me. My hair is hanging along my cheeks, my skirt is swaddled about me, I can feel the cold damp of my brow. I must look like something out of the Fall of the House of Usher. This sort of thing takes a fearful toll of a woman my age. And he worked up his little step himself, he with his degenerate cunning. And it was just a tiny bit tricky at first, but now I think I've got it. Two stumbles, slip, and a twenty-yard dash; yes, I've got it. I've got several other things, too, including a split shin and a bitter heart. I hate this creature I'm chained to. I hated him the moment I saw his leering, bestial face. And here I've been locked in his noxious embrace for the thirty-five years this waltz has lasted. Is that orchestra never going to stop playing? Or must this obscene travesty of a dance go on until hell burns out?

Oh, they're going to play another encore. Oh, goody. Oh, that's lovely. Tired? I should say I'm not tired. I'd like to go on like this forever.

I should say I'm not tired. I'm dead, that's all I am. Dead, and in what a cause! And the music is never going to stop playing, and we're going on like this, Double-Time Charlie and I, throughout eternity. I suppose I won't care any more, after the first hundred thousand years. I suppose nothing will matter then, not heat nor pain nor broken heart nor cruel, aching weariness. Well. It can't come too soon for me.

I wonder why I didn't tell him I was tired. I wonder why I didn't suggest going back to the table. I could have said let's just listen to the music. Yes, and if he would, that would be the first bit of attention he has given it all evening. George Jean Nathan said that the lovely rhythms of the waltz should be listened to in stillness and not be accompanied by strange gyrations of the human body. I think that's what he said. I think it was George Jean Nathan. Anyhow, whatever he said and whoever he was and whatever he's doing now, he's better off than I am. That's safe. Anybody who isn't waltzing with this Mrs. O'Leary's cow I've got here is having a good time.

Still, if we were back at the table, I'd probably have to talk to him. Look at him—what could you say to a thing like that! Did you go to the circus this year, what's your favorite kind of ice cream, how do you spell cat? I guess I'm as well off here. As well off as if I were in a cement mixer in full action.

I'm past all feeling now. The only way I can tell when

he steps on me is that I can hear the splintering of bones. And all the events of my life are passing before my eyes. There was the time I was in a hurricane in the West Indies, there was the day I got my head cut open in the taxi smash, there was the night the drunken lady threw a bronze ashtray at her own true love and got me instead, there was that summer that the sailboat kept capsizing. Ah, what an easy, peaceful time was mine, until I fell in with Swifty, here. I didn't know what trouble was, before I got drawn into this *danse macabre.* I think my mind is beginning to wander. It almost seems to me as if the orchestra were stopping. It couldn't be, of course; it could never, never be. And yet in my ears there is a silence like the sound of angel voices. . . .

Oh, they've stopped, the mean things. They're not going to play any more. Oh, darn. Oh, do you think they would? Do you really think so, if you gave them fifty dollars? Oh, that would be lovely. And look, do tell them to play this same thing. I'd simply adore to go on waltzing.

Dusk before
Fireworks

Dusk before Fireworks

*H*e was a very good-looking young man indeed, shaped to be annoyed. His voice was intimate as the rustle of sheets, and he kissed easily. There was no tallying the gifts of Charvet handkerchiefs, *art moderne* ash-trays, monogrammed dressing-gowns, gold keychains, and ciga-rette-cases of thin wood, inlaid with views of Parisian com-fort stations, that were sent him by ladies too quickly confident and were paid for with the money of unwitting husbands, which is acceptable any place in the world.

Every woman who visited his small, square apartment promptly flamed with the desire to assume charge of its redecoration. During his tenancy, three separate ladies had achieved this ambition. Each had left behind her, for her brief monument, much too much glazed chintz.

The glare of the latest upholstery was dulled, now, in an April dusk. There was a soft blur of mauve and gray over chairs and curtains, instead of the daytime pattern of heroic-sized double poppies and small, sad elephants. (The most recent of the volunteer decorators was a lady who added interest to her ways by collecting all varieties of elephants save those alive or stuffed; her selection of the chintz had been made less for the cause of contemporary design than in the hope of keeping ever present the wistful souvenirs of her hobby and, hence, of herself. Unhappily, the poppies, those flowers for forgetfulness, turned out to be predominant in the pattern.)

The very good-looking young man was stretched in a long chair, legless and short in the back. It was a strain to see in that chair any virtue save the speeding one of modernity. Certainly it was a peril to all who dealt with it; they were far from their best within its arms, and they could never have wished to be remembered as they appeared while easing into its depths or struggling out again. All, that is, save the young man. He was a long young man, broad at the shoulders and chest and narrow everywhere else, and his muscles obeyed him at the exact instant of command. He rose and lay, he moved and was still, always in beauty. Several men disliked him, but only one woman really hated him. She was his sister. She was stump-shaped, and she had straight hair.

On the sofa opposite the difficult chair there sat a young woman, slight and softly dressed. There was no more to her frock than some dull, dark silk and a little chiffon, but the recurrent bill for it demanded, in bitter black and white, a sum well on toward the second hundred. Once the very good-looking young man had said that he liked women in quiet and conservative clothes, carefully made. The young woman was of those unfortunates who remember every word. This made living peculiarly trying for her when it was later demonstrated that the young man was also partial to ladies given to garments of slap-dash cut and color like the sound of big brass instruments.

The young woman was temperately pretty in the eyes of most beholders; but there were a few, mainly hand-to-mouth people, artists and such, who could not look enough at her. Half a year before, she had been sweeter to see. Now there was tension about her mouth and unease along her brow, and her eyes looked puzzled and beseeching. The gentle dusk became her. The young man who shared it with her could not see these things.

She stretched her arms and laced her fingers high above her head.

"Oh, this is nice," she said. "It's nice being here."

"It's nice and peaceful," he said. "Oh, Lord. Why
can't people just be peaceful? That's little enough to ask,
isn't it? Why does there have to be so much hell, all the
time?"

She dropped her hands to her lap.

"There doesn't have to be at all," she said. She had
a quiet voice, and she said her words with every courtesy
to each of them, as if she respected language. "There's
never any need for hell."

"There's an awful lot of it around, sweet," he said.

"There certainly is," she said. "There's just as much
hell as there are hundreds of little shrill, unnecessary people. It's the second-raters that stir up hell; first-rate people
wouldn't. You need never have another bit of it in your
beautiful life if—if you'll pardon my pointing—you could
just manage to steel yourself against that band of spitting
hell-cats that is included in your somewhat overcrowded
acquaintance, my lamb. Ah, but I mean it, Hobie, dear.
I've been wanting to tell you for so long. But it's so rotten
hard to say. If I say it, it makes me sound just like one of
them—makes me seem inexpensive and jealous. Surely
you know, after all this time, I'm not like that. It's just that
I worry so about you. You're so fine, you're so lovely, it
nearly kills me to see you just eaten up by a lot of things
like Margot Wadsworth and Mrs. Holt and Evie Maynard
and those. You're so much better than that. You know

that's why I'm saying it. You know I haven't got a stitch
of jealousy in me. Jealous! Good heavens, if I were going
to be jealous, I'd be it about someone worth while, and not
about any silly, stupid, idle, worthless, selfish, hysterical,
vulgar, promiscuous, sex-ridden—"

"Darling!" he said.

"Well, I'm sorry," she said. "I guess I'm sorry. I
didn't really mean to go into the subject of certain of your
friends. Maybe the way they behave isn't their fault, said
she, lying in her teeth. After all, you can't expect them to
know what it's about. Poor things, they'll never know how
sweet it can be, how lovely it always is when we're alone
together. It is, isn't it? Ah, Hobie, isn't it?"

The young man raised his slow lids and looked at her.
He smiled with one end of his beautiful curly mouth.

"Uh-huh," he said.

He took his eyes from hers and became busy with an
ash-tray and a spent cigarette. But he still smiled.

"Ah, don't," she said. "You promised you'd forget
about—about last Wednesday. You said you'd never remember it again. Oh, whatever made me do it! Making
scenes. Having tantrums. Rushing out into the night. And
then coming crawling back. Me, that wanted to show you
how different a woman could be! Oh, please, please don't
let's think about it. Only tell me I wasn't as terrible as I
know I was."

"Darling," he said, for he was often a young man of simple statements, "you were the worst I ever saw."

"And doesn't that come straight from Sir Hubert!" she said. "Oh, dear. Oh, dear, oh, dear. What can I say? 'Sorry' isn't nearly enough. I'm broken. I'm in little bits. Would you mind doing something about putting me together again?"

She held out her arms to him.

The young man rose, came over to the sofa, and kissed her. He had intended a quick, good-humored kiss, a moment's stop on a projected trip out to his little pantry to mix cocktails. But her arms clasped him so close and so gladly that he dismissed the plan. He lifted her to her feet, and did not leave her.

Presently she moved her head and hid her face above his heart.

"Listen," she said, against cloth. "I want to say it all now, and then never say it any more. I want to tell you that there'll never, never be anything like last Wednesday again. What we have is so much too lovely ever to cheapen. I promise, oh, I promise you, I won't ever be like—like anybody else."

"You couldn't be, Kit," he said.

"Ah, think that always," she said, "and say it sometimes. It's so sweet to hear. Will you, Hobie?"

"For your size," he said, "you talk an awful lot." His

fingers slid to her chin and he held her face for his greater convenience.

After a while she moved again.

"Guess who I'd rather be, right this minute, than anybody in the whole world," she said.

"Who?" he said.

"Me," she said.

The telephone rang.

The telephone was in the young man's bedroom, standing in frequent silence on the little table by his bed. There was no door to the bedchamber; a plan which had disadvantages, too. Only a curtained archway sequestered its intimacies from those of the living-room. Another archway, also streaming chintz, gave from the bedroom upon a tiny passage, along which were ranged the bathroom and the pantry. It was only by entering either of these, closing the door behind, and turning the faucets on to the full that any second person in the apartment could avoid hearing what was being said over the telephone. The young man sometimes thought of removing to a flat of more sympathetic design.

"There's that damn telephone," the young man said.

"Isn't it?" the young woman said. "And wouldn't it be?"

"Let's not answer it," he said. "Let's let it ring."

"No, you mustn't," she said. "I must be big and

strong. Anyway, maybe it's only somebody that just died and left you twenty million dollars. Maybe it isn't some other woman at all. And if it is, what difference does it make? See how sweet and reasonable I am? Look at me being generous."

"You can afford to be, sweetheart," he said.

"I know I can," she said. "After all, whoever she is, she's way off on an end of a wire, and I'm right here."

She smiled up at him. So it was nearly half a minute before he went away to the telephone.

Still smiling, the young woman stretched her head back, closed her eyes and flung her arms wide. A long sigh raised her breast. Thus she stood, then she went and settled back on the sofa. She essayed whistling softly, but the issuing sounds would not resemble the intended tune and she felt, though interested, vaguely betrayed. Then she looked about the dusk-filled room. Then she pondered her finger nails, bringing each bent hand close to her eyes, and could find no fault. Then she smoothed her skirt along her legs and shook out the chiffon frills at her wrists. Then she spread her little handkerchief on her knee and with exquisite care traced the "Katherine" embroidered in script across one of its corners. Then she gave it all up and did nothing but listen.

"Yes?" the young man was saying. "Hello? Hello. I *told* you this is Mr. Ogden. Well, I *am* holding the wire.

I've *been* holding the wire. *You're* the one that went away. Hello? Ah, now listen—Hello? Hey. Oh, what the hell *is* this? Come back, will you? Operator! Hello. *Yes*, this is Mr. Ogden. Who? Oh, hello, Connie. How are you, dear? What? You're what? Oh, that's too bad. What's the matter? Why can't you? Where are you, in Greenwich? Oh, I see. When, now? Why, Connie, the only thing is I've got to go right out. So if you came in to town now, it really wouldn't do much—Well, I couldn't very well do that, dear, I'm keeping these people waiting as it is. I say I'm late now, I was just going out the door when you called. Why, I'd better not say that, Connie, because there's no telling when I'll be able to break away. Look, why don't you wait and come in to town tomorrow some time? What? Can't you tell me now? Oh— Well— Oh, Connie, there's no reason to talk like that. Why, of course I'd do anything in the world I could, but I tell you I can't tonight. No, no, no, no, no, it isn't that at all. No, it's nothing like that, I tell you. These people are friends of my sister's, and it's just one of those things you've got to do. Why don't you be a good girl and go to bed early, and then you'll feel better tomorrow? Hm? Will you do that? What? Of course I do, Connie. I'll try to later on if I can, dear. Well, all right, if you want to, but I don't know what time I'll be home. Of course I do. Of course I do. Yes, I *do*, Connie. You be a good girl, won't you? 'By, dear."

The young man returned, through the chintz. He had a rather worn look. It was, of course, becoming to him.

"God," he said, simply.

The young woman on the sofa looked at him as if through clear ice.

"And how *is* dear Mrs. Holt?" she said.

"Great," he said. "Corking. Way up at the top of her form." He dropped wearily into the low chair. "She says she has something she wants to tell me."

"It can't be her age," she said.

He smiled without joy. "She says it's too hard to say over the wire," he said.

"Then it may be her age," she said. "She's afraid it might sound like her telephone number."

"About twice a week," he said, "Connie has something she must tell you right away, that she couldn't possibly say over the telephone. Usually it turns out she's caught the butler drinking again."

"I see," she said.

"Well," he said. "Poor little Connie."

"Poor little Connie," she said. "Oh, my God. That saber-toothed tigress. Poor little Connie."

"Darling, why do we have to waste time talking about Connie Holt?" he said. "Can't we just be peaceful?"

"Not while that she-beast prowls the streets," she said. "Is she coming in to town tonight?"

"Well, she was," he said, "but then she more or less said she wouldn't."

"Oh, she will," she said. "You get right down out of that fool's paradise you're in. She'll shoot out of Greenwich like a bat out of hell, if she thinks there's a chance of seeing you. Ah, Hobie, you don't really want to see that old thing, do you? Do you? Because if you do—Well, I suppose maybe you do. Naturally, if she has something she must tell you right away, you want to see her. Look, Hobie, you know you can see me any time. It isn't a bit important, seeing me tonight. Why don't you call up Mrs. Holt and tell her to take the next train in? She'd get here quicker by train than by motor, wouldn't she? Please go ahead and do it. It's quite all right about me. Really."

"You know," he said, "I knew that was coming. I could tell it by the way you were when I came back from the telephone. Oh, Kit, what makes you want to talk like that? You know damned well the last thing I want to do is see Connie Holt. You know how I want to be with you. Why do you want to work up all this? I watched you just sit there and deliberately talk yourself into it, starting right out of nothing. Now what's the idea of that? Oh, good Lord, what's the matter with women, anyway?"

"Please don't call me 'women,' " she said.

"I'm sorry, darling," he said. "I didn't mean to use bad words." He smiled at her. She felt her heart go liquid, but she did her best to be harder won.

"Doubtless," she said, and her words fell like snow when there is no wind, "I spoke illadvisedly. If I said, as I must have, something to distress you, I can only beg you to believe that that was my misfortune, and not my intention. It seemed to me as if I were doing only a courteous thing in suggesting that you need feel no obligation about spending the evening with me, when you would naturally wish to be with Mrs. Holt. I simply felt that—Oh, the hell with it! I'm no good at this. Of course I didn't mean it, dearest. If you had said, 'All right,' and had gone and told her to come in, I should have died. I just said it because I wanted to hear you say it was me you wanted to be with. Oh, I need to hear you say that, Hobie. It's—it's what I live on, darling."

"Kit," he said, "you ought to know, without my saying it. You know. It's this feeling you *have* to say things—that's what spoils everything."

"I suppose so," she said. "I suppose I know so. Only—the thing is, I get so mixed up, I just—I just can't go on. I've got to be reassured, dearest. I didn't need to be at first, when everything was gay and sure, but things aren't—well, they aren't the same now. There seem to be so many others that— So I need so terribly to have you tell me that it's me and not anybody else. Oh, I *had* to have you say that, a few minutes ago. Look, Hobie. How do you

think it makes me feel to sit here and hear you lie to
Connie Holt—to hear you say you have to go out with
friends of your sister's? Now why couldn't you say you had
a date with me? Are you ashamed of me, Hobie? Is that it?"

"Oh, Kit," he said, "for heaven's sake! I don't know
why I did it. I did it before I even thought. I did it—well,
sort of instinctively, I guess, because it seemed to be the
easiest thing to do. I suppose I'm just weak."

"No!" she said. "You weak? Well! And is there any
other news tonight?"

"I know I am," he said. "I know it's weak to do
anything in the world to avoid a scene."

"Exactly what," she said, "is Mrs. Holt to you and
you to her that she may make a scene if she learns that you
have an engagement with another woman?"

"Oh, God!" he said. "I told you I don't give a damn
about Connie Holt. She's nothing to me. Now will you for
God's sake let it drop?"

"Oh, she's nothing to you," she said. "I see. Naturally, that would be why you called her 'dear' every other
word."

"If I did," he said, "I never knew I was saying it.
Good Lord, that doesn't mean anything. It's simply a—a
form of nervousness, I suppose. I say it when I can't think
what to call people. Why, I call telephone operators
'dear.' "

"I'm sure you do!" she said.

They glared. It was the young man who gave first. He went and sat close to her on the sofa, and for a while there were only murmurs. Then he said, "Will you stop? Will you stop it? Will you always be just like this—just sweet and the way you're meant to be and no fighting?"

"I will," she said. "Honest, I mean to. Let's not let anything come between us again ever. Mrs. Holt, indeed! Hell with her."

"Hell with her," he said. There was another silence, during which the young man did several things that he did extraordinarily well.

Suddenly the young woman stiffened her arms and pushed him away from her.

"And how do I know," she said, "that the way you talk to me about Connie Holt isn't just the way you talk to her about me when I'm not here? How do I know that?"

"Oh, my Lord," he said. "Oh, my dear, sweet Lord. Just when everything was all right. Ah, stop it, will you, ba-bay? Let's just be quiet. Like this. See?"

A little later he said, "Look, sweet, how about a cocktail? Mightn't that be an idea? I'll go make them. And would you like the lights lighted?"

"Oh, no," she said. "I like it better in the dusk, like this. It's sweet. Dusk is so personal, somehow. And this way you can't see those lampshades. Hobie, if you knew how I hate your lampshades!"

"Honestly?" he said, with less injury than bewilderment in his voice. He looked at the shades as if he saw them for the first time. They were of vellum, or some substance near it, and upon each was painted a panorama of the right bank of the Seine, with the minute windows of the buildings cut out, under the direction of some master mind, so that light might come through. "What's the matter with them, Kit?"

"Dearest, if you don't know, I can't ever explain it to you," she said. "Among other things, they're banal, inappropriate, and unbeautiful. They're exactly what Evie Maynard *would* have chosen. She thinks, just because they show views of Paris, that they're pretty darned sophisticated. She is that not uncommon type of woman that thinks any reference to la belle France is an invitation to the waltz. 'Not uncommon.' If that isn't the mildest word-picture that ever was painted of that—"

"Don't you like the way she decorated the apartment?" he said.

"Sweetheart," she said, "I think it's poisonous. You know that."

"Would you like to do it over?" he said.

"I should say not," she said. "Look, Hobie, don't you remember me? I'm the one that doesn't want to decorate your flat. Now do you place me? But if I ever *did*, the first thing I should do would be to paint these walls putty color—no, I guess first I'd tear off all this chintz and fling it to the winds, and then I'd—"

The telephone rang.

The young man threw one stricken glance at the young woman and then sat motionless. The jangles of the bell cut the dusk like vicious little scissors.

"I think," said the young woman, exquisitely, "that your telephone is ringing. Don't let me keep you from answering it. As a matter of fact, I really must go powder my nose."

She sprang up, dashed through the bedroom, and into the bathroom. There was the sound of a closed door, the grind of a firmly turned key, and then immediately the noise of rushing waters.

When she returned, eventually, to the living-room, the young man was pouring a pale, cold liquid into small glasses. He gave one to her, and smiled at her over it. It was his wistful smile. It was of his best.

"Hobie," she said, "is there a livery stable anywhere around here where they rent wild horses?"

"What?" he said.

"Because if there is," she said, "I wish you'd call up and ask them to send over a couple of teams. I want to show you they couldn't drag me into asking who that was on the telephone."

"Oh," he said, and tried his cocktail. "Is this dry enough, sweet? Because you like them dry, don't you? Sure it's all right? Really? Ah, wait a second, darling. Let *me* light your cigarette. There. Sure you're all right?"

"I can't stand it," she said. "I just lost all my strength of purpose—maybe the maid will find it on the floor in the morning. Hobart Ogden, who was that on the telephone?"

"Oh, that?" he said. "Well, that was a certain lady who shall be nameless."

"I'm sure she should be," she said. "She doubtless has all the other qualities of a—Well. I didn't quite say it, I'm keeping my head. Ah, dearest, was that Connie Holt again?"

"No, that was the funniest thing," he said. "That was Evie Maynard. Just when we were talking about her."

"Well, well, well," she said. "Isn't it a small world? And what's on her mind, if I may so flatter her? Is *her* butler tight, too?"

"Evie hasn't got a butler," he said. He tried smiling again, but found it better to abandon the idea and concentrate on refilling the young woman's glass. "No, she's just dizzy, the same as usual. She's got a cocktail party at her apartment, and they all want to go out on the town, that's all."

"Luckily," she said, "you had to go out with these friends of your sister's. You were just going out the door when she called."

"I never told her any such thing!" he said. "I said I had a date I'd been looking forward to all week."

"Oh, you didn't mention any names?" she said.

"There's no reason why I should, to Evie Maynard," he said. "It's none of her affair, any more than what she's doing and who she's doing it with is any concern of mine. She's nothing in my life. You know that. I've hardly seen her since she did the apartment. I don't care if I never see her again. I'd *rather* I never saw her again."

"I should think that might be managed, if you've really set your heart on it," she said.

"Well, I do what I can," he said. "She wanted to come in now for a cocktail, she and some of those interior decorator boys she has with her, and I told her absolutely no."

"And you think that will keep her away?" she said. "Oh, no. She'll be here. She and her feathered friends. Let's see—they ought to arrive just about the time that Mrs. Holt has thought it over and come in to town. Well. It's shaping up into a lovely evening, isn't it?"

"Great," he said. "And if I may say so, you're doing everything you can to make it harder, you little peach." He poured more cocktails. "Oh, Kit, why are you being so nasty? Don't do it, darling. It's not like you. It's so unbecoming to you."

"I know it's horrible," she said. "It's—well, I do it

300

in defense, I suppose, Hobie. If I didn't say nasty things, I'd cry. I'm afraid to cry; it would take me so long to stop. I—oh, I'm so hurt, dear. I don't know what to think. All these women. All these awful women. If they were fine, if they were sweet and gentle and intelligent, I shouldn't mind. Or maybe I should. I don't know. I don't know much of anything, any more. My mind goes round and round. I thought what we had was so different. Well—it wasn't. Sometimes I think it would be better never to see you any more. But then I know I couldn't stand that. I'm too far gone now. I'd do anything to be with you! And so I'm just another of those women to you. And I used to come first, Hobie—oh, I did! I did!"

"You did!" he said. "And you do!"

"And I always will?" she said.

"And you always will," he said, "as long as you'll only be your own self. Please be sweet again, Kit. Like this, darling. Like this, child."

Again they were close, and again there was no sound.

The telephone rang.

They started as if the same arrow had pierced them. Then the young woman moved slowly back.

"You know," she said, musingly, "this is my fault. I did this. It was me. I was the one that said let's meet here, and not at my house. I said it would be quieter, and I had so much I wanted to talk to you about. I said we could be quiet and alone here. Yes. I said that."

"I give you my word," he said, "that damn thing hasn't rung in a week."

"It was lucky for me, wasn't it?" she said, "that I happened to be here last time it did it. I am known as Little Miss Horseshoes. Well. Oh, please do answer it, Hobie. It drives me even crazier to have it ring like this."

"I hope to God," the young man said, "that it's a wrong number." He held her to him, hard. "Darling," he said. Then he went to the telephone.

"Hello," he said into the receiver. "Yes? Oh, hello there. How are you, dear—how are you? Oh, did you? Ah, that's too bad. Why, you see I was out with these friends of my—I was out till quite late. Oh, you did? Oh, that's too bad, dear, you waited up all that time. No, I did *not* say that, Margot, I said I'd come if I possibly could. That's exactly what I said. I did so. Well, then you misunderstood me. Well, you must have. Now, there's no need to be unreasonable about it. Listen, what I said, I said I'd come if it was possible, but I didn't think there was a chance. If you think hard, you'll remember, dear. Well, I'm terribly sorry, but I don't see what you're making so much fuss about it. It was just a misunderstanding, that's all. Why don't you calm down and be a good little girl? Won't you? Why, I can't tonight, dear. Because I *can't*. Well, I have a date I've had for a long time. Yes. Oh, no, it isn't anything like that! Oh, now, please, Margot! Margot, please don't! Now don't do that! I tell you I won't be here. All right, come ahead, but I won't be in. Listen, I can't talk to you when you're like this. I'll call you tomorrow, dear. I tell you I won't be IN, dear! Please be good. Certainly I do. Look, I have to run now. I'll call you, dear. 'By."

The young man came back to the living-room, and sent his somewhat shaken voice ahead of him.

"How about another cocktail, sweet?" he said. "Don't you think we really ought—" Through the thickening dark, he saw the young woman. She stood straight and tense. Her fur scarf was knotted about her shoulders, and she was drawing on her second glove.

"What's this about?" the young man said.

"I'm so sorry," the young woman said, "but I truly must go home."

"Oh, really?" he said. "May I ask why?"

"It's sweet of you," she said, "to be interested enough to want to know. Thank you so much. Well, it just happens, I can't stand any more of this. There is somewhere, I think, some proverb about a worm's eventually turning. It is doubtless from the Arabic. They so often are. Well, good night, Hobie, and thank you so much for those delicious cocktails. They've cheered me up wonderfully."

She held out her hand. He caught it tight in both of his.

"Ah, now listen," he said. "Please don't do this, Kit. Please don't, darling. Please. This is just the way you were last Wednesday. Remember?"

"Yes," she said. "And for exactly the same reason. Please give me back my hand. Thank you. Well, good night, Hobie, and good luck, always."

"All right," he said. "If this is what you want to do."

"Want to do!" she said. "It's nothing *I* want. I simply felt it would be rather easier for you if you could be alone, to receive your telephone calls. Surely you cannot blame me for feeling a bit *de trop*."

"My Lord, do you think I want to talk to those fools?" he said. "What can I do? Take the telephone receiver off? Is that what you want me to do?"

"It's a good trick of yours," she said. "I gather that was what you did last Wednesday night, when I kept trying to call you after I'd gone home, when I was in holy agony there."

"I did not!" he said. "They must have been calling the wrong number. I tell you I was alone here all the time you were gone."

"So you said," she said.

"I don't lie to you, Kit," he said.

"That," she said, "is the most outrageous lie you have ever told me. Good night, Hobie."

Only from the young man's eyes and voice could his

anger be judged. The beautiful scroll of his mouth never straightened. He took her hand and bowed over it.

"Good night, Kit," he said.

"Good night," she said. "Well, good night. I'm sorry it must end like this. But if you want—other things— well, they're what you want. You can't have both them and me. Good night, Hobie."

"Good night, Kit," he said.

"I'm sorry," she said. "It does seem too bad. Doesn't it?"

"It's what you want," he said.

"I?" she said. "It's what *you* do."

"Oh, Kit, can't you understand?" he said. "You always used to. Don't you know how I am? I just say things and do things that don't mean anything, just for the sake of peace, just for the sake of not having a feud. That's what gets me in trouble. You don't have to do it, I know. You're luckier than I am."

"Luckier?" she said. "Curious word."

"Well, stronger, then," he said. "Finer. Honester. Decenter. All those. Ah, don't do this, Kit. Please. Please take those things off, and come sit down."

"Sit down?" she said. "And wait for the ladies to gather?"

"They're not coming," he said.

"How do you know?" she said. "They've come here

before, haven't they? How do you know they won't come tonight?"

"I don't know!" he said. "I don't know what the hell they'll do. I don't know what the hell you'll do, any more. And I thought you were different!"

"I was different," she said, "just so long as you thought I was different."

"Ah, Kit," he said, "Kit. Darling. Come and be the way we were. Come and be sweet and peaceful. Look. Let's have a cocktail, just to each other, and then let's go out to some quiet place for dinner, where we can talk. Will you?"

"Well—" she said. "If you think—"

"I think," he said.

The telephone rang.

"Oh, my *God!*" shrieked the young woman. "Go answer it, you damned—you damned *stallion!*"

She rushed for the door, opened it, and was gone. She was, after all, different. She neither slammed the door nor left it stark open.

The young man stood, and he shook his remarkable head slowly. Slowly, too, he turned and went into the bedroom.

He spoke into the telephone receiver drearily at first, then he seemed to enjoy both hearing and speaking. He used a woman's name in address. It was not Connie; it was not Evie; it was not Margot. Glowingly he besought the unseen one to meet him; tepidly he agreed to await her coming where he was. He besought her, then, to ring his bell first three times and then twice, for admission. No, no, no, he said, this was not for any reason that might have occurred to her; it was simply that some business friend of his had said something about dropping in, and he wanted to make sure there would be no such intruders. He spoke of his hopes, indeed his assurances, of an evening of sweetness and peace. He said "good-by," and he said "dear."

The very good-looking young man hung up the receiver, and looked long at the dial of his wrist-watch, now delicately luminous. He seemed to be calculating. So long for a young woman to reach her home, and fling herself upon her couch, so long for tears, so long for exhaustion, so long for remorse, so long for rising tenderness. Thoughtfully he lifted the receiver from its hook and set it on end upon the little table.

Then he went into the living-room, and sped the dark before the tiny beams that sifted through the little open windows in the panoramas of Paris.

The Little Hours

The Little Hours

Now what's this? What's the object of all this darkness all over me? They haven't gone and buried me alive while my back was turned, have they? Ah, now would you think they'd do a thing like that! Oh, no, I know what it is. I'm awake. That's it. I've waked up in the middle of the night. Well, isn't that nice. Isn't that simply ideal. Twenty minutes past four, sharp, and here's Baby wide-eyed as a marigold. Look at this, will you? At the time when all decent people are just going to bed, I must wake up. There's no way things can ever come out even, under this system. This is as rank as injustice is ever likely to get. This is what brings about revolutions, that's what *this* does.

Yes, and you want to know what got me into this mess? Going to bed at ten o'clock, that's what. That spells ruin. T-e-n-space-o-apostrophe-c-l-o-c-k: ruin. Early to bed, and you'll wish you were dead. Bed before eleven, nuts before seven. Bed before morning, sailors give warning. Ten o'clock, after a quiet evening of reading. Reading—there's an institution for you. Why, I'd turn on the light and read, right this minute, if reading weren't what contributed toward driving me here. I'll show it. God, the bitter misery that reading works in this world! Everybody knows that—everybody who *is* everybody. All the best minds have been off reading for years. Look at the swing La Rochefoucauld took at it. He said that if nobody had ever learned to read, very few people would be in love. There was a man for you, and that's what *he* thought of it. Good for you, La Rochefoucauld; nice going, boy. I wish I'd never learned to read. I wish I'd never learned to take off my clothes. Then I wouldn't have been caught in this jam at half-past four in the morning. If nobody had ever learned to undress, very few people would be in love. No, his is better. Oh, well, it's a man's world.

La Rochefoucauld, indeed, lying quiet as a mouse,

and me tossing and turning here! This is no time to be getting all steamed up about La Rochefoucauld. It's only a question of minutes before I'm going to be pretty darned good and sick of La Rochefoucauld, once and for all. La Rochefoucauld this and La Rochefoucauld that. Yes, well, let me tell you that if nobody had ever learned to quote, very few people would be in love with La Rochefoucauld. I bet you I don't know ten souls who read him without a middleman. People pick up those rambling little essays that start off "Was it not that lovable old cynic, La Rochefoucauld, who said . . ." and then they go around claiming to know the master backwards. Pack of illiterates, that's all they are. All right, let them keep their La Rochefoucauld, and see if I care. I'll stick to La Fontaine. Only I'd be better company if I could quit thinking that La Fontaine married Alfred Lunt.

I don't know what I'm doing mucking about with a lot of French authors at this hour, anyway. First thing you know, I'll be reciting *Fleurs du Mal* to myself, and then I'll be little more good to anybody. And I'll stay off Verlaine too; he was always chasing Rimbauds. A person would be better off with La Rochefoucauld, even. Oh, damn La Rochefoucauld. The big Frog. I'll thank him to keep out of my head. What's he doing there, anyhow? What's La Rochefoucauld to me, or he to Hecuba? Why, I don't even know the man's first name, that's how close

I ever was to *him*. What am I supposed to be, a stooge for La Rochefoucauld? That's what *he* thinks. Sez he. Well, he's only wasting his time, hanging around here. I can't help him. The only other thing I can remember his saying is that there is always something a little pleasing to us in the misfortunes of even our dearest friends. That cleans me all up with Monsieur La Rochefoucauld. *Maintenant c'est fini, ça.*

Dearest friends. A sweet lot of dearest friends *I've* got. All of them lying in swinish stupors, while I'm practically up and about. All of them stretched sodden through these, the fairest hours of the day, when man should be at his most productive. Produce, produce, produce, for I tell you the night is coming. Carlyle said that. Yes, and a fine one *he* was, to go shooting off his face on the subject. *Oh,* Thomas Car*li*-yill, what *I* know about *you*-oo! No, that will be enough of that. I'm not going to start fretting about Carlyle, at this stage of the game. What did he ever do that was so great, besides founding a college for Indians? (That crack ought to flatten him.) Let him keep his face out of this, if he knows what's good for him. I've got enough trouble with that lovable old cynic, La Rochefoucauld— him and the misfortunes of his dearest friends!

The first thing I've got to do is get out and whip me up a complete new set of dearest friends; that's the first thing. Everything else can wait. And will somebody please kindly be so good as to inform me how I am ever going to meet up with any new people when my entire scheme of living is out of joint—when I'm the only living being awake while the rest of the world lies sleeping? I've got to get this thing adjusted. I must try to get back to sleep right now. I've got to conform to the rotten little standards of this sluggard civilization. People needn't feel that they have to change their ruinous habits and come my way. Oh, no, no; no, indeed. Not at all. I'll go theirs. If that isn't the woman of it for you! Always having to do what somebody else wants, like it or not. Never able to murmur a suggestion of her own.

And what suggestion has anyone to murmur as to how I am going to drift lightly back to slumber? Here I am, awake as high noon what with all this milling and pitching around with La Rochefoucauld. I really can't be expected to drop everything and start counting sheep, at my age. I hate sheep. Untender it may be in me, but all my life I've hated sheep. It amounts to a phobia, the way I hate them. I can tell the minute there's one in the room. They needn't think that I am going to lie here in the dark and count their unpleasant little faces for them; I wouldn't do it if I didn't fall asleep again until the middle of next August. Suppose they never get counted—what's the worst that can happen? If the number of imaginary sheep in this world remains a matter of guesswork, who is richer or poorer for it? No, sir; *I'm* not going to be the patsy. Let them count themselves, if they're so crazy mad after mathematics. Let them do their own dirty work. Coming around here, at this time of day, and asking me to count them! And not even *real* sheep, at that. Why, it's the most preposterous thing I ever heard in my life.

But there must be *something* I could count. Let's see. No, I already know by heart how many fingers I have. I could count my bills, I suppose. I could count the things I didn't do yesterday that I should have done. I could count the things I should do today that I'm not going to do. I'm never going to accomplish anything; that's perfectly clear to me. I'm never going to be famous. My name will never be writ large on the roster of Those Who Do Things. I don't do anything. Not one single thing. I used to bite my nails, but I don't even do that any more. I don't amount to the powder to blow me to hell. I've turned out to be nothing but a bit of flotsam. Flotsam and leave 'em—that's me from now on. Oh, it's all terrible.

Well. This way lies galloping melancholia. Maybe it's because this is the zero hour. This is the time the swooning soul hangs pendant and vertiginous between the new day and the old, nor dares confront the one or summon back the other. This is the time when all things, known and hidden, are iron to weight the spirit; when all ways, traveled or virgin, fall away from the stumbling feet, when all

before the straining eyes is black. Blackness now, everywhere is blackness. This is the time of abomination, the
dreadful hour of the victorious dark. For it is always darkest—Was it not that lovable old cynic, La Rochefoucauld,
who said that it is always darkest before the deluge?

There. Now you see, don't you? Here we are again,
practically back where we started. La Rochefoucauld, we
are here. Ah, come on, son—how about your going your
way and letting me go mine? I've got my work cut out for
me right here; I've got all this sleeping to do. Think how
I am going to look by daylight if this keeps up. I'll be a
seamy sight for all those rested, clear-eyed, fresh-faced
dearest friends of mine —the rats! Why, *Dotty,* whatever
have you been doing; I thought you were on the wagon.
Oh, I was helling around with La Rochefoucauld till all
hours; we couldn't stop laughing about your misfortunes.
No, this is getting too thick, really. It isn't right to have
this happen to a person, just because she went to bed at ten
o'clock once in her life. Honest, I won't ever do it again.
I'll go straight, after this. I'll never go to bed again, if I can
only sleep now. If I can tear my mind away from a certain
French cynic, *circa 1650,* and slip into lovely oblivion.
1650. I bet I look as if I'd been awake since then.

How do people go to sleep? I'm afraid I've lost the
knack. I might try busting myself smartly over the temple
with the night-light. I might repeat to myself, slowly and

317

soothingly, a list of quotations beautiful from minds pro-
found; if I can remember any of the damn things. That
might do it. And it ought effectually to bar that visiting
foreigner that's been hanging around ever since twenty
minutes past four. Yes, that's what I'll do. Only wait till I
turn the pillow; it feels as if La Rochefoucauld had crawled
inside the slip.

    Now let's see—where shall we start? Why—er—let's
see. Oh, yes, I know one. This above all, to thine own self
be true and it must follow, as the night the day, thou canst
not then be false to any man. Now they're off. And once
they get started, they ought to come like hot cakes. Let's
see. Ah, what avail the sceptered race and what the form
divine, when every virtue, every grace, Rose Aylmer, all
were thine. Let's see. They also serve who only stand and
wait. If Winter comes, can Spring be far behind. Lilies that
fester smell far worse than weeds. Silent upon a peak in
Darien. Mrs. Porter and her daughter wash their feet in
soda-water. And Agatha's Arth is a hug-the-hearth, but my
true love is false. Why did you die when lambs were crop-
ping, you should have died when apples were dropping.
Shall be together, breathe and ride, so one day more am I
deified, who knows but the world will end tonight. And he
shall hear the stroke of eight and not the stroke of nine.
They are not long, the weeping and the laughter; love and
desire and hate I think will have no portion in us after we

pass the gate. But none, I think, do there embrace. I think that I shall never see a poem lovely as a tree. I think I will not hang myself today. Ay tank Ay go home now.

Let's see. Solitude is the safeguard of mediocrity and the stern companion of genius. Consistency is the hobgoblin of little minds. Something is emotion remembered in tranquillity. A cynic is one who knows the price of everything and the value of nothing. That lovable old cynic is one who—oops, there's King Charles's head again. I've got to watch myself. Let's see. Circumstantial evidence is a trout in the milk. Any stigma will do to beat a dogma. If you would learn what God thinks about money, you have only to look at those to whom he has given it. If nobody had ever learned to read, very few people—

All right. That fixes it. I throw in the towel right now. I know when I'm licked. There'll be no more of this nonsense; I'm going to turn on the light and read my head off. Till the next ten o'clock, if I feel like it. And what does La Rochefoucauld want to make of that? Oh, he *will*, eh? Yes, he will! He and who else? La Rochefoucauld and *what* very few people?

Sentiment

Sentiment

Oh, anywhere, driver, anywhere—it doesn't matter. Just keep driving.

It's better here in this taxi than it was walking. It's no good my trying to walk. There is always a glimpse through the crowd of someone who looks like him—someone with his swing of the shoulders, his slant of the hat. And I think it's he, I think he's come back. And my heart goes to scalding water and the buildings sway and bend above me. No, it's better to be here. But I wish the driver would go fast, so fast that people walking by would be a long gray blur, and I could see no swinging shoulders, no slanted hat. It's bad stopping still in the traffic like this. People pass too slowly, too clearly, and always the next one might be— No, of course it couldn't be. I know that. Of course I know it. But it might be, it might.

And people can look in and see me, here. They can see if I cry. Oh, let them—it doesn't matter. Let them look and be damned to them.

Yes, you look at me. Look and look and look, you poor, queer tired woman. It's a pretty hat, isn't it? It's meant to be looked at. That's why it's so big and red and new, that's why it has these great soft poppies on it. Your poor hat is all weary and done with. It looks like a dead cat, a cat that was run over and pushed out of the way against the curbstone. Don't you wish you were I and could have a new hat whenever you pleased? You could walk fast, couldn't you, and hold your head high and raise your feet from the pavement if you were on your way to a new hat, a beautiful hat, a hat that cost more than ever you had? Only I hope you wouldn't choose one like mine. For red is mourning, you know. Scarlet red for a love that's dead. Didn't you know that?

She's gone now. The taxi is moving and she's left behind forever. I wonder what she thought when our eyes and our lives met. I wonder did she envy me, so sleek and safe and young. Or did she realize how quick I'd be to fling away all I have if I could bear in my breast the still, dead heart that she carries in hers. She doesn't feel, she doesn't even wish. She is done with hoping and burning, if ever she burned and she hoped. Oh, that's quite nice, it has a real lilt. She is done with hoping and burning, if ever she— Yes, it's pretty. Well—I wonder if she's gone her slow way a little happier, or, perhaps, a little sadder for knowing that there is one worse off than herself.

This is the sort of thing he hated so in me. I know what he would say. "Oh, for heaven's sake!" he would say. "Can't you stop that fool sentimentalizing? Why do you have to do it? Why do you *want* to do it? Just because you see an old charwoman on the street, there's no need to get sobbing about her. She's all right. She's fine. 'When your eyes and your lives met'—oh, come on, now. Why, she never even saw you. And her 'still, dead heart,' nothing! She's probably on her way to get a bottle of bad gin and have a roaring time. You don't have to dramatize *every-thing*. You don't have to insist that *everybody's* sad. Why are you always so sentimental? Don't *do* it, Rosalie." That's what he would say. I know.

But he won't say that or anything else to me, any more. Never anything else, sweet or bitter. He's gone away and he isn't coming back. "Oh, of course I'm coming back!" he said. "No, I don't know just when—I told you that. Ah, Rosalie, don't go making a national tragedy of it. It'll be a few months, maybe—and if ever two people needed a holiday from each other! It's nothing to cry about. I'll be back. I'm not going to stay away from New York forever."

But I knew. I knew. I knew because he had been far away from me long before he went. He's gone away and he won't come back. He's gone away and he won't come back, he's gone away and he'll never come back. Listen to the wheels saying it, on and on and on. That's sentimental, I suppose. Wheels don't say anything. Wheels can't speak. But I *hear* them.

I wonder why it's wrong to be sentimental. People are so contemptuous of feeling. "You wouldn't catch *me* sitting alone and mooning," they say. "Moon" is what they say when they mean remember, and they are so proud of not remembering. It's strange, how they pride themselves upon their lacks. "I never take anything seriously," they say. "I simply couldn't imagine," they say, "letting myself care so much that I could be hurt." They say, "No one person could be that important to *me.*" And why, why do they think they're right?

Oh, who's right and who's wrong and who decides? Perhaps it was I who was right about that charwoman. Perhaps she *was* weary and still-hearted, and perhaps, for just that moment, she knew all about me. She needn't have

been all right and fine and on her way for gin, just because
he said so. Oh. Oh, I forgot. He didn't say so. He wasn't
here; he isn't here. It was I, imagining what he would say.
And I thought I heard him. He's always with me, he and
all his beauty and his cruelty. But he mustn't be any more.
I mustn't think of him. That's it, don't think of him. Yes.
Don't breathe, either. Don't hear. Don't see. Stop the
blood in your veins.

I can't go on like this. I can't, I can't. I cannot stand
this frantic misery. If I knew it would be over in a day or
a year or two months, I could endure it. Even if it grew
duller sometimes and wilder sometimes, it could be borne.
But it is always the same and there is no end.

> "Sorrow like a ceaseless rain
> Beats upon my heart.
> People twist and scream in pain,—
> Dawn will find them still again;
> This has neither wax nor wane,
> Neither stop nor start."

Oh, let's see—how does the next verse go? Something, something, something, something, something to
rhyme with "wear." Anyway, it ends:

> "All my thoughts are slow and brown:
> Standing up or sitting down

327

Little matters, or what gown
Or what shoes I wear."

Yes, that's the way it goes. And it's right, it's so right. What is it to me what I wear? Go and buy yourself a big red hat with poppies on it—that ought to cheer you up. Yes—go buy it and loathe it. How am I to go on, sitting and staring and buying big red hats and hating them, and then sitting and staring again—day upon day upon day upon day? Tomorrow and tomorrow and tomorrow. How am I to drag through them like this?

But what else is there for me? "Go out and see your friends and have a good time," they say. "Don't sit alone and dramatize yourself." Dramatize yourself! If it be drama to feel a steady—no, a ceaseless rain beating upon my heart, then I do dramatize myself. The shallow people, the little people, how can they know what suffering is, how could their thick hearts be torn? Don't they know, the empty fools, that I could not see again the friends we saw together, could not go back to the places where he and I have been? For he's gone, and it's ended. It's ended, it's ended. And when it ends, only those places where you have known sorrow are kindly to you. If you revisit the scenes of your happiness, your heart must burst of its agony.

And that's sentimental, I suppose. It's sentimental to know that you cannot bear to see the places where once all was well with you, that you cannot bear reminders of a dead loveliness. Sorrow is tranquillity remembered in emotion. It—oh, I think that's quite good. "Remembered in emotion"—that's a really nice reversal. I wish I could say it to him. But I won't say anything to him, ever again, ever, ever again. He's gone, and it's over, and I dare not think of the dead days. All my thoughts must be slow and brown, and I must——

Oh, no, no, no! Oh, the driver shouldn't go through this street! This was our street, this is the place of our love and our laughter. I can't do this, I can't, I can't. I will crouch down here, and hold my hands tight, tight over my eyes, so that I cannot look. I must keep my poor heart still, and I must be like the little, mean, dry-souled people who are proud not to remember.

But oh, I see it, I see it, even though my eyes are blinded. Though I had no eyes, my heart would tell me this street, out of all streets. I know it as I know my hands, as I know his face. Oh, why can't I be let to die as we pass through?

We must be at the florist's shop on the corner now. That's where he used to stop to buy me primroses, little yellow primroses massed tight together with a circle of their silver-backed leaves about them, clean and cool and gentle. He always said that orchids and camellias were none of my affair. So when there were no spring and no

329

primroses, he would give me lilies-of-the-valley and little, gay rosebuds and mignonette and bright blue cornflowers. He said he couldn't stand the thought of me without flowers—it would be all wrong; I cannot bear flowers near me, now. And the little gray florist was so interested and so glad—and there was the day he called me "madam"! Ah, I can't, I can't.

And now we must be at the big apartment house with the big gold doorman. And the evening the doorman was holding the darling puppy on a big, long leash, and we stopped to talk to it, and he took it up in his arms and cuddled it, and that was the only time we ever saw the doorman smile! And next is the house with the baby, and he always would take off his hat and bow very solemnly to her, and sometimes she would give him her little starfish of a hand. And then is the tree with the rusty iron bars around it, where he would stop to turn and wave to me, as I leaned out the window to watch him. And people would look at him, because people always had to look at him, but he never noticed. It was our tree, he said; it wouldn't dream of belonging to anybody else. And very few city people had their own personal tree, he said. Did I realize that, he said.

And then there's the doctor's house, and the three thin gray houses and then—oh, God, we must be at our house now! Our house, though we had only the top floor.

And I loved the long, dark stairs, because he climbed them every evening. And our little prim pink curtains at the windows, and the boxes of pink geraniums that always grew for me. And the little stiff entry and the funny mail-box, and his ring at the bell. And I waiting for him in the dusk, thinking he would never come; and yet the waiting was lovely, too. And then when I opened the door to him—Oh, no, no, no! Oh, no one could bear this. No one, no one.

Ah, why, why, why must I be driven through here? What torture could there be so terrible as this? It will be better if I uncover my eyes and look. I will see our tree and our house again, and then my heart will burst and I will be dead. I will look, I will look.

But where's the tree? Can they have cut down our tree—*our* tree? And where's the apartment house? And where's the florist's shop? And where—oh, where's our house, where's——

Driver, what street is this? Sixty-Fifth? Oh. No, nothing, thank you. I—I thought it was Sixty-Third. . . .

331

A Young Woman in Green Lace

A Young Woman in Green Lace

*T*he young man in the sharply cut dinner jacket
crossed the filled room and stopped in front of the young
woman in green lace and possible pearls. He was, you must
have said, a young man of imagination, strength of purpose, and a likable receptivity of the new, for such garments as his do not come about by accident; thought goes
into their selection, and time, and both must be backed by
a fine self-belief. From the young man's coat, more surely
than from his palm, might be read the ingredients of his

character. Whimsy peeped around the lapels of that coat; balance showed in the double march of its buttons; and the color of its material, the dreamy blue of a spring midnight, confessed a deep strain of sentiment. The face above the jacket was neat and spare, and wore, at the moment, a look of pleading.

"Good evening," the young man said. "At least, I beg your pardon. At least, I wonder if you'd mind if I sat down here beside of you. If you wouldn't mind, that is. If you'd let me, at least."

"But certainly," the young woman said, for she had recently returned from France. "But of course."

She lent him room on the little sofa where she sat, light and languid, and he rested none too easily beside her. He set his gaze upon her face, nor did he take it away.

"You know, this is terribly nice of you to let me do this," he said. "It's—well, what I mean is, I was afraid maybe you wouldn't."

"But no!" she said.

"You see," he said, "I've been looking at you all evening. At least, I couldn't get my eyes off of you. Honest. First thing I saw you, I tried to get Marge to introduce me, but she's been so busy fixing drinks and everything, I couldn't get near her. And then I saw you come and sit here, all by yourself, and I've been trying to get up my nerve to come over and talk to you. I thought you might be sore or something, at least. I'd get all set to start over, and then I'd think, 'Oh, she's so sweet and pretty, she'll just give me the bum's rush.' I thought you'd be sore or something, me coming over and talking to you without an introduction, I mean."

"Oh, *non*," she said. "Why, I'd never dream of being sore. Abroad, you know, they say the roof is an introduction."

"Beg pardon?" he said.

"That's what they say abroad," she said. "In Paris and places. You go to a party, and the person that's giving the party doesn't introduce anybody to anybody. They just take it for granted that everybody will talk to everybody else, because they take it for granted that their friends are their friends' friends. *Comprenez-vous?* Oh, I'm sorry. Slips. I *must* stop talking French. Only it's so hard, once you get into the habit of rattling it off. I mean, see what I mean? Why, I'd forgotten all about people having to be introduced to other people at a party."

"Well, I'm certainly glad you aren't sore," he said. "At least, it's wonderful for me. Only maybe you'd rather be alone, here. Would you?"

"Oh, *non, non, non, non, non*," she said. "Goodness, no. I was just sitting here, watching everybody. I feel as if I don't know a soul since I've come back. But it's so interesting, just to sit and watch the way people behave and their clothes and everything. You feel as if you were in another world. Well, you know how you feel when you've come back from being abroad. Don't you?"

"I've never been abroad," he said.

"Oh, my," she said. "Oh, *là-là-là*. Haven't you really? Well, you must go, the very first minute you can. You'll adore it. I can tell just by looking at you you'll be crazy over it."

"Were you abroad long?" he said.

"I was in Paris over three weeks," she said.

"That's one place I'd like to go," he said. "I guess that must be tops."

"Oh, don't talk about it," she said. "It makes me so homesick I can't see straight. Oh, Paree, Paree, *ma chère* Paree. I just feel as though it's *my* city. Honestly, I don't know how I'm ever going to get along away from it. I'd like to go right straight back this minute."

"Hey, don't talk like that, will you?" he said. "We need you around here. At least, don't go back yet a while, will you please? I've only just met you."

"Oh, that's sweet of you," she said. "Goodness, so few American men know how to talk to a woman. I guess they're all too busy, or something. Everybody seems in such a hurry—no time for anything but money, money, money. Well, *c'est ça*, I suppose."

"We could find time for other things," he said.

"There's a lot of fun we could have. There's a lot of fun around New York, at least."

"This old New York!" she said. "I don't believe I'll ever get used to it. There's nothing to *do* here. Now in Paris, it's so picturesque and everything, you're never blue a second. And there are all these cute little places where you can go and have a drink, when you want. Oh, it's wonderful."

"I know any amount of cute little places where you can go and have a drink," he said. "I can take you to any one of them in ten minutes."

"It wouldn't be like Paris," she said. "Oh, every time I think of it, I get *terriblement triste*. Darn it, there I go again. Will I *ever* remember?"

"Look," he said, "can't I get you a drink now? Why, you haven't been doing a thing. What would you like?"

"Oh, *mon dieu,* I don't know," she said. "I've got so in the habit of drinking champagne that really— What have they got? What do people drink here, anyway?"

"Well, there's Scotch and gin," he said, "and I think maybe there's some rye out in the dining-room. At least there may be."

"How funny!" she said. "You forget about the terrible things that people drink. Well, when in Rome—Gin, I guess."

"With ginger ale?" he said.

"Quel horreur!" she said. "No, just plain, I think, just—what do you call it?—straight."

"I'll be right back," he said, "and it'll be too long."

He left her and quickly returned, bearing little full glasses. Carefully he presented one to her.

"Merci mille fois," she said. "Oh, darn me. Thank you, I mean."

The young man sat down again beside her. He drank, but he did not look at the glass in his hand. He looked at the young woman.

"J'ai soif," she said. *"Mon dieu.* I hope you don't think I swear terribly. I've got so in the way of doing it, I really don't realize what I'm saying. And in French, you know, they don't think anything of it at all. Everybody says it. It isn't even like swearing. Ugh. My goodness, this is strong."

"It's all right, though," he said. "Marge has a good man."

"Marge?" she said. "A good man?"

"At least," he said, "the stuff isn't cut."

"Stuff?" she said. "Isn't cut?"

"She's got a good bootlegger, at least," he said. "I wouldn't be much surprised if he really did get it off the boat."

"Oh, please don't talk about boats!" she said. "It makes me so homesick, I just nearly die. It makes me want to get right on a boat now."

"Ah, don't," he said. "Give me just a little chance. Lord, when I think I nearly passed up this party. Honestly, I wasn't going to come at first. And then the minute I saw you, I knew I'd never been so right in my life. At least, when I saw you sitting there and that dress and every-thing—well, I went for a loop, that's all."

"What, this old thing?" she said. "Why, it's old as the hills. I got it before I went abroad. I sort of didn't want to wear any of my French things tonight because—well, of course no one thinks anything of them over there, but I thought maybe these New York people might think they were pretty extreme. You know how Paris clothes are. They're so Frenchy."

"Would I like to see you in them," he said. "Boy! Why, I'd— Hey, there isn't anything in your glass. Here, let me fix that up for you. And don't move, will you?"

Again he went and came back, and again he bore glasses filled with colorless fluid. He resumed looking at the young woman.

"Well," she said. "*À votre santé*. Heavens, I wish I could stop that. I mean good luck."

"I've got it," he said, "ever since I met you. I wish— at least I wish we could get off somewhere away from here. Marge says they're going to roll back the rugs and dance, and everybody'll be wanting to dance with you, and I won't have a prayer."

"Oh, I don't want to dance," she said. "American

men dance so badly, most of them. And I don't want to
meet a lot of people, anyway. It's awfully hard for me to
talk to them. I can't seem to understand what they're
talking about, since I've been back. I suppose they think
their slang is funny, but I don't see it."

"You know what we might do," he said, "if you
would, at least? We might wait till they start dancing, and
then just ease out. We might do the town for a while. What
would you say, at least?"

"You know, that might be rather amusing," she said.
"I'd really like to see some of your new little *bistros*—
what do you call them?—oh, you know what I mean—
speakeasies. I hear some of them are really quite
interesting. I suppose this stuff is strong, but it doesn't
seem to do anything at all to me. It must be because I
haven't been used to anything but those wonderful French
wines."

"Can I get you some more?" he said.

"Well," she said, "I might have a little. One has to do
what everybody else does, don't you?"

"Same thing?" he said. "Straight gin?"

"*S'il vous plaît,*" she said. "But yes."

"Lady," he said, "can you take it! Are we going to
have an evening!"

For the third time he went and came. For the third
time he watched her though he drank.

"*Ce n'est pas mal,*" she said. "*Pas du tout,* at all. There's a little place in one of the Boulevards—they're those big avenues they have—that has a sort of cordial that tastes almost exactly like this. My, I'd like to be there now."

"Ah, no, you wouldn't," he said. "Would you, really? You won't after a little while, anyway. There's a little place on Fifty-Second Street I want to take you first. Look, when they start dancing, what do you say you get your coat, or at least whatever you have, and meet me in the hall? There's no sense saying good-night. Marge will never know. I can show you a couple of places might make you forget Paris."

"Oh, don't say that," she said. "Please. As if I could ever forget my Paree! You just can't know how I feel about it. Every time anybody says 'Paris,' I just want to cry and cry."

"You can even do that," he said, "at least as long as you do it on my shoulder. It's waiting right here for you. What do you say we get started, baby? Mind if I call you baby? Let's go get ourselves a couple of pretty edges. How are you coming with that gin? Finished? Atta girl. How about it we go out now and get stinking?"

"But oke!" said the young woman in green lace.

They went out.

Lady with a Lamp

Lady with a Lamp

*W*ell, Mona! Well, you poor sick thing, you! Ah,
you look so little and white and *little*, you do, lying there
in that great big bed. That's what you do—go and look so
childlike and pitiful nobody'd have the heart to scold you.
And I ought to scold you, Mona. Oh, yes, I should so, too.
Never letting me know you were ill. Never a word to your
oldest friend. Darling, you might have known I'd understand, no matter what you did. What do I mean? Well,
what do you *mean* what do I mean, Mona? Of course, if

347

you'd rather not talk about— Not even to your oldest friend. All I wanted to say was you might have known that I'm always for you, no matter what happens. I do admit, sometimes it's a little hard for me to understand how on earth you ever got into such—well. Goodness knows I don't want to nag you now, when you're so sick.

All right, Mona, then you're *not* sick. If that's what you want to say, even to me, why, all right, my dear. People who aren't sick have to stay in bed for nearly two weeks, I suppose; I suppose people who aren't sick look the way you do. Just your nerves? You were simply all tired out? I see. It's just your nerves. You were simply tired. Yes. Oh, Mona, Mona, why don't you feel you can trust me?

Well—if that's the way you want to be to me, that's the way you want to be. I won't say anything more about it. Only I do think you might have let me know that you had—well, that you were so *tired*, if that's what you want me to say. Why, I'd never have known a word about it if I hadn't run bang into Alice Patterson and she told me she'd called you up and that maid of yours said you had been sick in bed for ten days. Of course, I'd thought it rather funny I hadn't heard from you, but you know how you are—you simply let people go, and weeks can go by like, well, like *weeks,* and never a sign from you. Why, I could have been dead over and over again, for all you'd know. Twenty times over. Now, I'm not going to scold you when you're sick, but frankly and honestly, Mona, I said to myself this time, "Well, she'll have a good wait before I call her up. I've given in often enough, goodness knows. Now she can just call me first." Frankly and honestly, that's what I said!

And then I saw Alice, and I did feel mean, I really did. And now to see you lying there —well, I feel like a complete *dog*. That's what you do to people even when you're in the wrong the way you always are, you wicked little thing, you! Ah, the poor dear! Feels just so awful, doesn't it?

Oh, don't keep trying to be brave, child. Not with me. Just give in—it helps so much. Just tell me all about it. You know I'll never say a word. Or at least you ought to know. When Alice told me that maid of yours said you were all tired out and your nerves had gone bad, I naturally never said anything, but I thought to myself, "Well, maybe that's the only thing Mona could say was the matter. That's probably about the best excuse she could think of." And of course *I'll* never deny it—but perhaps it might have been better to have said you had influenza or ptomaine poisoning. After all, people don't stay in bed for ten whole days just because they're nervous. All right, Mona, then they *do*. Then they do. Yes, dear.

Ah, to think of you going through all this and crawl-

ing off here all alone like a little wounded animal or something. And with only that colored Edie to take care of you.
Darling, oughtn't you have a trained nurse, I mean really
oughtn't you? There must be so many things that have to
be done for you. Why, Mona! Mona, please! Dear, you
don't have to get so excited. Very well, my dear, it's just
as you say—there isn't a single thing to be done. I was
mistaken, that's all. I simply thought that after— Oh,
now, you don't have to do that. You never have to say
you're sorry, to *me*. I understand. As a matter of fact, I was
glad to hear you lose your temper. It's a good sign when
sick people are cross. It means they're on the way to
getting better. Oh, I know! You go right ahead and be
cross all you want to.

Look, where shall I sit? I want to sit some place where
you won't have to turn around, so you can talk to me. You
stay right the way you're lying, and I'll— Because you
shouldn't move around, I'm sure. It must be terribly bad
for you. All right, dear, you can move around all you want
to. All right, I must be crazy. I'm crazy, then. We'll leave
it like that. Only please, please don't excite yourself that
way.

I'll just get this chair and put it over—oops, I'm
sorry I joggled the bed—put it over here, where you can
see me. There. But first I want to fix your pillows before
I get settled. Well, they certainly are *not* all right, Mona.

After the way you've been twisting them and pulling them, these last few minutes. Now look, honey, I'll help you raise yourself ve-ry, ve-ry slo-o-ow-ly. Oh. Of course you can sit up by yourself, dear. Of course you can. Nobody ever said you couldn't. Nobody ever thought of such a thing. There now, your pillows are all smooth and lovely, and you lie right right down again, before you hurt yourself. Now, isn't that better? Well, I should think it was!

Just a minute, till I get my sewing. Oh, yes, I brought it along, so we'd be all cozy. Do you honestly, frankly and honestly, think it's pretty? I'm so glad. It's nothing but a traycloth, you know. But you simply can't have too many. They're a lot of fun to make, too, doing this edge—it goes so quickly. Oh, Mona dear, so often I think if you just had a home of your own, and could be all busy, making pretty little things like this for it. It would do so *much* for you. I worry so about you, living in a little furnished apartment, with nothing that belongs to you, no roots, no nothing. It's not right for a woman. It's all wrong for a woman like you. Oh, I wish you'd get over that Garry McVicker! If you could just meet some nice, sweet, considerate man, and get married to him, and have your own lovely place—and with your *taste*, Mona!—and maybe have a couple of children. You're so simply adorable with children. Why, Mona Morrison, are you crying? Oh, you've got a cold? You've got a cold, *too?* I thought you were crying, there for a second.

351

Don't you want my handkerchief, lamb? Oh, you have yours. Wouldn't you have a pink chiffon handkerchief, you nut! Why on earth don't you use cleansing tissues, just lying there in bed with no one to see you? You little idiot, you! Extravagant little fool!

No, but really, I'm serious. I've said to Fred so often, "Oh, if we could just get Mona married!" Honestly, you don't know the feeling it gives you, just to be all secure and safe with your own sweet home and your own blessed children, and your own nice husband coming back to you every night. That's a woman's *life*, Mona. What you've been doing is really horrible. Just drifting along, that's all. What's going to happen to you, dear, whatever is going to become of you? But no—you don't even think of it. You go and go falling in love with that Garry. Well, my dear, you've got to give me credit—I said from the very first, "He'll never marry her." You know that. What? There was never any thought of marriage, with you and Garry? Oh, Mona, now listen! Every woman on earth thinks of marriage as soon as she's in love with a man. Every woman, I don't care who she is.

Oh, if you were just married! It would be all the difference in the world. I think a child would do everything for you, Mona. Goodness knows, I just can't speak *decently* to that Garry, after the way he's treated you—well, you know perfectly well, *none* of your friends can—but I can frankly and honestly say, if he married you, I'd absolutely let bygones by bygones, and I'd be just as happy, as happy, for you. If he's what you want. And I will say, what with your lovely looks and what with good-looking as he is, you ought to have simply *gorgeous* children. Mona, baby, you really have got a rotten cold, haven't you? Don't you want me to get you another handkerchief? Really?

I'm simply sick that I didn't bring you any flowers. But I thought the place would be full of them. Well, I'll stop on the way home and send you some. It looks too dreary here, without a flower in the room. Didn't Garry send you any? Oh, he didn't know you were sick. Well, doesn't he send you flowers anyway? Listen, hasn't he called up, all this time, and found out whether you were sick or not? Not in ten days? Well, then, haven't you called him and told him? Ah, now, Mona, there *is* such a thing as being too much of a heroine. Let him worry a little, dear. It would be a very good thing for him. Maybe that's the trouble—you've always taken all the worry for both of you. Hasn't sent any flowers! Hasn't even telephoned! Well, I'd just like to talk to that young man for a few minutes. After all, this is all *his* responsibility.

He's away? He's *what?* Oh, he went to Chicago two weeks ago. Well, it seems to me I'd always heard that there were telephone wires running between here and Chicago, but of course— And you'd think since he's been back, the

least he could do would be to do something
yet? He's not *back* yet? Mona, what are y
me? Why, just night before last— Said I
the minute he got home? Of all the rotter
heard in my life, this is really the— Mc
down. Please. Why, I didn't mean any
what I was going to say, honestly I d
been anything. For goodness' sake,
thing else.

Let's see. Oh, you really ov
living-room, the way she's done
walls—not beige, you know,
brown—and these cream-colo
Mona, I tell you I absolutely d
to say, before. It's gone comp
see how unimportant it mus
lie quiet and try to relax. P'
a few minutes, anyway.
worked up about. Catch
expect to get well quick
You know that.

What doctor did y
to say? Your own? Y
mean it! Well, I cer
like—Yes, dear, o
dear. Yes, dear. '

I could do to make you see what that man really is! Only
do relax, darling. Just for me. Dear, Garry isn't in Chicago.
Fred and I saw him night before last at the Park Avenue,
dancing. And Alice saw him Tuesday night at El Patio.
And I don't know how many people have said they've seen
him around at the theater and restaurant and things. Why,
he couldn't have stayed in Chicago more than a day or
so—if he went at all.

Well, he was with *her* when we saw him, honey. Apparently he's with her all the time; nobody ever sees him
with anyone else. You really must make up your mind to
it, dear; it's the only thing to do. I hear all over that he's
just simply *pleading* with her to marry him, but I don't
know how true that is. I'm sure I can't see why he'd want
to, but then you never can tell what a man like that will d
It would be just good enough *for* him if he got her, tha
what I say. Then he'd see. She'd never stand for any of
nonsense. She'd make him toe the mark. She's a s
woman.

But, oh, so *ordinary*. I thought, when we saw
the other night, "Well, she just looks cheap, that's
looks." That must be what he likes, I suppose.
admit he looked very well. I never saw him look be
course you know what I think of him, but I alwa
say he's one of the handsomest men I ever saw i
I can understand how any woman would be at

him—at first. Until they found out what he's really like. Oh, if you could have seen him with that awful, common creature, never once taking his eyes off her, and hanging on every word she said, as if it was pearls! It made me just——

Mona, angel, are you *crying?* Now, darling, that's just plain silly. That man's not worth another thought. You've thought about him entirely too much, that's the trouble. Three years! Three of the best years of your life you've given him, and all the time he's been deceiving you with that woman. Just think back over what you've been through—all the times and times and times he promised you he'd give her up; and you, you poor little idiot, you'd believe him, and then he'd go right back to her again. And *everybody* knew about it. Think of that, and then try telling me that man's worth crying over! Really, Mona! I'd have more pride.

You know, I'm just glad this thing happened. I'm just glad you found out. This is a little too much, this time. In Chicago, indeed! Let you know the minute he came home! The kindest thing a person could possibly have done was to tell you, and bring you to your senses at last. I'm not sorry I did it, for a second. When I think of him out having the time of his life and you lying here deathly sick all on account of him, I could just— Yes, it is on account of him. Even if you didn't have an—well, even if I was mistaken about what I naturally thought was the matter with you when you made such a secret of your illness, he's driven you into a nervous breakdown, and that's plenty bad enough. All for that man! The skunk! You just put him right out of your head.

Why, of course you can, Mona. All you need to do is to pull yourself together, child. Simply say to yourself, "Well, I've wasted three years of my life, and that's that." Never worry about *him* any more. The Lord knows, darling, he's not worrying about you.

It's just because you're weak and sick that you're worked up like this, dear. I know. But you're going to be all right. You can make something of your life. You've got to, Mona, you know. Because after all—well, of course, you never looked lovelier, I don't mean that; but you're— well, you're not getting any younger. And here you've been throwing away your time, never seeing your friends, never going out, never meeting anybody new, just sitting here waiting for Garry to telephone, or Garry to come in—if he didn't have anything better to do. For three years, you've never had a thought in your head but that man. Now you just forget him.

Ah, baby, it isn't good for you to cry like that. Please don't. He's not even worth talking about. Look at the woman he's in love with, and you'll see what kind he is. You were much too good for him. You were much too sweet to him. You gave in too easily. The minute he had you, he didn't want you any more. That's what he's like. Why, he no more loved you than——

Mona, don't! Mona, stop it! Please, Mona! You mustn't talk like that, you mustn't say such things. You've got to stop crying, you'll be terribly sick. Stop, oh, stop it, oh, please stop! Oh, what am I going to do with her? Mona, dear—Mona! Oh, where in heaven's name is that fool maid?

Edie. Oh, Edie! Edie, I think you'd better get Dr. Britton on the telephone, and tell him to come down and give Miss Morrison something to quiet her. I'm afraid she's got herself a little bit upset.

Glory in the Daytime

Glory in the Daytime

$\mathcal{M}$r. Murdock was one who carried no enthusiasm whatever for plays and their players, and that was too
bad, for they meant so much to little Mrs. Murdock. Always she had been in a state of devout excitement over the
luminous, free, passionate elect who serve the theater. And
always she had done her wistful worshiping, along with the
multitudes, at the great public altars. It is true that once,
when she was a particularly little girl, love had impelled
her to write Miss Maude Adams a letter beginning "Dear-

est Peter," and she had received from Miss Adams a minia-
ture thimble inscribed "A kiss from Peter Pan." (That was
a day!) And once, when her mother had taken her holiday
shopping, a limousine door was held open and there had
passed her, as close as *that*, a wonder of sable and violets
and round red curls that seemed to tinkle on the air; so,
forever after, she was as good as certain that she had been
not a foot away from Miss Billie Burke. But until some
three years after her marriage, these had remained her only
personal experiences with the people of the lights and the
glory.

Then it turned out that Miss Noyes, newcome to little
Mrs. Murdock's own bridge club, knew an actress. She
actually knew an actress; the way you and I know collectors
of recipes and members of garden clubs and amateurs of
needlepoint.

The name of the actress was Lily Wynton, and it
was famous. She was tall and slow and silvery; often she
appeared in the rôle of a duchess, or of a Lady Pam or an
Honorable Moira. Critics recurrently referred to her as
"that great lady of our stage." Mrs. Murdock had attended, over years, matinée performances of the Wynton
successes. And she had no more thought that she would
one day have opportunity to meet Lily Wynton face to
face than she had thought—well, than she had thought
of flying!

Yet it was not astounding that Miss Noyes should walk at ease among the glamorous. Miss Noyes was full of depths and mystery, and she could talk with a cigarette still between her lips. She was always doing something difficult, like designing her own pajamas, or reading Proust, or modeling torsos in plasticine. She played excellent bridge. She liked little Mrs. Murdock. "Tiny one," she called her.

"How's for coming to tea tomorrow, tiny one?" she said, at a therefore memorable meeting of the bridge club. "Lily Wynton's going to drop up. You might like to meet her."

The words fell so easily that she could not have realized their weight. Lily Wynton was coming to tea. Mrs. Murdock might like to meet her. Little Mrs. Murdock walked home through the early dark, and stars sang in the sky above her.

Mr. Murdock was already at home when she arrived. It required but a glance to tell that for him there had been no singing stars that evening in the heavens. He sat with his newspaper opened at the financial page, and bitterness had its way with his soul. It was not the time to cry happily to him of the impending hospitalities of Miss Noyes; not the time, that is, if one anticipated exclamatory sympathy. Mr. Murdock did not like Miss Noyes. When pressed for a reason, he replied that he just plain didn't like her.

365

Occasionally he added, with a sweep that might have commanded a certain admiration, that all those women made
him sick. Usually, when she told him of the temperate
activities of the bridge club meetings, Mrs. Murdock kept
any mention of Miss Noyes's name from the accounts. She
had found that this omission made for a more agreeable
evening. But now she was caught in such a sparkling swirl
of excitement that she had scarcely kissed him before she
was off on her story.

"Oh, Jim," she cried. "Oh, what do you think! Hallie
Noyes asked me to tea tomorrow to meet Lily Wynton!"

"Who's Lily Wynton?" he said.

"Ah, Jim," she said. "Ah, really, Jim. Who's Lily
Wynton! Who's Greta Garbo, I suppose!"

"She some actress or something?" he said.

Mrs. Murdock's shoulders sagged. "Yes, Jim," she
said. "Yes. Lily Wynton's an actress."

She picked up her purse and started slowly toward the
door. But before she had taken three steps, she was again
caught up in her sparkling swirl. She turned to him, and
her eyes were shining.

"Honestly," she said, "it was the funniest thing you
ever heard in your life. We'd just finished the last rubber—oh, I forgot to tell you, I won three dollars, isn't that
pretty good for me?—and Hallie Noyes said to me, 'Come
on in to tea tomorrow. Lily Wynton's going to drop up,'

she said. Just like that, she said it. Just as if it was anybody."

"Drop up?" he said. "How can you drop *up?*"

"Honestly, I don't know what I said when she asked me," Mrs. Murdock said. "I suppose I said I'd love to—I guess I must have. But I was so simply— Well, you know how I've always felt about Lily Wynton. Why, when I was a little girl, I used to collect her pictures. And I've seen her in, oh, everything she's ever been in, I should think, and I've read every word about her, and interviews and all. Really and truly, when I think of *meeting* her—Oh, I'll simply die. What on earth shall I say to her?"

"You might ask her how she'd like to try dropping down, for a change," Mr. Murdock said.

"All right, Jim," Mrs. Murdock said. "If that's the way you want to be."

Wearily she went toward the door, and this time she reached it before she turned to him. There were no lights in her eyes.

"It—it isn't so awfully nice," she said, "to spoil somebody's pleasure in something. I was so thrilled about this. You don't see what it is to me, to meet Lily Wynton. To meet somebody like that, and see what they're like, and hear what they say, and maybe get to know them. People like that mean—well, they mean something different to me. They're not like this. They're not like me. Who do I ever see? What do I ever hear? All my whole life, I've wanted to know—I've almost prayed that some day I could meet—Well. All right, Jim."

She went out, and on to her bedroom.

Mr. Murdock was left with only his newspaper and his bitterness for company. But he spoke aloud.

" 'Drop up!' " he said. " 'Drop *up*,' for God's sake!"

The Murdocks dined, not in silence, but in pronounced quiet. There was something straitened about Mr. Murdock's stillness; but little Mrs. Murdock's was the sweet, far quiet of one given over to dreams. She had forgotten her weary words to her husband, she had passed through her excitement and her disappointment. Luxuriously she floated on innocent visions of days after the morrow. She heard her own voice in future conversations. . . .

I saw Lily Wynton at Hallie's the other day, and she was telling me all about her new play—no, I'm terribly sorry, but it's a secret, I promised her I wouldn't tell anyone the name of it. . . . Lily Wynton dropped up to tea yesterday, and we just got to talking, and she told me the most interesting things about her life; she said she'd never dreamed of telling them to anyone else. . . . Why, I'd love to come, but I promised to have lunch with Lily Wynton. . . . I had a long, long letter from Lily Wynton. . . . Lily Wynton called me up this morning. . . . Whenever I feel blue, I just go and have a talk with Lily Wynton, and then I'm all right again. . . . Lily Wynton told me . . . Lily Wynton and I . . . "Lily," I said to her . . .

The next morning, Mr. Murdock had left for his office before Mrs. Murdock rose. This had happened several times before, but not often. Mrs. Murdock felt a little queer about it. Then she told herself that it was probably just as well. Then she forgot all about it, and gave her mind to the selection of a costume suitable to the afternoon's event. Deeply she felt that her small wardrobe included no dress adequate to the occasion; for, of course, such an occasion had never before arisen. She finally decided upon a frock of dark blue serge with fluted white muslin about the neck and wrists. It was her style, that was the most she could say for it. And that was all she could say for herself. Blue serge and little white ruffles—that was she.

The very becomingness of the dress lowered her spirits. A nobody's frock, worn by a nobody. She blushed and went hot when she recalled the dreams she had woven the night before, the mad visions of intimacy, of equality with Lily Wynton. Timidity turned her heart liquid, and she thought of telephoning Miss Noyes and saying she had a bad cold and could not come. She steadied, when she planned a course of conduct to pursue at teatime. She would not try to say anything; if she stayed silent, she could not sound foolish. She would listen and watch and worship and then come home, stronger, braver, better for an hour she would remember proudly all her life.

Miss Noyes's living-room was done in the early modern period. There were a great many oblique lines and acute angles, zigzags of aluminium and horizontal stretches of mirror. The color scheme was sawdust and steel. No seat was more than twelve inches above the floor, no table was made of wood. It was, as has been said of larger places, all right for a visit.

Little Mrs. Murdock was the first arrival. She was glad of that; no, maybe it would have been better to have come after Lily Wynton; no, maybe this was right. The maid motioned her toward the living-room, and Miss Noyes greeted her in the cool voice and the warm words that were her special combination. She wore black velvet trousers, a red cummerbund, and a white silk shirt, opened at the throat. A cigarette clung to her lower lip, and her eyes, as was her habit, were held narrow against its near smoke.

"Come in, come in, tiny one," she said. "Bless its little heart. Take off its little coat. Good Lord, you look easily eleven years old in that dress. Sit ye doon, here beside of me. There'll be a spot of tea in a jiff."

Mrs. Murdock sat down on the vast, perilously low divan, and, because she was never good at reclining among cushions, held her back straight. There was room for six like her, between herself and her hostess. Miss Noyes lay back, with one ankle flung upon the other knee, and looked at her.

"I'm a wreck," Miss Noyes announced. "I was modeling like a mad thing, all night long. It's taken everything out of me. I was like a thing bewitched."

"Oh, what were you making?" cried Mrs. Murdock.

"Oh, Eve," Miss Noyes said. "I always do Eve. What else is there to do? You must come pose for me some time, tiny one. You'd be nice to do. Ye-es, you'd be very nice to do. My tiny one."

"Why, I——" Mrs. Murdock said, and stopped. "Thank you very much, though," she said.

"I wonder where Lily is," Miss Noyes said. "She said she'd be here early—well, she always says that. You'll adore her, tiny one. She's really rare. She's a real person. And she's been through perfect hell. God, what a time she's had!"

"Ah, what's been the matter?" said Mrs. Murdock.

"Men," Miss Noyes said. "Men. She never had a man that wasn't a louse." Gloomily she stared at the toe of her flat-heeled patent leather pump. "A pack of lice, always. All of them. Leave her for the first little floozie that comes along."

"But——" Mrs. Murdock began. No, she couldn't have heard right. How could it be right? Lily Wynton was a great actress. A great actress meant romance. Romance

371

meant Grand Dukes and Crown Princes and diplomats touched with gray at the temples and lean, bronzed, reckless Younger Sons. It meant pearls and emeralds and chinchilla and rubies red as the blood that was shed for them. It meant a grim-faced boy sitting in the fearful Indian midnight, beneath the dreary whirring of the *punkahs,* writing a letter to the lady he had seen but once; writing his poor heart out, before he turned to the service revolver that lay beside him on the table. It meant a golden-locked poet, floating face downward in the sea, and in his pocket his last great sonnet to the lady of ivory. It meant brave, beautiful men, living and dying for the lady who was the pale bride of art, whose eyes and heart were soft with only compassion for them.

A pack of lice. Crawling after little floozies; whom Mrs. Murdock swiftly and hazily pictured as rather like ants.

"But—" said little Mrs. Murdock.

"She gave them all her money," Miss Noyes said. "She always did. Or if she didn't, they took it anyway. Took every cent she had, and then spat in her face. Well, maybe she's beginning to learn a little sense now. Oh, there's the bell—that'll be Lily. No, sit ye doon, tiny one. You belong there."

Miss Noyes rose and made for the archway that separated the living-room from the hall. As she passed Mrs.

Murdock, she stooped suddenly, cupped her guest's round chin, and quickly, lightly kissed her mouth.

"Don't tell Lily," she murmured, very low.

Mrs. Murdock puzzled. Don't tell Lily what? Could Hallie Noyes think that she might babble to the Lily Wynton of these strange confidences about the actress's life? Or did she mean— But she had no more time for puzzling. Lily Wynton stood in the archway. There she stood, one hand resting on the wooden molding and her body swayed toward it, exactly as she stood for her third-act entrance of her latest play, and for a like half-minute.

You would have known her anywhere, Mrs. Murdock thought. Oh, yes, anywhere. Or at least you would have exclaimed, "That woman looks something like Lily Wynton." For she was somehow different in the daylight. Her figure looked heavier, thicker, and her face—there was so much of her face that the surplus sagged from the strong, fine bones. And her eyes, those famous dark, liquid eyes. They were dark, yes, and certainly liquid, but they were set in little hammocks of folded flesh, and seemed to be set but loosely, so readily did they roll. Their whites, that were visible all around the irises, were threaded with tiny scarlet veins.

"I suppose footlights are an awful strain on their eyes," thought little Mrs. Murdock.

Lily Wynton wore, just as she should have, black

satin and sables, and long white gloves were wrinkled luxuriously about her wrists. But there were delicate streaks of grime in the folds of her gloves, and down the shining length of her gown there were small, irregularly shaped dull patches; bits of food or drops of drink, or perhaps both, sometime must have slipped their carriers and found brief sanctuary there. Her hat—oh, her hat. It was romance, it was mystery, it was strange, sweet sorrow; it was Lily Wynton's hat, of all the world, and no other could dare it. Black it was, and tilted, and a great, soft plume drooped from it to follow her cheek and curl across her throat. Beneath it, her hair had the various hues of neglected brass. But oh, her hat.

"Darling!" cried Miss Noyes.

"Angel," said Lily Wynton. "My sweet."

It was that voice. It was that deep, soft, glowing voice. "Like purple velvet," someone had written. Mrs. Murdock's heart beat visibly.

Lily Wynton cast herself upon the steep bosom of her hostess, and murmured there. Across Miss Noyes's shoulder she caught sight of little Mrs. Murdock.

"And who is this?" she said. She disengaged herself.

"That's my tiny one," Miss Noyes said. "Mrs. Murdock."

"What a clever little face," said Lily Wynton. "Clever, clever little face. What does she do, sweet Hallie? I'm sure she writes, doesn't she? Yes, I can feel it. She writes beautiful, beautiful words. Don't you, child?"

"Oh, no, really I——" Mrs. Murdock said.

"And you must write me a play," said Lily Wynton. "A beautiful, beautiful play. And I will play in it, over and over the world, until I am a very, very old lady. And then I will die. But I will never be forgotten, because of the years I played in your beautiful, beautiful play."

She moved across the room. There was a slight hesitancy, a seeming insecurity, in her step, and when she would have sunk into a chair, she began to sink two inches, perhaps, to its right. But she swayed just in time in her descent, and was safe.

"To write," she said, smiling sadly at Mrs. Murdock, "to write. And such a little thing, for such a big gift. Oh, the privilege of it. But the anguish of it, too. The agony."

"But, you see, I——" said little Mrs. Murdock.

"Tiny one doesn't write, Lily," Miss Noyes said. She threw herself back upon the divan. "She's a museum piece. She's a devoted wife."

"A wife!" Lily Wynton said. "A wife. Your first marriage, child?"

"Oh, yes," said Mrs. Murdock.

"How sweet," Lily Wynton said. "How sweet, sweet, sweet. Tell me, child, do you love him very, very much?"

"Why, I——" said little Mrs. Murdock, and blushed. "I've known him for ages," she said.

"You love him," Lily Wynton said. "You love him.

375

And is it sweet to go to bed with him?"

"Oh——" said Mrs. Murdock, and blushed till it hurt.

"The first marriage," Lily Wynton said. "Youth, youth. Yes, when I was your age I used to marry, too. Oh, treasure your love, child, guard it, live in it. Laugh and dance in the love of your man. Until you find out what he's really like."

There came a sudden visitation upon her. Her shoulders jerked upward, her cheeks puffed, her eyes sought to start from their hammocks. For a moment she sat thus, then slowly all subsided into place. She lay back in her chair, tenderly patting her chest. She shook her head sadly, and there was grieved wonder in the look with which she held Mrs. Murdock.

"Gas," said Lily Wynton, in the famous voice. "Gas. Nobody knows what I suffer from it."

"Oh, I'm so sorry," Mrs. Murdock said. "Is there anything——"

"Nothing," Lily Wynton said. "There is nothing. There is nothing that can be done for it. I've been everywhere."

"How's for a spot of tea, perhaps?" Miss Noyes said. "It might help." She turned her face toward the archway and lifted up her voice. "Mary! Where the hell's the tea?"

"You don't know," Lily Wynton said, with her grieved eyes fixed on Mrs. Murdock, "you don't know what stomach distress is. You can never, never know, unless you're a stomach sufferer yourself. I've been one for years. Years and years and years."

"I'm terribly sorry," Mrs. Murdock said.

"Nobody knows the anguish," Lily Wynton said. "The agony."

The maid appeared, bearing a triangular tray upon which was set an heroic-sized tea service of bright white china, each piece a hectagon. She set it down on a table within the long reach of Miss Noyes and retired, as she had come, bashfully.

"Sweet Hallie," Lily Wynton said, "my sweet. Tea—I adore it. I worship it. But my distress turns it to gall and wormwood in me. Gall and wormwood. For hours, I should have no peace. Let me have a little, tiny bit of your beautiful, beautiful brandy, instead."

"You really think you should, darling?" Miss Noyes said. "You know——"

"My angel," said Lily Wynton, "it's the only thing for acidity."

"Well," Miss Noyes said. "But do remember you've got a performance tonight." Again she hurled her voice at the archway. "Mary! Bring the brandy and a lot of soda and ice and things."

"Oh, no, my saint," Lily Wynton said. "No, no, sweet Hallie. Soda and ice are rank poison to me. Do you want to freeze my poor, weak stomach? Do you want to kill poor, poor Lily?"

"Mary!" roared Miss Noyes. "Just bring the brandy and a glass." She turned to little Mrs. Murdock. "How's for your tea, tiny one? Cream? Lemon?"

"Cream, if I may, please," Mrs. Murdock said. "And two lumps of sugar, please, if I may."

"Oh, youth, youth," Lily Wynton said. "Youth and love."

The maid returned with an octagonal tray supporting a decanter of brandy and a wide, squat, heavy glass. Her head twisted on her neck in a spasm of diffidence.

"Just pour it for me, will you, my dear?" said Lily Wynton. "Thank you. And leave the pretty, pretty decanter here, on this enchanting little table. Thank you. You're so good to me."

The maid vanished, fluttering. Lily Wynton lay back in her chair, holding in her gloved hand the wide, squat glass, colored brown to the brim. Little Mrs. Murdock lowered her eyes to her teacup, carefully carried it to her lips, sipped, and replaced it on its saucer. When she raised her eyes, Lily Wynton lay back in her chair, holding in her gloved hand the wide, squat, colorless glass.

"My life," Lily Wynton said, slowly, "is a mess. A stinking mess. It always has been, and it always will be. Until I am a very, very old lady. Ah, little Clever-Face, you writers don't know what struggle is."

"But really I'm not—" said Mrs, Murdock.

"To write," Lily Wynton said. "To write. To set one word beautifully beside another word. The privilege of it. The blessed, blessed peace of it. Oh, for quiet, for rest. But do you think those Jew bastards would close that play while it's doing a nickel's worth of business? Oh, no. Tired as I am, sick as I am, I must drag along. Oh, child, child, guard your precious gift. Give thanks for it. It is the greatest thing of all. It is the only thing. To write."

"Darling, I told you tiny one doesn't write," said Miss Noyes. "How's for making more sense? She's a wife."

"Ah, yes, she told me. She told me she had perfect, passionate love," Lily Wynton said. "Young love. It is the greatest thing. It is the only thing." She grasped the decanter; and again the squat glass was brown to the brim.

"What time did you start today, darling?" said Miss Noyes.

"Oh, don't scold me, sweet love," Lily Wynton said. "Lily hasn't been naughty. Her wuzzunt naughty dirl 't all. I didn't get up until late, late, late. And though I parched, though I burned, I didn't have a drink until after my breakfast. 'It is for Hallie,' I said." She raised the glass to her mouth, tilted it, and brought it away, colorless.

"Good Lord, Lily," Miss Noyes said. "Watch yourself. You've got to walk on that stage tonight, my girl."

"All the world's a stage," said Lily Wynton. "And all the men and women merely players. They have their entrance and their exitses, and each man in his time plays many parts, his act being seven ages. At first, the infant, mewling and puking——"

"How's the play doing?" Miss Noyes said.

"Oh, lousily," Lily Wynton said. "Lousily, lousily, lousily. But what isn't? What isn't, in this terrible, terrible world? Answer me that." She reached for the decanter.

"Lily, listen," said Miss Noyes. "Stop that. Do you hear?"

"Please, sweet Hallie," Lily Wynton said. "Pretty please. Poor, poor Lily."

"Do you want me to do what I had to do last time?" Miss Noyes said. "Do you want me to strike you, in front of tiny one, here?"

Lily Wynton drew herself high. "You do not realize," she said, icily, "what acidity is." She filled the glass and held it, regarding it as though through a lorgnon. Suddenly her manner changed, and she looked up and smiled at little Mrs. Murdock.

"You must let me read it," she said. "You mustn't be so modest."

"Read——" said little Mrs. Murdock.

"Your play," Lily Wynton said. "Your beautiful, beautiful play. Don't think I am too busy. I always have time. I have time for everything. Oh, my God, I have to go to the dentist tomorrow. Oh, the suffering I have gone through with my teeth. Look!" She set down her glass, inserted a gloved forefinger in the corner of her mouth, and dragged it to the side. "Oogh!" she insisted. "Oogh!"

Mrs. Murdock craned her neck shyly, and caught a glimpse of shining gold.

"Oh, I'm so sorry," she said.

"As wah ee id a me ass ime," Lily Wynton said. She took away her forefinger and let her mouth resumed its shape. "That's what he did to me last time," she repeated. "The anguish of it. The agony. Do you suffer with your teeth, little Clever-Face?"

"Why, I'm afraid I've been awfully lucky," Mrs. Murdock said. "I———"

"You don't know," Lily Wynton said. "Nobody knows what it is. You writers—you don't know." She took up her glass, sighed over it, and drained it.

"Well," Miss Noyes said. "Go ahead and pass out, then, darling. You'll have time for a sleep before the theater."

"To sleep," Lily Wynton said. "To sleep, perchance to dream. The privilege of it. Oh, Hallie, sweet, sweet Hallie, poor Lily feels so terrible. Rub my head for me, angel. Help me."

"I'll go get the eau de Cologne," Miss Noyes said. She left the room, lightly patting Mrs. Murdock's knee as she passed her. Lily Wynton lay in her chair and closed her famous eyes.

"To sleep," she said. "To sleep, perchance to dream."

"I'm afraid," little Mrs. Murdock began. "I'm afraid," she said, "I really must be going home. I'm afraid I didn't realize how awfully late it was."

"Yes, go, child," Lily Wynton said. She did not open her eyes. "Go to him. Go to him, live in him, love him. Stay with him always. But when he starts bringing them into the house—get out."

"I'm afraid—I'm afraid I didn't quite understand," Mrs. Murdock said.

"When he starts bringing his fancy women into the house," Lily Wynton said. "You must have pride, then. You must go. I always did. But it was always too late then. They'd got all my money. That's all they want, marry them or not. They say it's love, but it isn't. Love is the only thing. Treasure your love, child. Go back to him. Go to bed with him. It's the only thing. And your beautiful, beautiful play."

"Oh, dear," said little Mrs. Murdock. "I—I'm afraid it's really terribly late."

There was only the sound of rhythmic breathing from the chair where Lily Wynton lay. The purple voice rolled along the air no longer.

Little Mrs. Murdock stole to the chair upon which she had left her coat. Carefully she smoothed her white muslin frills, so that they would be fresh beneath the jacket. She felt a tenderness for her frock; she wanted to protect it. Blue serge and little ruffles—they were her own.

When she reached the outer door of Miss Noyes's apartment, she stopped a moment and her manners conquered her. Bravely she called in the direction of Miss Noyes's bedroom.

"Good-bye, Miss Noyes," she said. "I've simply got to run. I didn't realize it was so late. I had a lovely time— thank you ever so much."

"Oh, good-by, tiny one," Miss Noyes called. "Sorry Lily went by-by. Don't mind her—she's really a real person. I'll call you up, tiny one. I want to see you. Now where's that damned cologne?"

"Thank you ever so much," Mrs. Murdock said. She let herself out of the apartment.

Little Mrs. Murdock walked homeward, through the clustering dark. Her mind was busy, but not with memories of Lily Wynton. She thought of Jim; Jim, who had left for his office before she had arisen that morning, Jim, whom she had not kissed good-by. Darling Jim. There were no others born like him. Funny Jim, stiff and cross and silent; but only because he knew so much. Only because he knew the silliness of seeking afar for the glamour and beauty and romance of living. When they were right at home all the time, she thought. Like the Blue Bird, thought little Mrs. Murdock.

Darling Jim. Mrs. Murdock turned in her course, and entered an enormous shop where the most delicate and esoteric of foods were sold for heavy sums. Jim liked red caviar. Mrs. Murdock bought a jar of the shiny, glutinous eggs. They would have cocktails that night, though they had no guests, and the red caviar would be served with them for a surprise, and it would be a little, secret party to celebrate her return to contentment with her Jim, a party to mark her happy renunciation of all the glory of the world. She bought, too, a large, foreign cheese. It would give a needed touch to dinner. Mrs. Murdock had not given much attention to ordering dinner, that morning. "Oh, anything you want, Signe," she had said to the maid. She did not want to think of that. She went on home with her packages.

Mr. Murdock was already there when she arrived. He was sitting with his newspaper opened to the financial page. Little Mrs. Murdock ran in to him with her eyes a-light. It is too bad that the light in a person's eyes is only the light in a person's eyes, and you cannot tell at a look what causes it. You do not know if it is excitement about you, or about something else. The evening before, Mrs. Murdock had run in to Mr. Murdock with her eyes a-light.

"Oh, hello," he said to her. He looked back at his paper, and kept his eyes there. "What did you do? Did you drop up to Hank Noyes's?"

Little Mrs. Murdock stopped right where she was.

"You know perfectly well, Jim," she said, "that Hallie Noyes's first name is Hallie."

"It's Hank to me," he said. "Hank or Bill. Did what's-her-name show up? I mean drop up. Pardon me."

"To whom are you referring?" said Mrs. Murdock, perfectly.

"What's-her-name," Mr. Murdock said. "The movie star."

"If you mean Lily Wynton," Mrs. Murdock said, "she is not a movie star. She is an actress. She is a great actress."

"Well, did she drop up?" he said.

Mrs. Murdock's shoulders sagged. "Yes," she said. "Yes, she was there, Jim."

"I suppose you're going on the stage now," he said.

"Ah, Jim," Mrs. Murdock said. "Ah, Jim, please. I'm not sorry at all I went to Hallie Noyes's today. It was — it was a real experience to meet Lily Wynton. Something I'll remember all my life."

"What did she do?" Mr. Murdock said. "Hang by her feet?"

"She did no such thing!" Mrs. Murdock said. "She recited Shakespeare, if you want to know."

"Oh, my God," Mr. Murdock said. "That must have been great."

"All right, Jim," Mrs. Murdock said. "If that's the way you want to be."

Wearily she left the room and went down the hall. She stopped at the pantry door, pushed it open, and spoke to the pleasant little maid.

"Oh, Signe," she said. "Oh, good evening, Signe. Put these things somewhere, will you? I got them on the way home. I thought we might have them some time."

Wearily little Mrs. Murdock went on down the hall to her bedroom.